2/5/84

A friend of

As a friend of yours

Ed Frankel

Ferns

Also by Edward Frankel

DNA—Ladder of Life, 2nd Edition
(McGraw-Hill, 1979)

FERNS

A Natural History

by

Edward Frankel

Illustrated by

Edgar M. Paulton

The Stephen Greene Press
BRATTLEBORO, VERMONT

This book has been produced in the United States of America.
It is published by The Stephen Greene Press,
Fessenden Road, Brattleboro, Vermont 05301.

Library of Congress Cataloging in Publication Data

Frankel,Edward.
  Ferns: a natural history.

  Bibliography: p.
  Includes index.

  Summary: Discusses fern structures, life cycles,
classification, folklore, evolution, and ecology, and
instructs the gardener on outdoor and indoor cultivation
of ferns.

  1. Ferns. 2. Ferns, Ornamental.   [1. Ferns]
I. Paulton, Edgar M., ill.   II. Title.
QK522.F7   587'.31   81-6700
ISBN 0-8289-0429-4   AACR2

To, all my ferns friends
and
all friends of ferns

Contents

Preface

*T*he fern fraternity has the distinction of being one of the smallest and oldest of the botanical groups on earth today. Living inconspicuously in the shadows of flowering plants, ferns and their allies command relatively little attention. They are looked down upon as second class citizens in the plant kingdom and considered of little importance in the web of life.

This is far from the facts. The pteridophytes, that is, the ferns and fern allies, had their beginning in the distant geological past and for over a hundred million years dominated the plant world. Gradually they declined in size and numbers leaving behind a handful of dwarf descendants and stupendous stores of fossils as coal deposits. These "skeletons" of ancient pteridophytes sparked and fueled the industrial revolution which created today's energy-hungry society. Fossil fuels also gave rise to growing environmental problems of worldwide proportions and are the boon and bane of human existence today.

Although there is a steady stream of books about ferns and their allies, most focus on the identification and cultivation of these plants. This book has a broader scope. Not only does it tell how to know and grow ferns but it also considers the environmental impact and the problems created by pteridophyte fossil remains, coal. Energy alternatives to the faltering "fouling" fossil fuels are discussed with emphasis on solar sources.

This book attempts to present the story of pteridophytes, past, present, and future. The initial chapters endeavor to kindle flames of interest in ferns and fern allies by acquainting beginners with the place of pteridophytes in the plant kingdom, the structure and modes of reproduction of ferns and their evolution.

For those with an out-of-doors, down-to-earth inclination, this book tries to transmit the excitement of seeking and finding ferns in fields and forests, greeting them by name as you would a friend and introducing your fern friends to fellow travelers and converts.

Fern tables and folklore—some fact, most fiction, are included for your entertainment.

For fern farmers, indoors and outdoors, ways and means are presented for growing pteridophytes from spores, parts and whole plants in plots, pots, and terrariums. There is also something for collectors and hobbyists who prefer to putter rather than plant pteridophytes.

The unique feature of this book are the last two chapters on fossil fern fuels; especially coal, the energy crisis and energy alternatives. The theme developed in these chapters is that coal, although the most abundant, is the "dirtiest" and the most dangerous of the fossil fuels. It has the potential of poisoning the earth and killing off its inhabitants by cumulative contamination of the environment. Nuclear energy as an alternative is also discussed. The growing disenchantment with nuclear reactors which generate power and pollution by atomic fission and the present experimental status of atomic fusion technology are examined critically. Living ferns hold the secret of trapping and storing solar energy by the process of photosynthesis; they are ideal models that beg to be studied intensively. The future is in solar energy which is our cleanest, safest and unlimited power source.

Literary license has been taken in the use of some words which will probably not meet the approval of the entire botanical brotherhood. The intention is to simplify the way for newcomers into the world of pteridophytes rather than confuse them with scientific exactitude.

If you should meet some words in the text that have not been included in the latest Webster's Collegiate Dictionary, don't let it disturb you. It is just a way of expressing a thought in what it is hoped is an entertaining manner; these verbal calisthenics are self explanatory.

On the other hand, for the unintentional and seemingly inevitable errors that creep into print despite heroic efforts of writers and proofreaders, the author accepts complete responsibility and would be a most happy fellow to stand corrected.

The guidelines in writing this book, stated simply, are that life is a rare phenomenon, unique in our solar system and as far as we know not yet discovered elsewhere in the universe. Its existence depends upon delicately balanced fragile ecological re-lationships. Homo sapiens, one among a million or so known species, is stretching the limits of the earth's life sustaining mech-anisms and fast approaching the point of no return. It is predicted that by the end of this century, two million species, known and unknown, may be added to the growing list of extinct organisms, most being placed there by man's inhumanity to man and to other living things. A serious question to ask is "Will Homo sapiens appear on future lists?"

However, humans are not lemmings bent on self destruction. There is a growing trend to control and curtail activities that are contaminating and poisoning the environment. There is also the realization that green plants are not something just to please the eye and the palate but are indispensible for survival. They are the basic source of food, oxygen and most of our energy, the vital link in the chain of life and pteridophytes are a part of it.

This book is not the last testament of a prophet of doom. It is written to make more people aware of the fragility of the en-vironment and the need to preserve it. Its purpose and message is one of hope for a better, brighter future in a green world.

Edward Frankel
Bronxville, New York

Acknowledgments

*I*t would be impossible to acknowledge all the people who directly or indirectly contributed to the preparation of this book. It would be equally impossible not to mention the many friends and colleagues who played a significant part in the production of this pteridophyte tome.

First and foremost, my gratitude and appreciation go to Edgar Paulton, friend, fellow pteridophile, collaborator and illustrator extraordinaire. His experience as illustrator of fern publications, and art director of "Fiddlehead Forum", bulletin of the American Fern Society, together with his critical eye, lively creative imagination, quick wit and dedication to pteridology made him the ideal partner in this venture.

Dr. John T. Mickel, Curator of Ferns at the New York Botanical Garden, author of several books and innumerable articles on ferns, editor of "Fiddlehead Forum" and dynamic leader of the New York Chapter of the American Fern Society was most generous and supportive throughout; his review of the technical aspects of the final draft helped immeasurably in improving the accuracy and the content of this book.

Stimulation, encouragement and help came from several members of the New York Chapter of the American Fern Society where the idea for the book was born. Thanks go to Charles Anderson, Mary Eybers, Dorothy and Ed Linde, Charles Neidorf, Virginia and Bob Otto and Ethelyn Williams among others.

I would also like to acknowledge the contributions of the staff members of the Stephen Greene Press; especially Wilbur F. Eastman, with whom I was in constant communication from the very beginning and who was most enthusiastic about the book.

Dr. Regina Rumstein, dear friend and colleague, proofread the final draft of the manuscript and offered kind, helpful suggestions.

To all, I am most grateful.

Ferns

CHAPTER I

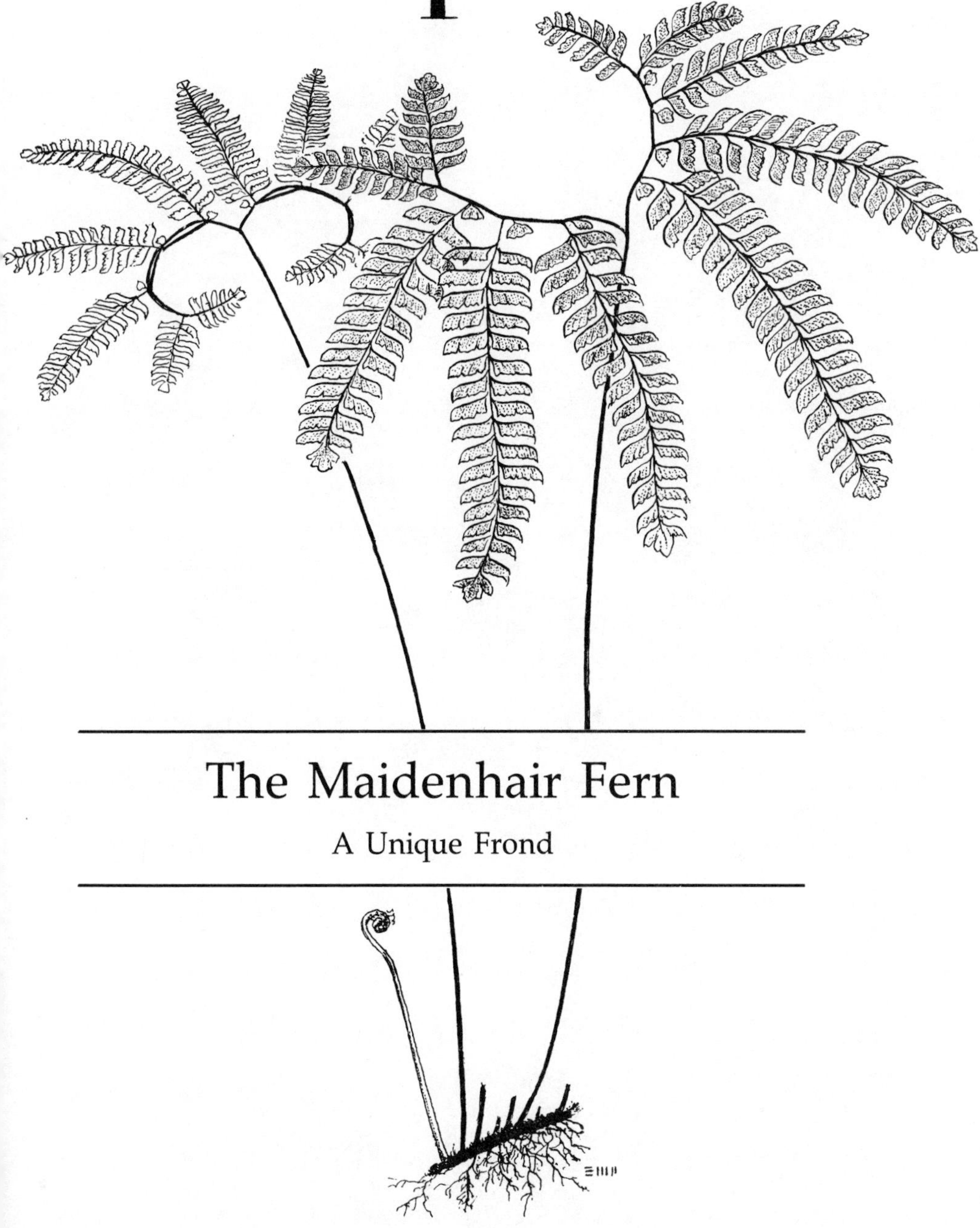

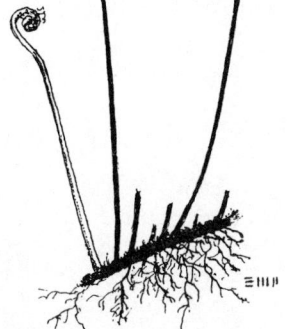

The Maidenhair Fern

A Unique Frond

I

Why Ferns?

$\mathcal{A}$s far as we know, our planet Earth is the only place in this solar system and beyond that is inhabited by living beings. We humans share this world with at least a million kinds of animals and a half-million species of plants. Each species has its niche and lives within it, except one: *Homo sapiens*. We challenge all other living organisms that stand in the way of our expanding, exploding population. Not only do we dispossess other organisms and re-possess their homes, but we destroy them at an incredible rate for food, clothing, housing, and amusement. Unless we learn to live in peaceful coexistence with other organisms and ourselves, we are heading toward the complete annihilation of all life on earth. Forces as destructive to the environment as the most powerful atomic bombs are being released by us. So long as there are green plants their color is the "go" sign of life; no green plants, no life. Among the potential victims of our biocidal (life-killing) holocaust are ferns. They, no less than other forms of life, are not long for this world unless we recognize their right to life and to a homeland. In this struggle there are no victors, only victims.

But you may ask, "Why all this fuss about ferns?" A compelling answer is that ferns are a very important strand in the web of life that reaches back almost 400 million years. Ferns were among the pioneers that first invaded lifeless land and then dominated it for eons. A record of their reign has come down to us as coal, the fossil fuel that ushered in the industrial revolution and is the center of controversy in today's power struggle. The solar energy locked up in ferns hundreds of millions of years ago is profoundly affecting contemporary human society and its future.

The living descendants of the ancient and honorable fern fraternity are relatively few in number and small in stature. In addition, because they lack colorful, showy flowers and hide in shady nooks and crannies, ferns are generally overlooked or ig-nored. To many, "a fern is a fern," "all ferns looks alike," or "if you've seen one fern you've seen them all"; these are confessions of how little such belittlers know about these plants. It must be said to their credit that what ferns lack in size and number, they make up in their will to live. Every part of the earth—except the darkest caves, the coldest ice caps, and the driest deserts—is home to ferns. You can find them wallowing in water and wetlands, flourishing in forests and fields, tightly clutching and climbing tree trunks and limbs.

Most ferns reside in tropical rain forests, which are present-day replicas of their ancestral abodes. Considering the rate at which tropical rain forests are being leveled, the future of ferns is not too bright. They may join the growing list of "has-beens," those phantom ferns of extinct species that are known to us through fossil "footprints," the only evidence we have that they were once among the living.

With the growing awareness of our shrinking natural environment, we are beginning to question what we lose when an open field becomes a parking lot, a wooded area is traded for a housing development, or a wetland is replaced by a marina. Instead of talking about "nature" or "the environment" abstractly, we are starting to think of the kinds of plants and animals that live in natural areas and the consequences of destroying their homes. Becoming aware of ferns, seeing them in their natural habitats, and being able to identify them may make us think twice before allowing a natural area to disappear. A forest without ferns is as incomplete as a daisy without petals.

Once you "discover" ferns it is difficult to resist or ignore them. Apparently there is a fern ferment in the land causing "fernitis," a condition that develops in susceptible individuals when they are exposed to ferns. The chief symptom is the desire to raise ferns, indoors and outdoors, day and night, all year round. This love for ferns (pteridophilia) is being spread by other "carriers" of the amiable affliction. It is being encouraged by professional and amateur fern growers who are providing an endless array of new materials and new methods for growing them.

Ferns may be viewed as environmental barometers, indicators of the present state of our planet and predictors of its future. Having survived so long on this restless earth, through its ups and downs, droughts and drizzles, frosts and fires, ferns are well qualified as weather vanes. Sensitive to changes in temperature, humidity, light, air, soil, water, and invading organisms, they keep us posted on what is happening in the environment. What is good for ferns is good for us. By protecting and preserving ferns we are protecting and preserving ourselves.

CHAPTER II

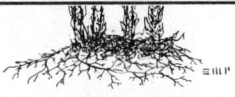

The Cinnamon Fern

Hair tuft on underside at base
of pinnae; separate fertile frond

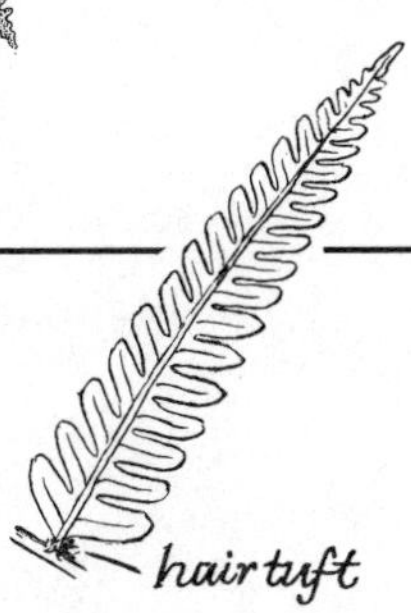

hair tuft

II

Ferns Among the Flora

From outer space, the Earth appears as a shiny blue agate marble, a jewel suspended against a jet black background. From a few hundred miles away, a pattern of colors becomes visible: the whites of swirling clouds, ice caps, and snow fields; the browns of bare mountain tops and sandy deserts; the blues of oceans, seas, and lakes; and the greens of forests, fens, and fields. The flora give the earth its green glow, making it the garden spot of the solar system, the planet of plants.

Half-a-million species of plants have been found, named and catalogued in an orderly, logical manner. Before beginning our study of the fern fraternity, an overview of the plant kingdom is in order to show the place of ferns and their allies in the floral fraternity. Various schemes of classifying plants have been proposed and used; a simple system, adequate for our needs, divides all plants into four major groups:

Green algae   Non green plants

1. Algae and fungi, formerly referred to collectively as the *thallophytes* (THALL-owe-fights; from the Greek *thallos:* young branch, and *phyton:* plant); these are the simplest green and non-green plants.

7

Liverworts   Mosses

2. Liverworts and mosses, the *bryophytes* (BRY-owe-fights, from the Greek *bryon:* moss, and *phyton:* plant); these are primitive wetland plants.

Ferns   Fern Allies

3. Ferns and fern allies, the *pteridophytes* (teh-RID-owe-fights; from the Greek *pteris:* fern, and *phyton:* plant); these are more complex wetland-dryland plants.

Evergreens   Flowers

4. Cone-bearing and flowering plants, collectively known as *spermatophytes* (spur-MAT-owe-fights; from the Greek *sperma:* seed, and *phyton:* plant or seed plants); these are the land plants: evergreens, and flowers.

Thallophytes:
Simple Green and Nongreen Plants

The simplest and most varied group of plants is the thallophytes. Included in this group are about 150,000 species of green and nongreen plants, roughly one-third of the world's flora. Thallophytes range in size from microscopic microbes to giant seaweeds hundreds of feet long. Extreme conditions of drought, heat, and cold do not stop thallophytes from establishing themselves on bare rocks, in deserts, on glaciers, and in hot springs. They are recyclers of the dead, the basic food of aquatic life, and the source of free oxygen that is indispensable for almost all life on earth. Thallophytes are conveniently divided into two subgroups based on how they get their food: green plants (the algae) make it, nongreen plants (the fungi) take it.

Fungi:
Nongreen plants

It may come to you as a surprise, but a fifth of all known
plants, 100,000 species, are not
green. These are the *fungi* (singular *fungus:* FUN-guss; plural
fungi: FUN-jee). The best-known
fungi are bacteria, molds, and
mushrooms. Fungi come in all
shades of black and white and
in all the colors of the rainbow.
Their common denominator is a
lack of **chlorophyll** (CLOR-owe-
fill), the coloring material present in green plants. Although
there are green molds—the
makers of penicillin—their green
pigment is not chlorophyll.
Fungi cannot do what chlorophyll-carrying green plants do:
capture solar energy and use it
to convert air, water, and minerals into food and oxygen. Unable to make their own food,
fungi feed on other organisms,
dead or alive.

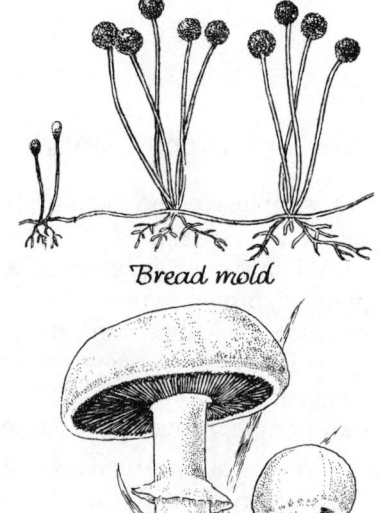

Bread mold

Common edible mushroom

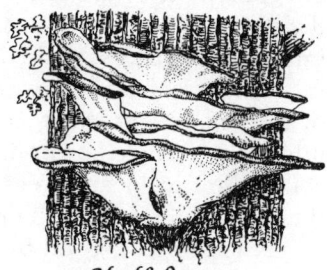

Shelf fungus

Some fungi devour the dead and decompose their remains.
The chemicals in the disintegrated bodies of the dead are thus
returned to the soil as fertilizer and reused by the living. Nothing
is wasted in nature, even the dead are recycled; by dining on the
dead, fungi feed the living. These decomposers of the dead are
called **saprophytes** (SAP-row-fights; from the Greek *sapros:* rotten,
and *phyton:* plant, which describes their role as "rotters" or
decayers).

Other fungi prey on the living, bringing death and disease
to their victims, which may be other plants, including ferns; or
animals, including humans. Fungi that feed on the living are called
parasites (PAR-ah-sights; from the Greek *para:* besides, and *sitos:*
food, one that eats at another's table).

9

Algae:
Primitive Green Plants

The simplest green plants are the *algae* (singular *alga:* AL-gah; plural *algae:* AL-gee). Estimates place their species number at 30,000, and they range in size from microscopic one-celled green plants to brown seaweeds hundreds of feet long. Algae, regardless of color, contain chlorophyll, enabling them to be independent food- and oxygen-makers. Their chlorophyll may be mixed with or masked by other pigments; hence algae may be yellow, gold, red, orange, brown, blue, green, or combinations of these colors.

Diatoms

Green Alga

Blue-green Alga

Giant Kelp

Sea Lettuce

The most primitive among these green plants, at the bottom of the floral ladder, are blue-green algae, often described as chlorophyll-carrying bacteria. About 8,000 species with a world-wide distribution are known. They are at home in the most unlikely and seemingly inhospitable places: in the boiling water of hot springs, on top of glaciers, in salt water, in polluted lakes; as well as in moist soil and on rocks and trees. Blue-green algae have the rare ability to enrich the soil by changing inert and hence useless nitrogen gas in the air to useful nitrates, compounds which plants must have to live and grow.

Approximately 25,000 kinds of green, yellow, and gold algae inhabit the fresh and salt waters of the world. These algae are the basic food of water dwellers, and the source of the dissolved oxygen in the water and at least half the free oxygen present in the air. The greater part of the free-floating masses of microscopic sea life called **plankton** (PLANK-ton) contains algae, such as diatoms. Referred to as the "grass of the sea," aquatic animals from one-celled protozoa to giant whales graze on plankton.

The giants among the algae are the seaweeds; 10,000 species of red, brown and green seaweeds are known the world over. Most are marine; they live in salt water, attached to rocks between the high and low tide zones. Seaweed culture and farming are developing sources of food and fuel.

Lichens:
An Algae-Fungi Combine

An unusual group of primitive plants are the *lichens* (LIE-kinz), of which there are 25,000 different kinds. Lichens are two plants in one, a perfect partnership between two entirely different organisms, an alga and a fungus. The fungus provides the alga with housing, anchorage, water, and minerals. The green or blue-green alga makes food by photosynthesis which it shares with the fungus. These odd but very happy couples are pioneer plants; gaining footholds on bare rock and paving the way for other plants. Resistant to drought, heat, and cold, these slow-growing, sun-loving, long-lived plants thrive on mountain peaks, open polar plains (tundras), deserts, and tropical jungles. Lichens come in all colors, from black to brilliant red, and in a variety of shapes. Some appear as painted flakes and spots pressed tightly against tree trunks and rock surfaces; others are attached more loosely with curled edges like leaves; and still others are branching and may hang from branches or grow upright.

Lichens on tree bark.

Upright Lichen: "British soldiers" wear red berets

Lichens are very sensitive and susceptible to air pollutants, especially sulfur dioxide, a highly toxic substance released when low grade coal or oil is burned. Smoke from industrial areas has all but wiped out the lichens in neighboring regions. Their presence or absence is a good measure of the degree of air pollution.

11

Bryophytes:
Liverworts and Mosses

The second group of green plants are the bryophytes: the mosses and their lesser-known cousins, the liverworts. About 25,000 of these wetland lodgers are on register, 10,000 species of liverworts and 15,000 species of mosses. Among land-living green plants, they are the simplest in structure and the smallest in size. Lacking roots, stems, leaves, and a conducting system, they absorb moisture from wet, shaded surroundings through all parts of their body, like a sponge.

Liverworts are green, flat, paper-thin, liver-shaped plants about one to two inches long. Inhabiting a shady setting and being small, they are inconspicuous, seen by few people and known to fewer.

Mosses are the green carpets covering forest floors, rocks, tree trunks, and logs. A single moss plant, which is no more than an inch or two in height, looks like a tiny pine tree or a fern. In spite of their appearance, mosses are very primitive and are strongly dependent on shade and water for survival. They, like lichens, are indicators of air pollution. "Where there is smog and smoke, mosses and lichens choke."

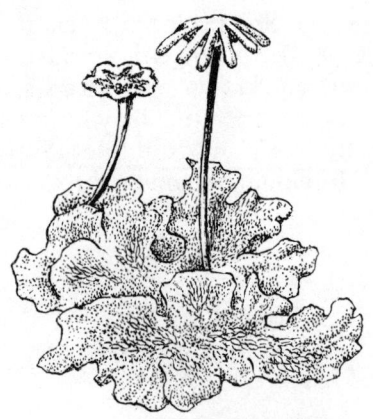

Liverworts

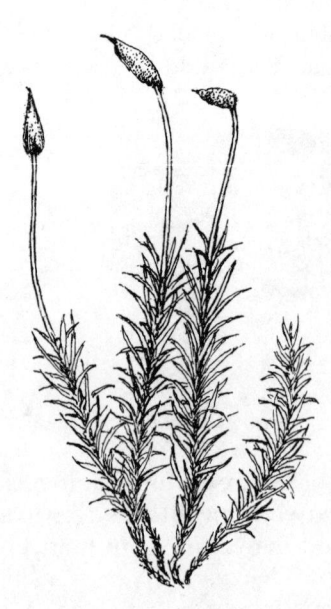

Mosses

Pteridophytes:
Ferns and Their Allies

The third group are the pteridophytes, the ferns and their relatives. A world-wide census places the pteridophyte population at 12,000 species of ferns and about 1,000 species of fern allies. The pteridophyte family is the smallest of the four major plant groups, constituting 2 percent of the world plant population. The majority live in tropical and subtropical rain forests, where some species are tree ferns 80 feet tall and others grow attached to tree trunks and branches. In the continental United States, there are less than 400 native species, mostly in wet, wooded areas, including one bog resident, a few inches tall and easily mistaken for a tuft of grass, the curly grass fern.

Pteridophytes are the first true **vascular** (VASS-cue-lar) plants; they have internal circulation systems consisting of two sets of channels, one for conducting materials up from their roots, and the other, down from their stems, and leaves. In all

Tree ferns soar to 80 feet above the floor of the tropical rain forest.

Ferns of the forest floor.

13

important respects but one, pteridophytes resemble the spermatophyte group: they lack flowers, fruits, and seeds.

Fern allies are relatively scarce and largely unknown to most people. Lacking broad leaves with branching veins, most show no resemblance to the ferns. Two of the most common fern relatives are the horsetails and the clubmosses.

Horsetails grow along the side of railroad tracks and appear as two different kinds of plants. One is flesh colored and looks like a miniature bamboo shoot with a cone-shaped head. The other is weedy and bushy with rings of long, deep-green spiny branches.

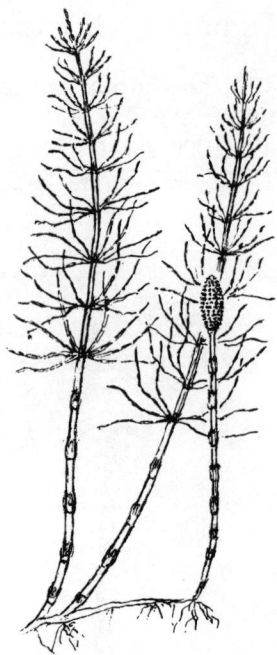

Horsetails

Clubmosses are evergreens that grow along a single branched or unbranched stem on shaded forest floors. Tiny green leaves cover the stiff, straight stem tipped with club-shaped cones. These clubs together with their superficial resemblance to mosses have given them the misleading name, clubmoss; they are not mosses.

Three other comparatively rare and seldom mentioned groups round out the fern allies. They are whiskbroom ferns (one native species) living in warm regions; spikemoss growing in moist, open fields; and quillworts wallowing in water. Despite differences among and between members of the fabulous fern flock, all follow the same basic life style: alternating generations of spore-producing plants and gamete-generating plants.

Clubmosses

Spermatophytes
(Seed Plants): Cones and Flowers

The spermatophytes or seed plants are the largest and best-known plants. Over 250,000 species cover and dominate the land, a number greater than all other plant species combined. Success as land lords is attributed to three structural developments: a very efficient conducting system, sexual reproduction without water, and the seed. The seed provides the key to understanding how this plant group conquered and still dominates dry land, a feat beyond the ability of almost all seedless plants. Seeds are capable of withstanding long periods of drought and extreme temperatures; they can remain dormant sometimes for years, until conditions favor their growth. Spermatophytes fall into two major subgroups: seed plants without flowers, and seed plants with flowers.

Pine cone and seeds

Gymnosperms:
Naked Seeds

The nonflowering seed plants are the *gymnosperms* (JIM-no-sperms; from the Greek: *gymno:* naked, and *sperma:* seed); the name "naked seed" indicates

The Giant Sequoia King of the Seed Plants stands up to thirty three stories tall

15

that the seeds in this plant are not enclosed in a fruit as they are in flowering plants. The best known gymnosperms are the conifers, the cone-bearing trees: pines, spruces, hemlocks, and firs. Most conifers are evergreens producing two kinds of cones, male and female. The seeds develop between the scales of the female cones; shake a mature cone vigorously and winged seeds will fall out. There are about 650 species of gymnosperms.

Angiosperms:
Covered Seeds

The flowering seed plants are the *angiosperms* (AN-gee-ah-sperms; from the Greek *angion:* case, and *sperma:* seed), a term describing seeds in a protective covering. This subgroup constitutes about half of all the known plant species today. Trees, shrubs, herbs, and grasses are angiosperms.

The Rose
Queen of the Seed Plants

All have flowers which are sometimes not recognized as such, particularly in grasses, sedges, and some trees. The flower when fertilized develops into a fruit which contains seeds, like the seeds in an apple, the peas in a pod, and the kernels on corn.

SUMMARY:

The Plant Ladder of Life

The half-million known species of plants populating this planet may be arranged as a four-runged ladder of life, from the simple to the complex and from water to land. The lowest rung is occupied by the thallophytes, the algae and fungi; the next by the bryophytes, the liverworts and mosses in wetland residence; the third rung by the pteridophytes, the ferns and fern allies, amphibians among plants; and the top rung by spermatophytes, the seed-bearers, especially flowering plants, the land plants. The algae live in the water, the bryophytes at its edge, the pteridophytes on wet land, and the spermatophytes on dry land. The fern flock, the smallest of the four groups, is the in-between group, the link between the "wets" below and the "drys" above on this ladder of plant life.

Pteridophytes, in common with seed-bearers, are vascular plants. They have internal conducting and supporting tissues. It is these tissues that enable ferns and seed plants with their roots, stems, and leaves to attain great heights and stature and to dominate the land. Plants on the lower rungs are nonvascular, which keeps them close to the ground and water.

In today's world, ferns are far less successful than flowers as land plants, judging by their relative numbers. Only 5 percent of the vascular plants are ferns and 95 percent are flowers. A reason for their minority status in the world of land plants may be ascribed in part to the dependence of ferns on water for sexual reproduction, a topic which will be discussed later.

17

CHAPTER III

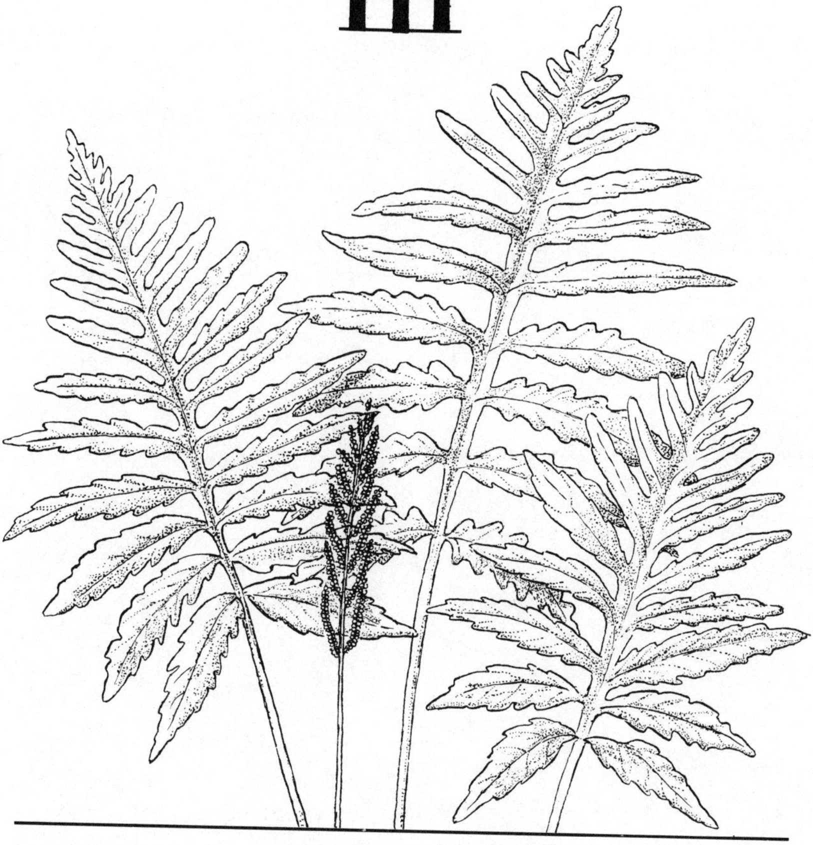

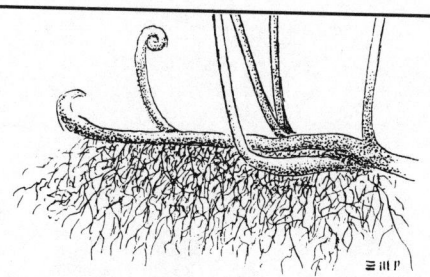

Sensitive Fern

Once-cut sterile frond
Beaded fertile frond

III

Structure of Ferns

$\mathcal{N}$ow that you have been introduced to some of the members of the plant kingdom and have some understanding of the place of ferns in the botanical scheme of things, we can discuss the fern family in depth. We will begin with the question, "What is a fern?"

The word "fern" comes from the old Anglo-Saxon *fearn* which means "feather," an apt description of the delicate plume-like appearance of most ferns. Botanists classify ferns with the pteridophytes (see page 13). The prefix *pterido* (teh-RID-owe) can be traced back to the ancient Greek word for "feather," and *phytes* meaning "plants" also has a Greek origin. Whether you call it by its Anglo-Saxon derivation or by its Greek counterpart, it's the same plant. A fern is a fern is a fern.

Calling a plant a fern does not automatically entitle it to membership in the fern fraternity. The asparagus fern and the sweet-fern are flowering plants, and ferns in name only. On the other hand, plants with a ferny, feathery appearance are not necessarily ferns. Such common and well-known flowering plants as Queen Anne's lace, yarrow, rue, buttercup, butter-and-eggs, and ragweed have that ferny look and are often mistaken for ferns. You cannot distinguish a fern from a flowering plant by its name or appearance. To know what makes a fern a fern you should learn "fernese," the language used by botanists in speaking about ferns (see Appendix B for a glossary of "fernese").

"Fern" Defined

To the **pteridologist** (ter-eh-DOLL-oh-jist), the fern expert, a fern is a vascular plant with roots, stem, and green leaves but no flowers, fruits, or seeds. What does this definition tell us? First, ferns are flowerless, fruitless, and seedless. You can be sure that a plant with flowers, fruit, or seeds is not a fern. The absence of these reproductive structures is a feature ferns share with thallophytes and bryophytes. However, all these nonflowering plants have one thing in common, they reproduce by spores (but more about spores in the next chapter). Unlike the other flowerless flora, both ferns and seed plants are proud possessors of a vascular system, a network of conducting tubes that transports water, minerals, and food up and down the roots, stem, and leaves of these plants. In addition, the stems of vascular plants also contain thick, strong tissues enabling them to grow vertically sometimes eighty feet toward the sun.

Fern Fiddlers: The Spring Symphony

Early spring is a good time to start finding and fiddling with ferns. This is the season of the year when a young fern's fancy lightly turns to unrolling its bud. Peeking through the damp, drab forest floors and fallow fields are fern buds which look like the heads of violins or fiddles; hence the name "fiddleheads." Some fiddleheads wear a white or tan wooly cloak that covers and protects a tightly rolled-up fernlet. Slowly the fiddleheads uncoil upward and unfurl their folded leaflets outward until the ferns reach their full height and breadth. Unfurling fronds is the fern's way of greeting the spring. This uncoiling method of growth is unique to ferns. Although not all ferns grow in fiddlehead fashion, a sure sign of a fern is the unfurling fiddleheads.

A curled-up frond is in each pinnae-packed Fiddlehead

Fiddleheads unfurling

Fern Feet: Rhizomes and Roots

Another fern feature is a fiddle-head growing directly from a stem called the **rootstock** or **rhizome** (RYE-zome). This structure usually grows horizontally either on or just below the surface of the soil. In addition to sprouting fiddleheads, rhizomes are storehouses of fern food made in the leaves and stem. Food-filled rhizomes are covered by thin, black, hairlike roots that anchor the plant to the soil from which they imbibe mineral water.

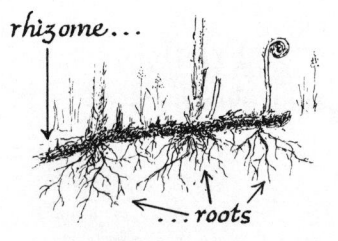

Rock-cap Polypody

At the end of the growing season, most ferns lose their leaves; they die right down to the roots and rhizomes which continue to live and grow from year to year, like the roots, trunk, and branches of a tree. Practically all ferns are perennials by virtue of their long-lived rhizomes that continuously produce new leaves each year.

Ferns that live in swamps, such as the cinnamon fern, grow large clumps of surface rootstocks and rhizomes that look like big, old shoe-brushes half submerged in mud. Some of these rootstock masses are as much as one hundred years old and look it—shabby, partially decayed, and withered, but with enough vitality to put forth beautiful bunches of tall, bright-green fern fronds every spring.

Because the annual crop of fiddleheads sprouts from the buds at one end of the rhizome while the other end dies, ferns appear to move to new quarters each season. The rockcap or common polypody fern, with a name that accurately describes its abode, is usually found sprawling over the top of a shaded rock. From exposed, spreading rhizomes, densely covered with a cinnamon colored fuzz, strings of bright, evergreen leaves are seen creeping in all directions.

Within the rhizome-root complex are groups of conducting tubes, the vascular bundles through which food, water, and min-

23

erals circulate. Vascular bundles in varying patterns can be seen by cutting across a rhizome with a sharp knife.

Fern Fronds:
Green Feathers

The green leaves or **fronds** (rhymes with ponds) are the most conspicuous and most beautiful part of the fern; they are also its food factory. Some of the frond-fabricated food is sent down to the rhizomes to be stored for the future, and some is used immediately for growing more and bigger fronds. Not all ferns are frondless in winter or the dry season. Some are evergreen; they hold on to their green fronds throughout the year. Evergreen ferns stand out as beautiful, bright green bouquets against the brown leaves and earth in late fall and the white snow and ice in the winter. The Christmas fern, common polypody, and marginal shield ferns are good examples of common perennial ferns you can enjoy year round.

A fern frond consists of a short stem or **stipe** (rhymes with pipe) and an enlarged green leafy portion, the **blade.** The stipe connects the blade to the rhizome and extends through the middle of the blade as the midrib or **rachis** (RAY-kiss); it is the backbone of the frond. From the rachis, veins extend to the margin of the blade forming distinctive patterns. In most ferns the veins are free, they do not connect with other veins to form a network; in others they do, forming beautiful patterns. Vein patterns are helpful hints in identifying ferns. Also, the stipe, rachis, and veins contain vascular bundles. By cutting across the stipe, these bundles can be seen in a variety of distinctive patterns helpful in recognizing some of the main groups of ferns. The stipe is frequently clothed in brownish, flaky scales, and may even have a light coat of hair.

Fern Fashions: Cut and Uncut Fronds

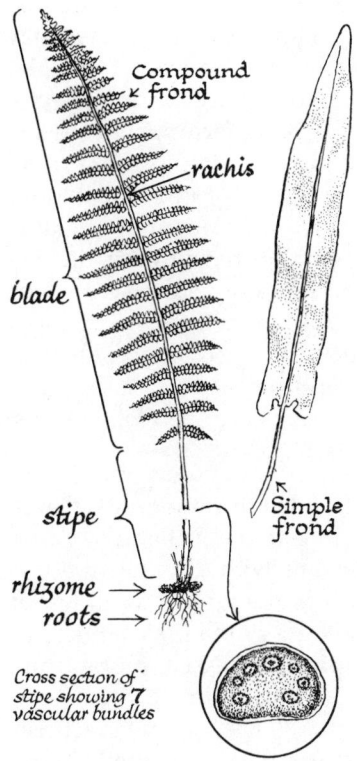

Compound frond

rachis

blade

stipe

Simple frond

rhizome →
roots →

Cross section of stipe showing 7 vascular bundles

Up to a certain point fronds follow the fern family formula: They grow from a stem; starting at the rhizome and extending into a broad, green, many veined frond. Beyond that, they may exhibit forms so unfernlike as to make you wonder about their fernness. They may be neither delicate in texture, nor finely cut, nor feathery in form. An example of a nonconformist is the walking fern, which has long, narrow, finely pointed, undivided fronds shaped like an arrowhead. Furthermore, where the tip of its arching fronds touches the earth, baby walkers, "toddlers," sprout. It is not unusual to see the "mother" plant out for a "walk," surrounded by her family of fernlets still attached to her "frond strings."

Another fern rebel is the climbing or Hartford fern, which neither looks nor acts like a fern. Its small fronds are ivy shaped with several extending, fingerlike lobes. It grows like a vine, turning, twisting, twining, and climbing over anything in its path.

The Climbing Fern climbs

The Walking Fern "walks"

25

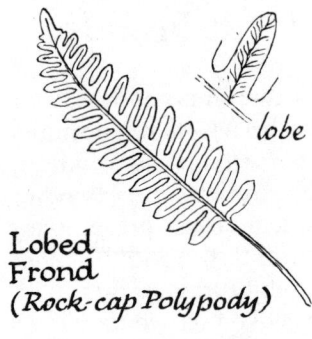

Lobed Frond
(Rock-cap Polypody)

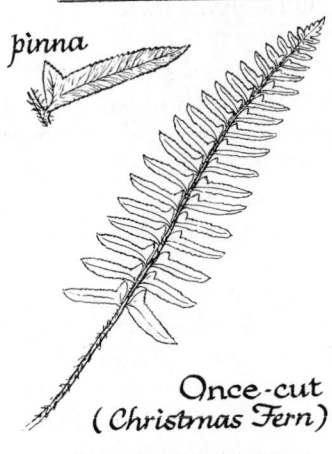

Once-cut
(Christmas Fern)

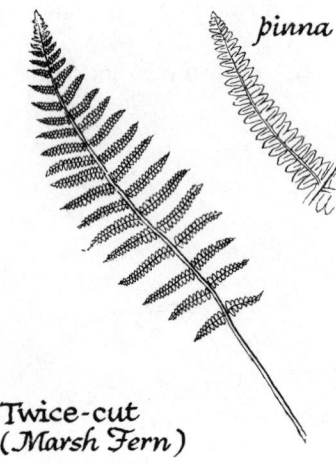

Twice-cut
(Marsh Fern)

"Fernlike" ferns are usually thought of as plants with finely divided, lacy, delicate fronds. However, fern blades may grade from undivided, **simple,** to once-, twice- and thrice-cut. The walking fern previously discussed has a simple entire frond giving it that unfernlike form. Ferns a little more fernlike in appearance have fronds divided into **lobes** on either side which do not reach the midrib. The rock-sitting common polypody and the sun-loving sensitive ferns are such lobed ferns.

In another group, the fronds are **compound,** that is cut into distinct and separate leaflets with divisions that extend to the midrib. Each leaflet is called a **pinna** (PIN-ah, singular; **pinnae:** PIN-ee, plural) from the Latin word meaning "feather." The evergreen Christmas fern with its stuffed Christmas stocking-shaped pinna, and the ebony spleenwort with its dark-brown, shiny stipe and its Christmas fern-looking pinnae have once-cut fronds.

The pinna may be divided again; these subleaflets are **pinnules** (PIN-yules, small feathers) or segments. The marsh fern that thrives in sunny, moist meadows, and the cinnamon fern that grows in clusters in almost every swamp in this country are representatives of the twice-cut ferns.

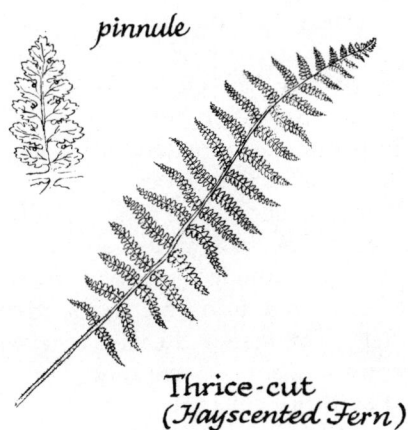

pinnule

Thrice-cut
(*Hayscented Fern*)

Then there are thrice-cut ferns, the laciest and ferniest of the ferns. Their pinnules are further dissected into **pinnulets.** The hay-scented fern grows like a weed in dry woods and fields, and the lady fern prefers moist, shaded and unshaded settings; they are both thrice cut.

SUMMARY:

Fern Structure

A fern is a large-leafed green plant that reproduces by spores. It has a vascular system that conducts food, water and minerals throughout its leaves, stems and roots. The leaves or fronds of most ferns develop in a distinctive and characteristic manner; the immature fronds are tightly packed in fiddleheads which unroll and unfold as the fronds grow upward and outward.

The fronds arise directly from stems or rhizomes which usually grow horizontally either on or just below the surface of the ground. Rhizomes are covered with fine roots which anchor the fern and also absorb water and minerals from the soil. Ferns, for the most part, are perennials; most lose their fronds at the end of the growing season but retain roots and rhizomes from which new fronds grow the following year; a few retain fronds, rhizomes and roots; these are the evergreen ferns.

The most prominent part of a fern is the frond which makes food and produces spores. A fern frond consists of a short stem or stipe connected to a broad leafy portion, the blade. The stipe runs through the middle of the blade as the midrib or rachis. Veins are slender bundles of conducting tubes, extending from the rachis to the edge of the blade in distinctive patterns.

Fern fronds vary considerably in size and shape. They range from tiny grasslike structures to large finely divided ones. The blade may be simple, that is, undivided or divided into lobes that do not extend to the rachis. The blade may also be compound, cut into distinct and separate leaflets or pinnae and called twice-cut fronds. The pinnae in lacy ferns are again dissected into sub-leaflets or pinnulets, and grouped as thrice-cut ferns.

Now to answer the question, "What is a fern?" look for a combination of the following features:

1. A network of vascular bundles connecting roots, stem and leaves.

2. Uncoiling fiddleheads growing from rhizomes either at or near the ground.

3. A pattern of (a) simple, (b) forking, or (c) netted frond veins.

4. Spores present either on the underside or on separate fronds (to be discussed in the next chapter).

CHAPTER
IV

Lady Fern

Thrice-cut blade with lax tips;
pinnules toothed

*straight or hooked sori
on veins of pinnules*

IV

Life Cycles of Ferns

*U*ntil the middle of the last century, the sex life of ferns was a complete mystery. Unlike most of the plants around us, ferns are flowerless and seedless, and therefore regarded as unusual. The discovery that ferns lead a double life, one public and the other private, solved this puzzle and revealed that they lead a secret sex life. It was found that there are two separate and distinctly different stages in the life of a fern. The first phase centers around the ferns you see and know. On their underside or on separate fronds, brown spots or masses develop. These are the source of the second phase, which was the missing link—and for very good reasons. It involves a tiny green plant completely hidden or camouflaged by the bed of green mosses in which it frequently "hides," and is not recognized as a link in the life of a fern. It is during this heretofore undiscovered stage that ferns enjoy a sex life and sexual activities. Most astonishing was the revelation that the pattern of sexual reproduction in ferns is strikingly similar to that in animals, including humans. There are sex organs, sex cells, fertilization, a developing young attached and fed by the "mother," and finally an independent adult capable of repeating the cycle of fern life.

Sori: Stacks of Spore Sacs

Now let us go back and fill in the details of fern fertility starting with the developing fronds. As spring unfolds, green fern fronds uncoil and unfurl and stand up straight and tall. Fernlets grow into adolescents and begin to show signs of maturity. Tiny green bumps which soon turn brown appear on the underside of most fronds or on separate fronds. They are not developing acne (pim-

31

Indusia

 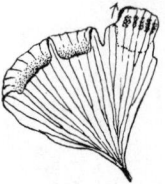  

*indusium attached
at one side*   *false indusium
(curled margin)*   *indusium
missing*   *indusium attached
centrally*

ples) or a rash or a fatal fern disease; these spots are **sori** (SAW-rye, plural; **sorus:** SAW-russ, singular; from the Greek word meaning "heap") or fruiting dots. This common name is a mistake; it is misleading since ferns do not bear fruit.

To the naked eye, sori are fuzzy brown spots or streaks. With a magnifying glass you can see that some sori are covered by a thin membrane called the *indusium* (in-DEW-zee-yum singular: *indusia:* in-DEW-zee-a, plural; from the Latin word meaning "undergarment" or covering). This covering may take the shape of a shield, a kidney, a crescent, or it may be missing. It may be attached on one side like an ear, or in the middle like an

Sorus

*Cross section showing
sporangia with indusium
covering*

umbrella; or the edge of the frond may be folded over the sori forming a false indusium. These indusium features are important clues in identifying ferns.

Spore Cases and Spores:
Storing and Scattering Spores

Closer examination discloses that sori consist of masses of spore cases or **sporangia** (spaw-RAN-gee-ah, plural; **sporangium:** spaw-RAN-gee-yum, singular; from the Greek *spora:* seed and *angeion:* vessel), another misnomer from the past when spores were thought to be seeds. With a more powerful magnifier, a sporangium appears to be a sac filled with microscopic spherical objects, **spores.**

SPORANGIUM SLING-SHOT

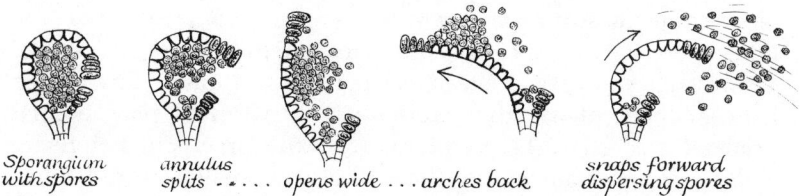

Sporangium with spores   *annulus splits* - • . . . *opens wide* . . . *arches back*   *snaps forward dispersing spores*

Sporangia not only store spores, but some have an ingenious mechanism for discharging and dispersing them. When the spores are ripe, the vertical belt of thick-walled cells around the spore case, the **annulus** (AN-you-liss) breaks at one point and slowly bends backward, tearing the case apart. Most of the spores stick to the pouch-shaped section of the split sporangium at the extended end of the annulus. Then suddenly the annulus snaps forward and like a slingshot, hurls the spores into the air, where they are scattered by the winds.

You can witness this spore-scattering spectacle by placing a frond fragment containing ripe, brown sori on a piece of white paper under a microscope and shining a light on it. As the heat of the light dries the sori, you can see sporangia popping one after the other like a string of silently exploding firecrackers. The released spores are too small and move too quickly to be seen under the microscope. However, if you place a container over the fern frond, with the sori face down on white paper for a few hours, you will observe an accumulation of brown dust. This consists of thousands of fern spores scattered about by the snapping sporangia.

The shape, size, color, and location of sporangia are basic in the identification of ferns. A single fern produces millions of microscopic spores which are airborne and float about at the mercy of the slightest breeze. Eventually they drift to earth; what happens to them next depends upon the landing field. Unless a spore finds a warm, moist haven, it remains a spore. Being a single cell enclosed in a tough, weatherproof covering, a spore can withstand extremes in temperature and drought for long periods of time, sometimes years. Most spores never make it and eventually die. The spore that touches down at the right time and in the right place comes to life and begins to grow.

33

Sprouting Spores and Sexy Prothalli

Now comes a surprise. You would expect that great ferns from little spores grow, if for no other reason than ferns sire spores. This is not the case. Instead, a spore grows into a tiny, green, heart-shaped plant, the **prothallus** (pro-THALL-us, singular; **prothalli:** pro-THALL-eye, plural; from the Greek *pro:* before and *thallus:* young branch). Prothalli are very small, about 1/4 inch across, and frequently live in mud or beds of mosses where they can easily be missed or mistaken for a bit of green fluff.

Few people have seen them and fewer know what they are. When prothalli are found, it is hard to believe that they are in any way related to ferns, since they are so unlike their parent.

A prothallus is a simple green plant without true roots, stem, or leaves, or a conducting system. It looks and lives like a little liverwort, for which it is often mistaken. The underside is covered with a mat of hairlike structures, **rhizoids** (RYE-zoids); they anchor the prothallus to the moist soil and absorb water and minerals for photosynthesis. The sex organs of this love symbol are also hidden on the underside. Near the base of the prothallus are the male sex organs, the **antheridia** (an-thur-ID-ee-ah, plural; **antheridium:** an-thur-ID-ee-yum, singular) where **sperms,** the male gametes or sex cells are generated. Fern sperms are corkscrew-shaped microscopic cells with a tuft of hairlike structures at one end for swimming. When the sperms mature, the antheridia open, releasing these cells,

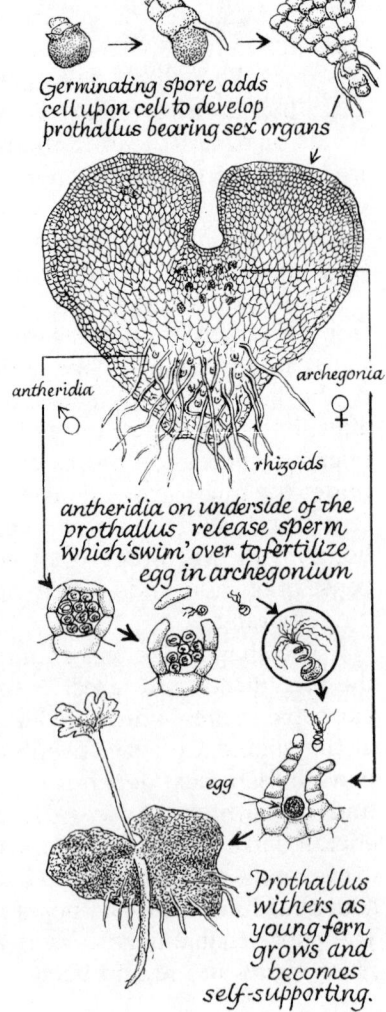

Germinating spore adds cell upon cell to develop prothallus bearing sex organs

antheridia

archegonia

rhizoids

antheridia on underside of the prothallus release sperm which 'swim' over to fertilize egg in archegonium

egg

Prothallus withers as young fern grows and becomes self-supporting.

which begin to swim spirally toward the notch of the prothallus. This is the locale of the female sex organs, the **archegonia** (arc-kah-GO-knee-ah, plural; **archegonium:** arc-kah-GO-knee-yum, singular). At the base of each flask-shaped archegonium sits the **egg,** the female gamete. As eggs mature, a chemical is released into the water that excites the sperms and enables them to locate the archegonia and swim directly toward them. The first sperm to reach the entrance of the chimney-shaped archegonial neck swims down it, fusing with the waiting egg and winning the reproduction race. The slower sperms, the "also-rans," quickly die. Out of this happy union of sperm and egg, a baby fern is born. At first the fernlet is attached to and fed by the parent prothallus. The green fernlet soon grows its own roots, stem, and fronds, and becomes self-sufficient and independent of "Mother Prothallus."

Alternating Generations in Ferns:
The Double Life

The life history of ferns is long and complicated. Ferns lead a double life, a conspicuous stage followed by an inconspicuous stage. The large, familiar fern is the spore-producing plant and is therefore called the **sporophyte** (SPO-row-fight; from the Greek *sporo:* seed and *phyton:* plant), a misnomer since ferns do not have seeds. The spores grow into tiny prothalli, the **gametophyte** (ga-ME-tow-fight; from the Greek *gameto:* marriage and *phyton:* plant), the gamete-generating plant where sperms fertilize eggs and begin the next generation. Thus, the frond makes spores, the spores make the prothalli, the prothalli make gametes, the gametes make the new plant, and the new plants repeat the cycle. In short, the sporophyte gives rise to the gametophyte which in turn gives rise to the next generation of sporophytes. This is what is meant by alternation of generation, the sporophyte-gametophyte sequence.

Fronds:
Sporeless and Sporefull

The fronds of most ferns look alike and act alike; they make food and bear spores. However, if you look on the underside of mature fronds you find that some species have sori and some do not. Those with sori are the **fertile** or reproductive fronds; those with-

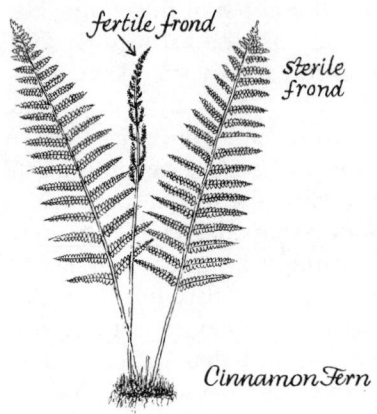

fertile frond

sterile frond

Cinnamon Fern

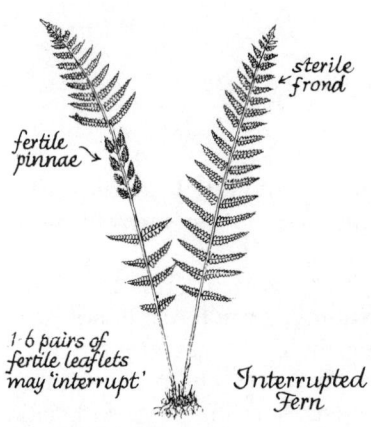

fertile pinnae

sterile frond

1 6 pairs of fertile leaflets may 'interrupt'

Interrupted Fern

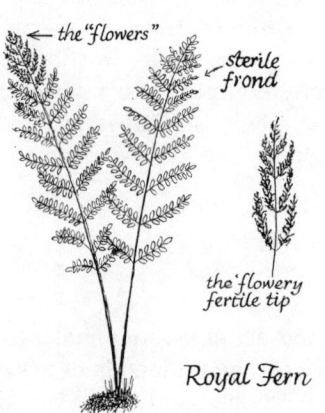

the "flowers"

sterile frond

the flowery fertile tip

Royal Fern

THE OSMUNDAS

36

out sori are the **sterile** or vegetative fronds. Sterile and fertile fronds may be slightly or strikingly different in appearance. In some ferns, the fertile fronds or the fertile parts of a frond are masses of sori brown or gold in color and easily distinguished from the green sterile sporeless fronds or leaflets. In others, the spores are on the underside of the upper pinnae.

The interrupted fern gets its name from the fact that there are a few pairs of brown fertile pinnae near the middle of the frond that stand out vividly between the sterile green pinnae above and below. In the royal fern, the fertile pinnae are at the top of the frond and appear as a terminal cluster of light brown "flowers." This fern is mistakenly called the "flowering fern," a botanical blunder since ferns are ferns, flowers are flowers, and never the twain mix.

The fronds of the ostrich, sensitive, and cinnamon ferns are either entirely fertile or sterile, either brown or green. The fertile fronds of the cinnamon fern are cinnamon-colored "sticks" standing erect in the middle of a clump of bright-green, sterile fronds. The dark-brown, fertile fronds of the ostrich fern are also surrounded by a circle of tall, dark-green plume-shaped fronds.

Numerous short chains of brown, bead-shaped sporangia make up the fertile fronds of the sensitive fern, entirely unlike the green, sterile fronds with their winged lobes. The fertile ostrich and sensitive fronds continue to live long after the green sterile fronds have died, and may be found almost any time of the year.

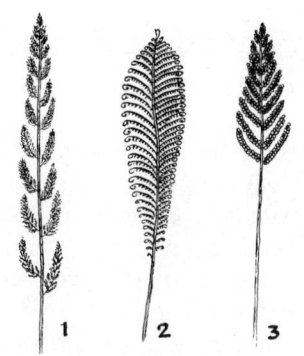

The Cinnamon (1), Ostrich (2), and Sensitive Ferns (3) all have separate fertile fronds.

Sexual Short Cuts:
Without Spores and Without Gametes

The sporophyte-gametophyte sexual cycle of ferns is extremely complex and beset by many dangers. There may be many slips twixt spore and sporophyte. Spores may not find suitable growing quarters; and when they do, there might not be enough water for fern sperms to "swim" to the egg and fertilize it. Such generation gaps break the sex cycle and may spell death for the plant.

Ferns have devised ingenious alternatives for cutting reproductive red tape. In some species, spores grow into sterile prothalli; they develop sexless sex organs unable to produce eggs or sperms. Instead, the prothalli produce buds, usually on the underside near the notch where archegonia, female sex organs, normally develop. The bud grows directly into a fern frond, a sporophyte. This variation on the sex story is called **apogamy** (ah-POG-ah-me; from the Greek *apo:* away from, and *gamy:* marriage). The new sporophyte develops from a bud produced by a sterile gametophyte without sex.

Another variation on the alternation of generation theme is **apospory** (ah-POS-pa-ree; from the Greek *apo:* away from, and *spory:* seeds). In this process, the fronds produce prothalli directly and the prothalli produce archegonia with eggs that grow into sporophytes without fertilization. Both sporophyte spores and gametophyte sperms are bypassed.

Apogamy and apospory are alternate asexual reproductive routes traveled by many ferns at least part of the time, especially when sexual methods are not favored: in dry, cold, dark settings or conditions.

Vegetative Reproduction:
A Chip Off the Old Fern

Most ferns are perennials; they live from year to year, skipping the gametophyte stage entirely and producing new sporophytes asexually from parts of the parent plant. A snip of the old sporophyte grows into a complete new sporophyte. In this method called vegetative reproduction, or natural cloning, the offspring is a carbon copy of the single parent. The vegetative road is more rapid and more certain than the sporophyte-gametophyte route.

A very common natural method of asexual reproduction among ferns is the repeated branching of rhizomes. As the older parts die, the rhizome separates into independent plants by runners and root buds. The ostrich fern sends out long underground runners (rhizomes) which take root some distance from the parent and up pops a bevy of new plants. The walking fern frond touches the ground with its long tip on which there is a bud, and as if by magic a new "walker" appears. The bulblet bladder fern grows little buds called bulblets on the underside of the frond; these fall off and take root. This fern can also reproduce by rhizomes and by spores; it has triple life insurance.

The subterranean rhizomes of the Ostrich Fern extend in all directions

pinna

bulblet

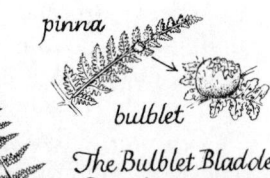

The Bulblet Bladder Fern insures reproduction with a "bud" on the underside of some of its pinnae

Obviously, ferns have backup systems of reproduction. If one fails, there are alternatives. Reproduction is much too important to be left to spores alone.

The Walking Fern develops baby ferns at its leaf tips

Sexual and Asexual Reproduction:
Today and Tomorrow

The reproductive repertoire of ferns includes sexual and asexual acts, both of which play a part in the story of the species' struggle for survival over long periods of time. In asexual reproduction, "chips" off the old fern appear as exact duplicates of the single parent fern. This sameness is not a problem as long as the environment remains the same. Other things being equal, what is good for the single parent is good for its clone. However, things do not remain the same or equal for very long. The "chip" may fall on hard times or unfriendly places; and what was good for the single parent may not be good for the clone.

Sexual reproduction in ferns promotes differences between parent and offspring, in contrast to asexual reproduction, which maintains sameness. Differences between male and female parents or parts are built into their sex cells, combined and recombined in the fertilized egg, and expressed in the offspring. These differences become more evident when the sperms come from one kind of fern, the eggs from another close relative, and the offspring is a product of such mixed marriages, a hybrid.

Sex insures variety, which is the spice of life. Being different is an asset when the environment changes; new approaches and new faces are necessary to meet new situations. Thus, to meet the sameness of the day-to-day existence, asexual reproduction provides the *modus operandi*. To deal with the inevitable long-range changes, sexual reproduction is the answer. Both are indispensable for survival: asexual for the present and sexual for the future.

SUMMARY:

The Life History of Ferns

Ferns reproduce both sexually and asexually. The sex life cycle consists of two consecutive connected generations of plants. One is the large, familiar fern whose mature fronds bear spores; this is the sporophyte, the spore-generating generation. The spores are shed, fall to the ground, and develop into tiny, green, heart-shaped, independent plants, the prothalli. They develop male and female sex organs in which sperms and eggs, the gametes, are produced. The gamete-generating prothallus is the gametophyte generation. Fertilization, the fusion of sperms and eggs, occurs on the underside of the prothalli in the archegonium. The fertilized egg grows into the next generation sporophyte, which at maturity produces spores and repeats the alternation of generation—the sporophyte-gametophyte cycle.

Although most ferns develop spores on the underside of their green fronds, some have completely separate sterile and fertile fronds or fertile parts of sterile fronds.

There are modifications of the alternation of generation cycle which cut through reproductive red tape. One is apogamy, the development of the sporophyte from a bud on the gametophyte rather than from a fertilized egg. Another is apospory, the development of a gametophyte directly from the sporophyte, bypassing the spore stage. These alternate reproductive routes are more common than is generally realized.

Finally, ferns do not depend completely on sexual reproduction; most are perennials. New plants grow asexually from parts of the "mother" plant, from rhizomes by runners and root buds, from fronds by buds, bulblets, and rooting tips. Natural cloning produces an offspring identical with the single parent plant.

Both asexual and sexual methods of reproduction are essential for the survival of ferns. Asexual reproduction produces clones, carbon copies of their single parent, capable of living under constant conditions. Sexual reproduction promotes variety among offspring capable of adapting and surviving under changing conditions; it is life insurance for the future.

LIFE CYCLE OF A FERN

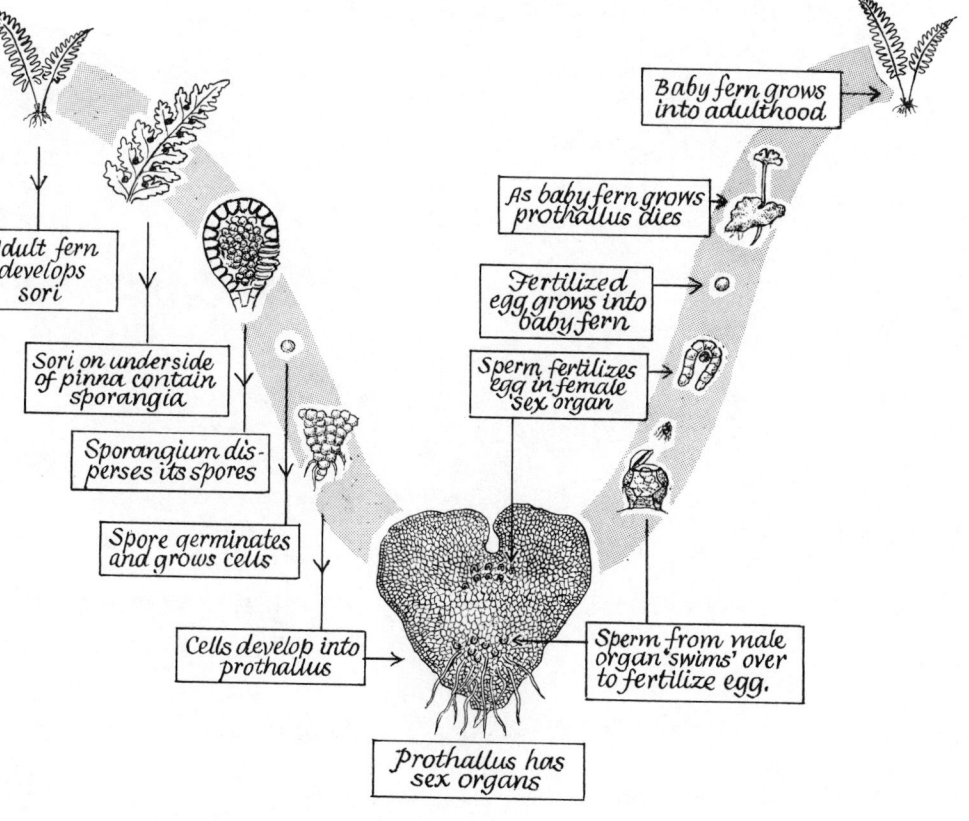

Adult fern develops sori

Sori on underside of pinna contain sporangia

Sporangium disperses its spores

Spore germinates and grows cells

Cells develop into prothallus

Prothallus has sex organs

Sperm from male organ 'swims' over to fertilize egg.

Sperm fertilizes egg in female sex organ

Fertilized egg grows into baby fern

As baby fern grows prothallus dies

Baby fern grows into adulthood

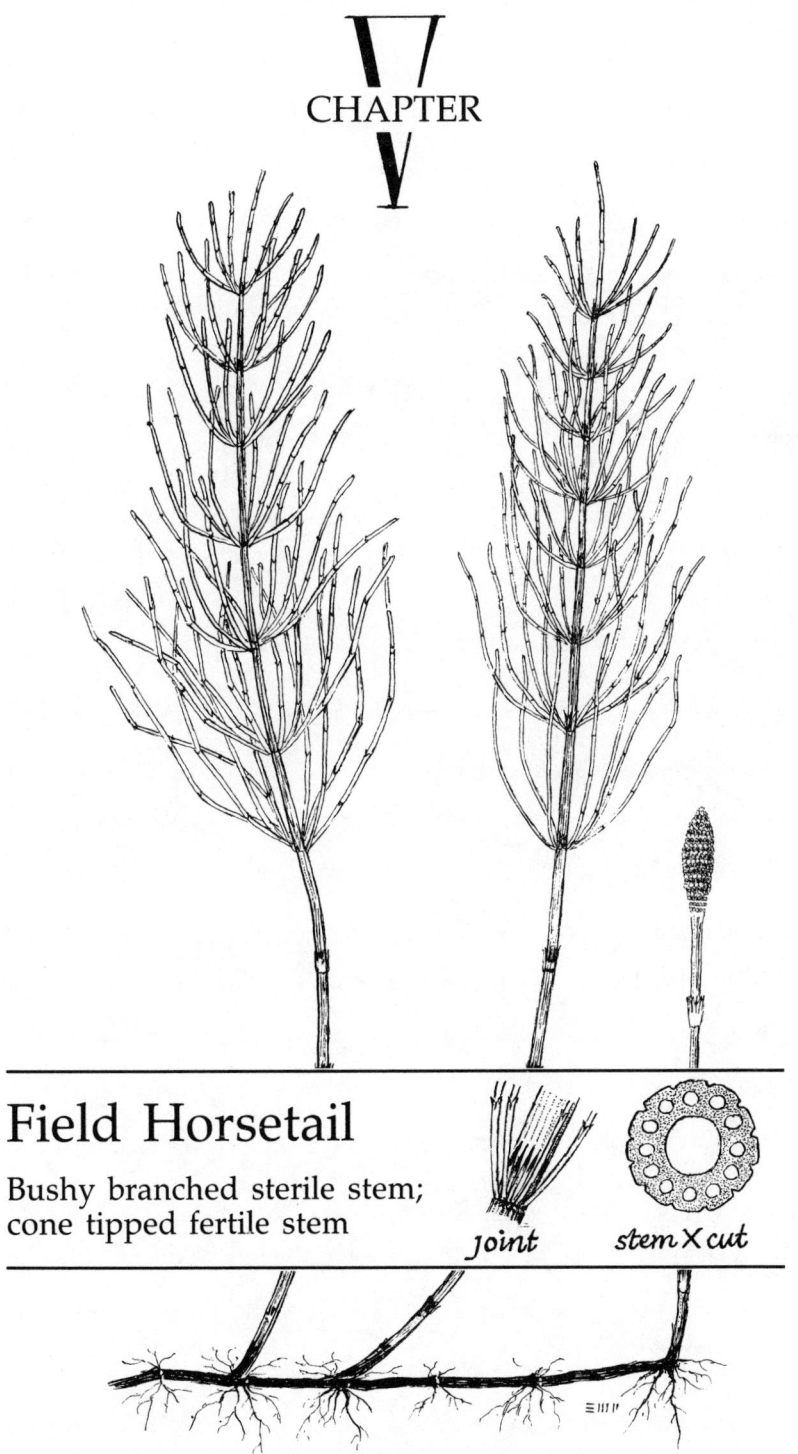

CHAPTER V

Field Horsetail

Bushy branched sterile stem;
cone tipped fertile stem

joint

stem X cut

V

Fern Relatives

The fern fraternity, the pteridophytes, may be divided into two major subgroups: the **true ferns** and the **fern allies.** The easiest way to tell them apart is by their fronds. True ferns put forth large, flat fronds with branching veins; the fern allies display small needlelike or scalelike leaves with a single unbranched vein. Despite differences in appearance, true ferns and their allies have a common pteridophyte tie. Both are vascular with the same life history of alternating generations; a large sporophyte plant produces spores which grow into small, inconspicuous, gamete-producing gametophytes where eggs fertilized by sperms develop into the next generation sporophyte. The repeating life pattern is a sporophyte-gametophyte-sporophyte-gametophyte sequence.

The fern allies are classified into five botanical families: **horsetails, clubmosses, spikemosses, quillworts,** and **whiskbroom ferns.** Another group, the **water ferns,** which are classified as true ferns is added. Although water ferns have flat fronds and forked veins, they are so unfernlike in appearance, habitat, and spore formation, they seem to fit better with fern allies (see page 55).

As their common names reveal, these distant relatives of the true ferns are unfernlike in appearance. Clubmosses have a mossy look, with club-shaped sporangia, and are mistakenly called mosses. Some clubmosses resemble strings of pygmy pines; others

  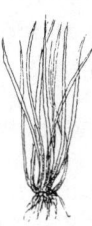 

Horsetail   *Clubmoss*   *Spikemoss*   *Quillwort*   *Whiskbroom Fern*

45

look like miniature cedar trees, inspiring such names as running pine and ground cedar. Quillworts are shaped like porcupine spines or quills; and horsetails were probably named by a horseman. Water ferns are easily mistaken for floating mats of mosses or four-leaved clovers. The most unusual are the whiskbroom ferns.

Whiskbroom Ferns:
Simplest Vascular Plants

It is out of respect for their rarity and simplicity that the whiskbroom ferns, *Psilotum* (sigh-LOW-tum) are discussed. Their alleged ancestors were found among the earliest known vascular plants. However, only one species grows in the United States, and it resides in the damp woods and swamps of the South. No fossils connecting this species to its presumed forebears have been found as yet. The lack of such links raises some questions about the origin and evolution of whiskbroom ferns.

The stem of this primitive pteridophyte, which is about one foot tall (30 centimeters), is green, wiry, and repeatedly forked, giving it the appearance of a green whiskbroom or a bunch of green twigs. Tiny, green scale-like bracts grow alternately along the upper stems. Roots and leaves are lacking, and its vascular system is simple.

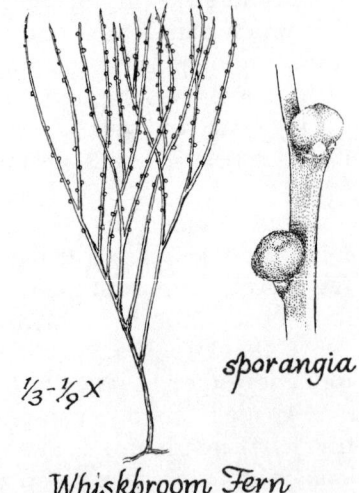

⅓-⅑ X

sporangia

Whiskbroom Fern

Its claim to pteridophyte status are the spores it produces and the gametophytes into which the spores germinate. Three chambered, solitary sporangia are borne on the upper branches. Its spores sprout underground into nongreen, long-lived prothalli, fed by soil fungi with which they take up company. Puny, primitive prothalli produce both sperms and eggs; the sperms equipped with many whiplike structures "swim" to the egg, fertilize it, and a new generation of whiskbroom ferns is born. Whiskbroom ferns are the simplest of the pteridophytes and the most primitive of the vascular plants alive today.

Horsetails and Scouring Rushes:
Rushes and Brushes

Horsetails, *Equisetum* (eh-kwa-SEAT-um), are the survivors of a long line of pteridophytes that trace their lineage back to the Coal Age. Hundreds of millions of years ago their giant ancestors filled the primeval forests. So numerous were they that in some parts of the world their fossilized spores and spore cases alone formed the coal deposits. Except for shrinking in size, horsetails have not changed very much since the Coal Age and are thought of as living fossils.

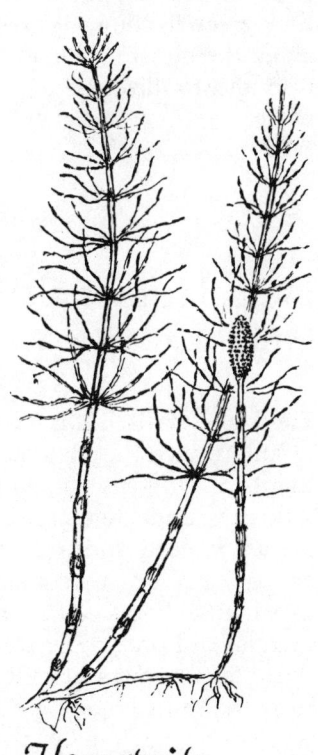

You can recognize horsetails by their erect, hollow, bamboo-like grooved stems with joints ringed by a collar of black and white, tiny, toothlike leaves. Some species display whorls of long, needlelike, bushy branches around the base of the joints between the ring of the leaves. Species without these branches are usually called scouring rushes to distinguish them from the bushy branched horsetails.

Horsetails grow in "herds" from underground, horizontally spreading systems of jointed rhizomes. At these joints, roots push downward, and aerial stems stretch upward above the ground. Aerial stems may be green or nongreen, with or without cone-shaped sporangia at their tips. The rhizomes are perennial, whereas the aerial stems are annuals and die down every year.

Horsetails

Horsetail spores are unusually short-lived, thin-walled, and green since they contain chlorophyll. They have just a few days to get out of the sporangium and begin to grow, otherwise they die. Four long elastic strips sensitive to humidity, **elaters** are attached to each spore and coil around it in damp weather and uncoil when it is dry. The coiling and uncoiling help the spores to break out of the spore case quickly. The elaters also hold together several spores that develop into either male or female gametophytes. This togetherness promotes mating; that is, sperms and eggs are in close contact, assuring fertilization. Horsetails produce only one kind of spore from which two kinds of gametophytes or prothalli develop, male and female.

Horsetail prothalli are very small. The male prothallus is a tiny, ribbon-shaped, yellow-green plant whose **antheridia** (sperm-producing organs) turn out hundreds of spoon-shaped sperms armed with many whiplike structures for swimming. The female prothallus is larger, about 1/2 inch (1 centimeter) in length, and dark green in color. Its **archegonia** (egg-making organs) are located along the moist underside of the prothallus. The liberated sperms find and fertilize the egg, and the baby horsetail enters the race of life.

Field Horsetails:
Fertile and Sterile Stems

Field horsetails is the species you are most likely to encounter. Living in moist fields and meadows, and along railroad embankments, they "graze" contentedly in large, spreading "herds." Two kinds of aerial stems arise from the underground network of rhizomes. In early spring, appearing first, are the fertile stems, which are pink, topped by cone-shaped sporangia, and resemble jointed asparagus shoots. After attaining a height of 6 inches (15 centimeters) and producing and dispersing millions of horsetail spores, these fertile stems quickly "fade" away. The sterile stems arising from the same creeping rhizomes follow; they are pale green with whirls of long, bushy, needlelike branches at each joint, giving them that "horsetail" look. In some localities, horsetails spread so rapidly and aggressively that they become annoying weeds.

Scouring Rushes:
Nature's Sandpaper for Pots and Pipes

Another interesting species of horsetails is the common **scouring rushes.** Tiny, cone-shaped sporangia cover the tips of some of the branchless, hollow, jointed green stems that produce both food and spores on the same stalk. The ridged, grooved stems of scouring rushes contain deposits of sand. Early American colonists used these plants to scrub and scour pots and pans, as do campers today, who know "scouring rushes" when they see them. This natural sandpaper is also used to polish wood, file fingernails and trim reeds for woodwind instruments. Musicians know scouring rushes as "Dutch rushes" and to campers they are "dish washings." It may sound like a "horse tale," but young horsetails are poisonous to horses and cattle.

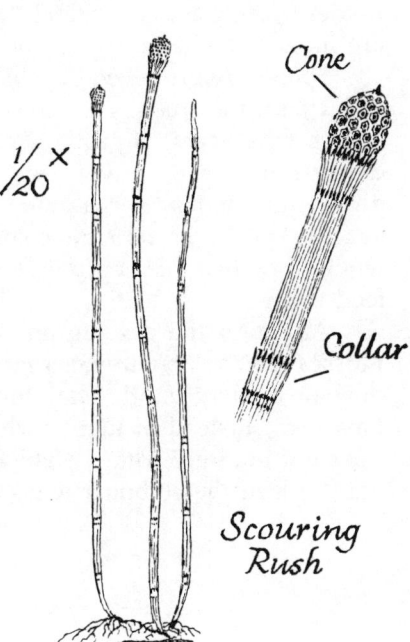

$\frac{1}{20} \times$

Cone

Collar

Scouring Rush

Clubmosses:
Pygmy Pines and Christmas Candles

The **clubmoss** clan (lycopods), *Lycopodium* (lie-koe-POE-dee-yum), is probably the best known among the fern allies. Their ancestors shared the Coal Age forests with horsetails; they, too, are just shrunken shadows of their forefathers. Fossilized clubmoss spores and sporangia are also a good part of today's coal deposits. Many clubmosses flourish on the floor of fertile forests, living as small, creeping, evergreen plants. Crowded, tiny, stemless, undivided leaves cover their stems in rows. The most common method of reproduction is by runners, stems that "run" along the ground slightly below or at the surface. The stem becomes longer each year as it grows faster at one end than it does at the other and the plants grow along the stem strung out in a row.

Club-shaped sporangia originate at the tips of the upright stems. Some sporangia are on slender stalks that resemble a candle holder bearing one to several "candles." In others, the sporangia are hidden, tucked away at the base of the upper leaves.

Spores are produced in prodigious quantities as a yellow powder. Unlike the green, short-lived, horsetail spores, some clubmoss spores take years to grow into a prothallus and more years to develop into a sporophyte. Two decades may elapse before a spore grows into the next generation sporophyte. In such slow-growing species, spores develop into colorless gametophytes underground, where they live like saprophytes or team up with soil fungi that feed them.

Although the sex life and life style of horsetails and club-mosses are similar, clubmoss gametophytes are colorless, and most develop underground. They tend to be smaller, and the sperms have two, instead of many, whiplike swimming structures. This does not interfere with the ability of the clubmoss sperms to find and fertilize the clubmoss eggs.

Common Clubmosses:
With and Without Clubs

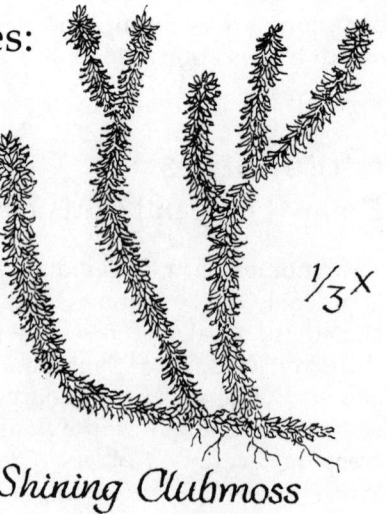

The **shining clubmoss** has hidden sporangia; they are concealed at the base of the upper leaves. Also found here are special buds which drop off and grow directly into new sporophytes asexually, without sexual entanglements. This lycopod without visible cones has 6-inch (15 centimeter) erect stems bristling with tiny, pointed, shiny evergreen leaves.

$\frac{1}{3}$ X

Shining Clubmoss

In the **stiff clubmoss,** another species of about the same height, slim, pointed, 1-inch (2.5 centimeter) "clubs" (cones) sit on top of the stiff, erect stem, which arises from thin, surface-running rhizomes.

Running cedar is a lycopod that holds four 1-inch to 2-inch (2.5-centimeter to 5-centimeter) "clubs" or "candles" on a long, slender-branched candle holder. Its stems spread out in fan fashion and are covered by short, flat, overlapping, scalelike leaves, similar to the leaves of cedar trees. This creeping, crawling, evergreen plant which grows irregularly in tangled masses, runs riot over the forest floor and is aptly called "running cedar." Used extensively for Christmas decorations, the running cedar has been all but wiped out by the wreath-makers (see page 197).

Ground pine, another lycopod which looks very much like running cedar displays two or three 1/2-inch to 1-inch (1-centimeter to 2.5-centimeter) candles in its candle holder. It also differs in that the horizontal and vertical stems are covered with pinelike evergreen leaves that stick out in all directions like tiny needles, instead of lying flat as they do in running cedar. Ground pine is also not running fast enough to outdistance the Christmas wreath shoppers.

½-¼X

Stiff Clubmoss

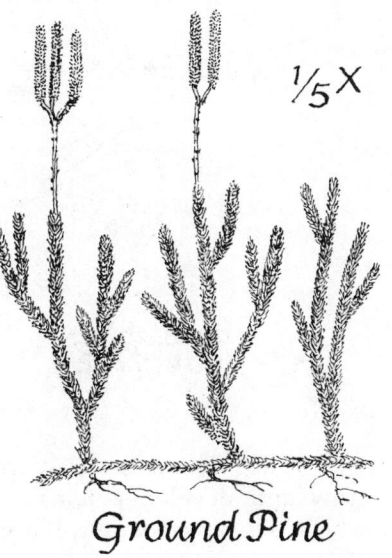

⅕X

Ground Pine

51

Spikemosses:
Male Microspores and Female Megaspores

The **spikemosses**, *Selaginella* (Sell-ah-je-NELL-ah), are first cousins to the clubmosses. Both have the same mossy, leafy appearance. The spikemosses, however, are smaller than their clubmoss cousins and lie closer to the ground. A few live in the dry areas of the West and Southwest, but most thrive in wet places and are easily confused with mosses and liverworts. Their ancestors also appear to be of Coal Age vintage.

Unlike the horsetails and clubmosses which make only one kind of spore, spikemosses generate two kinds: large female **megaspores** (MEG-ah-spores) and small male **microspores** (MY-crah-spores). These are found in separate sporangia at the base of the upper side of spikelike leaves at the tip of fertile stems. Also, the sporangia are square, instead of round as they are in clubmosses. Mature microspore cases (**microsporangia**) are filled with hundreds of thin-walled microspores which look like a fine orange powder. The megaspore cases (**megasporangia**) hold only four white or light-yellow thick-walled megaspores large enough to be seen with the naked eye.

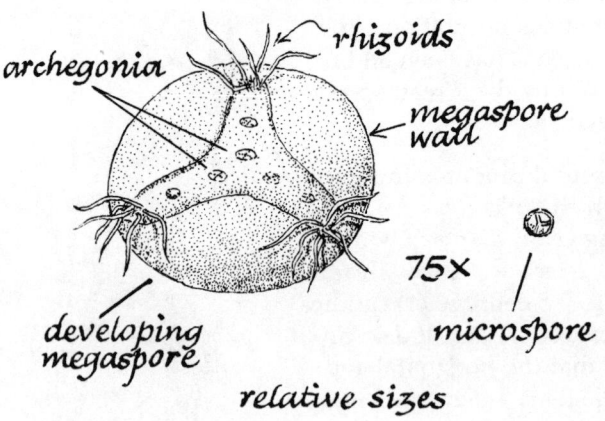

archegonia

rhizoids

megaspore wall

developing megaspore

75×

microspore

relative sizes

While still inside the sporangium, each megaspore begins to grow and develop a female gametophyte without chlorophyll which is retained within the megaspore wall for most of its life. However, continued growth causes the megaspore wall to crack, exposing a portion of the female gametophyte. It is on this exposed area that several egg-bearing archegonia develop.

Microspores also begin to develop while still in the sporangium. Each microspore (also without chlorophyll) forms a male gametophyte consisting of a single antheridium filled with many sperms. The microspores are shed at maturity; if they fall on a moist spot, the microspores absorb water, swell and their walls burst liberating the sperms. Equipped with two whiplike swimming structures, the sperm seek out the female gametophyte with its exposed archegonia and fertilize the egg. Protected by the thick megaspore wall and fed by the food stored in it, the fertilized egg begins its development inside the archegonium.

In some species, the megaspore containing the developing spikemoss is not shed until its roots and stem begin to appear. It then breaks loose, falls to the ground, and becomes an independent plant. The spikemoss saga reads in part like the Greek myth describing the birth of the goddess Athena, who sprang from the head of her father, the great god Zeus.

In general, the gametophytes of the spikemosses are extremely small, especially the male gametophyte, which is reduced to a single antheridium. The spores and the gametophytes they contain are held in the sporangium until fairly well advanced in their development. The gametophytes which are without chlorophyll are dependent upon the sporophyte "mother" plant. Life for the embryo spikemoss begins in a cradle, the archegonium of the female gametophyte, where it is protected and fed.

Spikemosses:
Wet and Dry

The **meadow spikemoss** is a moisture-seeking, creeping plant frequently found living in wet woods, swamps, meadows, and lawns. Its threadlike, spreading stems and branches are covered with tiny, very thin leaves in two sizes and in four rows. The sporangia are found at the base of special leaves at the tips of its semi-erect stems.

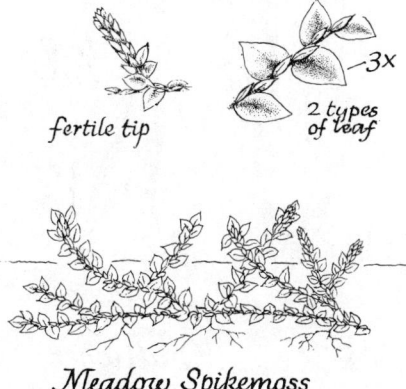

fertile tip

2 types of leaf —3x

Meadow Spikemoss

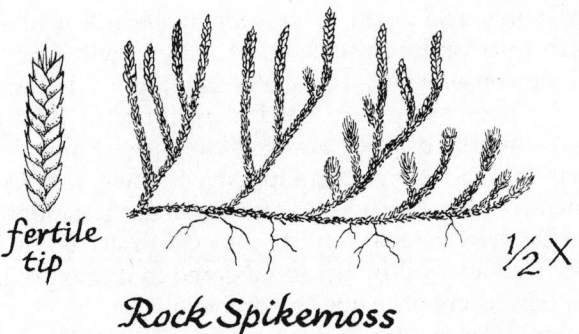

fertile tip

½ X

Rock Spikemoss

The **rock spikemoss,** in contrast, is less common and lives on dry rocks and sand. It frequently forms dense mats of gray-green, rigid, mosslike plants. Its stems are covered with crowded, overlapping, spiny leaves. The four-sided, erect stems bear sporangia on the upper surface, at the base of those leaves forming a terminal spike.

Quillworts:
Also with Microspores and Megaspores

In appearance the **quillworts,** *Isoetes* (eye-SEW-ah-teas), are the most unfernlike among the fern allies. Easily mistaken for tufts of grass or young onions, they grow either in or near water. Their long, stiff, hollow, slender, unbranched leaves are spoon-shaped at the bottom where they overlap in bulblike fashion. The youngest leaves are inside and the oldest outside. At the base is a fleshy, brownish, woody structure from which these leaves grow up and long, fleshy, forking roots grow down. Although their Coal Age ancestors were among the tallest trees in those extinct forests, modern quillworts rarely grow taller than 2 feet (60 centimeters). Like the spikemosses, quillworts have two kinds of spores: tiny male microspores and large female megaspores. Separate

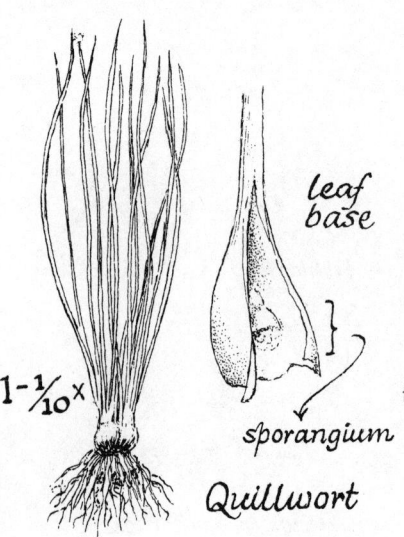

leaf base

1-¹⁄₁₀ˣ

sporangium

Quillwort

sex spore cases are located in pockets at the base of the leaves. Microspore cases are usually located in the pockets of the inner leaves and contain about a million microscopic microspores. Megaspore cases are in the pockets of outer leaves and contain fewer and larger spores, large enough to be seen with the naked eye. As in the spikemoss, each kind of spore develops its own kind of gametophyte with its own sex organs and sex cells.

The male gametophyte develops within the microspore and contains one antheridium that gives rise to four sperm cells. The female gametophyte also growing within the megaspore, forms several archegonia on the upper surface exposed by the rupturing of the spore wall.

Fertilization takes place when the walls of the microspore split open, releasing millions of spiral-shaped sperms, and the walls of the megaspore rupture, exposing the egg-containing archegonia to the sex-starved sperms. Life for the quillwort embryo begins in the archegonium of the female gametophyte where it is protected and fed by the "mother" sporophyte. It is not too long before the "baby" quillwort breaks out and becomes an independent sporophyte. However, liberation does not take place until the leaves holding these spore cases die and decay. Despite the great differences in appearance, the sex life of the quillworts and the spikemosses is strikingly similar and makes them close relatives.

Water Ferns:
Anchored and Free-Floating Ferns

Another uniquely different and unfernlike group are the **water ferns.** They are water dwellers with fronds that are either free-floating or anchored in mud by slender stalks. The flat, branched leaves and veins of the water fern places them with the true ferns. A reason for considering them with the fern allies is that they, like the spikemosses and quillworts, produce two kinds of spores: microspores and megaspores; true ferns make only one kind of spore. The spores of water ferns are produced in special chambers borne on special stalks.

Perhaps the most unusual members of this group are the **water clover** ferns, *Marsilea* (mar-SILL-ee-ah), which look like and are mistaken for four-leaved clovers or shamrocks. Creeping rhizomes rooted in the mud of shallow, fresh-water ponds and lakes send up slender stalks bearing sterile leaves divided into four leaflets. The leaves float on or just below the surface like water lilies. Spore cases resembling little beans contain microspore and megaspore compartments; they are attached by short, submerged stalks near the base of the floating fronds.

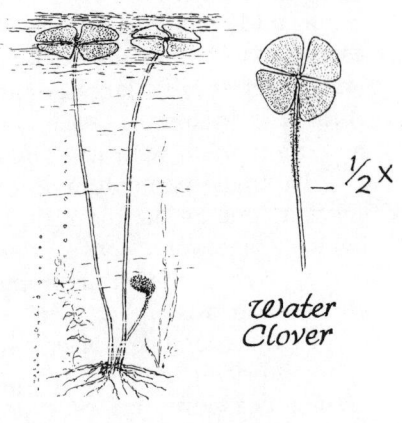

$\frac{1}{2}$X

Water Clover

Water spangles, *Salvinia* (sal-VIN-ee-ah), are free-floating, fast-growing plants that form thick mats on the surface of ponds, lakes, ditches, and dikes in the Southeast. Its fronds are a pair of roundish leaflets about 1/2 inch (1 centimeter) in diameter. The upper surfaces of the leaflets are covered with silvery, stiff hairs which make them waterproof. The third leaflet is divided into feathery, hairy, rootlike parts hanging below the surface of the water, between the two floating leaflets. From this junction, male and female sporangia of the same size and shape also dangle.

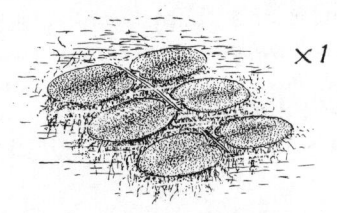

X1

Water Spangles

The third member of the water fern flotilla is the **mosquito fern,** *Azolla* (ah-ZOLL-ah), also a free-floater. Frequently they cover the surface of ponds, lakes, canals, and sluggish streams along the Atlantic coastline, forming mats so dense that presumably they smother mosquito larvae breeding in these waters. They are mossy-looking ferns with tiny, delicate, deeply-cleft,

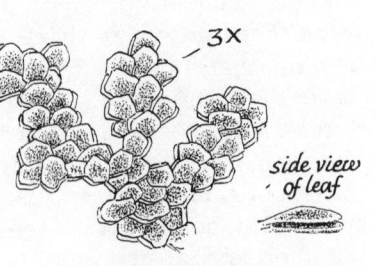

3X

side view of leaf

Mosquito Fern

overlapping leaflets arranged in two layers, like tiles on a roof. The upper leaflets which float are green, while the lower ones are submerged and colorless. Growing on fan-shaped branches, the leaflets often turn red in direct sunlight and bright green in the shade. Spore cases develop on the underside of the lower leaflets and come in two sizes: large, acorn-shaped cases that hold many microspores and smaller, spherical cases containing a single large megaspore. The tiny, upper, floating leaflets have a tiny compartment always occupied by a tenant, threads of blue-green algae. This algae "fixes" nitrogen; that is, it converts inert atmospheric nitrogen into active compounds that can be used by plants. The floating fern has the potential of decreasing the mosquito population and increasing our food supply.

SUMMARY:

Fern Allies

The pteridophytes may be divided into a large, well-known group of true ferns and five smaller groups of fern allies. True ferns are recognized by their broad leaves with branching veins; fern allies by needlelike or scaly leaves with single, unbranched veins.

The fern allies families are the whiskbrooms, horsetails, clubmosses, spikemosses, and quillworts. Water ferns which are true ferns, have been added. All are unfernlike in appearance and different from one another, but all have the same life cycle of alternating gametophyte-sporophyte generations.

The whiskbroom ferns are the simplest vascular plants known, with tiny, scalelike bracts, a simple conducting system, and no true roots or leaves. The only species alive today, grows in the South.

Horsetails are recognized by their hollow, ridged stems, with joints ringed by tiny black and white leaves. Above ground stems, green and nongreen, with and without terminal, cone-shaped sporangia, grow and spread from a network of underground rhizomes. Only one kind of green, short-lived spore is produced, which develops either into a tiny male or a female gametophyte. Field horsetails produce two kinds of stems: pink, fertile ones with cone-shaped sporangia; and green, sterile ones with whirls of long, green, bushy branches at each node. Scouring rushes are branchless with sandy stems, some of which are tipped with tiny sporangia.

Clubmosses are mossy, evergreen creepers. The sporangia are either at the base of tiny leaves near the tip of upright stems; in cone-shaped structures at the end of the stem; or on stalks above the stem, shaped like clubs or candles. The spores are slow growers; it may take more than two decades for spores to grow into sporophytes.

Spikemosses strongly resemble clubmosses, but unlike their close relatives, they have two kinds of spores, large female megaspores and small male microspores, in separate sporangia at the base of leaves. A female gametophyte develops within the megaspore and a male gametophyte within the microspore. Fertilization occurs in the archegonium of the megaspore where the baby spikemoss grows, develops, and is protected and fed by "mother" until it can take care of itself.

Quillworts, which resemble tufts of grass growing on or near water, also generate megaspores and microspores in separate sporangia. Fertilization and development within the megaspore follow the patterns of the spikemosses.

Water ferns which are aquatic true ferns, also produce microspores and megaspores in special, separate sporangia. Mosquito ferns and water spangles are free-floaters that form thick mats on the surface of ponds and lakes. Water clovers look like floating four-leaved clovers or shamrocks. They are rooted in the mud by slender stalks from which sporangia grow.

As a group, modern fern allies are the survivors of ancient species that filled the Coal Age forests for more than a hundred million years. They range from the simple whiskbroom ferns to the complex spikemosses and quillworts, with two kinds of spores, microscopic gametophytes, fertilization and development within sporangial walls, and dependent young sporophytes all of which point to the next higher group on the evolutionary ladder, the seed plants.

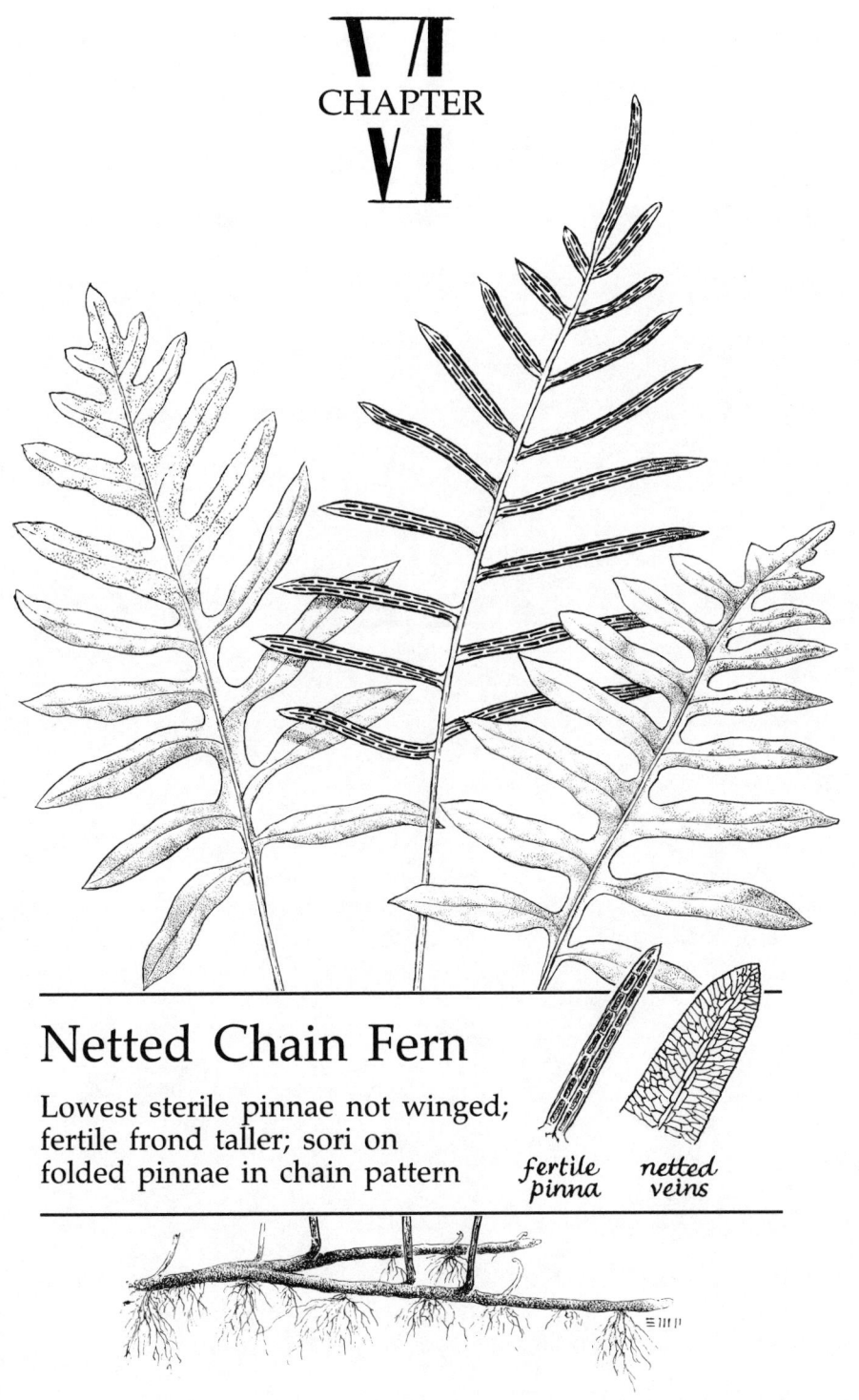

fertile
pinna

netted
veins

Netted Chain Fern

Lowest sterile pinnae not winged;
fertile frond taller; sori on
folded pinnae in chain pattern

VI

Ferns in the Evolution of Living Things

*W*e have explored the place of living ferns and their allies in the plant kingdom. It appears that as a group, pteridophytes are just about holding their own. Their comparatively small species-number may be an indication that ferns are a fading family. And yet at one time, the fern fraternity dominated the earth, just as flowering plants do today. A review of the history of life on this planet will help place pteridophytes in a proper perspective within the fourth dimension, time. A journey into the past may help us to understand how ferns came to be, how they rose to supreme heights, how they arrived at their present shrinking status, and possibly, what the future holds for them.

Birth of the Earth:
The Beginning

The Bible tells us that "In the beginning, the earth was without form and void, and darkness was upon the face of the deep." Scientists hypothesize that in the beginning there was no sun, no earth, and the universe was a huge cloud of gases whirling around in space. Slowly, over billions of years, the clouds contracted into denser and smaller masses which got hotter as they condensed. About 10 billion years ago, one of these glowing globes became our sun: and so a star was born. The remaining gases and dust around the newly-formed sun also clustered into several smaller, spinning spheres; these became the planets of our solar system. One of these hot, gyrating globes, about 100 million miles from the sun, was our planet Earth. To the best of our present knowledge, the solar system with its planets and satellites came into being about 4.5 billion years ago.

First Life: Water Inhabitants

Over the next billion years the earth slowly cooled down enough to acquire a thin crust. Our planet Earth could easily be mistaken for a steaming, shriveled sphere, suspended in space. Sometime

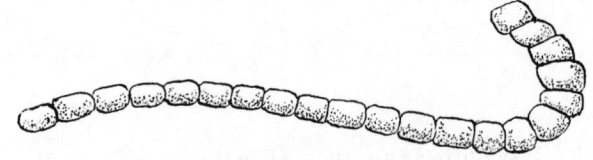

Microfossil cell chains indicate life is over 3.5 billion years old

toward the end of the first billion years, life appeared—primitive, bacteria-like beings. Exactly when this took place is not known, but it was more than 3.5 billion years ago. This estimate is based on very recent discoveries in northwestern Australia of fossils believed to be the remains of photosynthetic bacteria found in rocks 3.5 billion years old. It is assumed, therefore, that simpler forms of life, nonphotosynthetic bacteria, existed and predated these solar-energy-trapping organisms. Similar fossils in rocks somewhat younger were found in Ontario, Canada, and in South Africa. Seemingly, life may have arisen in several places early in the history of the earth.

During the next billion years, the earth underwent continuous changes and its inhabitants multiplied and diversified. A billion years ago, the shallow seas and ocean inlets were crowded with all kinds of algae—green, gold, red, and brown—and many kinds of primitive, soft-bodied animals. But they were all water-bound and remained so until about 500 million years ago when plants began to invade the barren, lifeless land. For at least 90 percent of the time since the first organisms appeared on earth, living things led a strictly aquatic life.

Ancient Atmosphere: No Oxygen

Why did it take so long for plants to find their way out of the water on to the land? We really do not know the answer, but we can make several educated guesses. There is some evidence suggesting that the ancient atmosphere may have contained water

(H_2O), ammonia (NH_3), methane (CH_4), and some hydrogen (H_2). Unlike the present atmosphere, there was no free oxygen (O_2), the gas vital to practically all living things on earth today. However, this atmosphere did contain the chemical elements essential for life: carbon (C), oxygen (O), nitrogen (N), and hydrogen (H). Combinations of these chemical elements make up over 95 percent of the compounds present in all living things. Carbon, oxygen, hydrogen, and nitrogen are the four basic building blocks of life.

Endless chemical reactions among these chemicals, sparked by the heat of the earth and energized by solar radiations, led to the formation of increasingly complex molecules and to the first forms of life, which were cradled in water. These primitive organisms just managed to survive in an oxygen-free environment. The breakthrough came with the appearance of blue-green algae more than 3.5 billion years ago. These organisms were photosynthesizers who kicked off a chain of chemical and biological events that revolutionized the earth, its atmosphere, and its inhabitants. They introduced solar energy harnessing systems which meant that living things could be independent, capable of making food and oxygen from air and water by photosynthesis.

Blue Green Algae: Oxygen Generators

The energy trap introduced by blue-green algae was chlorophyll, which absorbs and uses solar radiations to split water (H_2O) into hydrogen (H) and oxygen (O). The oxygen is released into the environment, and the hydrogen is joined with carbon dioxide to make the carbon compounds which are the building materials and the food for all living things.

Oxygen, as gas, the byproduct of photosynthesis, slowly and steadily began to accumulate in the water and atmosphere, making dramatic changes in the environment. Primitive organisms living in oxygen-free water were being killed off by the oxygen which is poison to them. It is surmised that blue-green algae, which could live in the new oxygen-rich air, began to displace the nonphotosynthesizers.

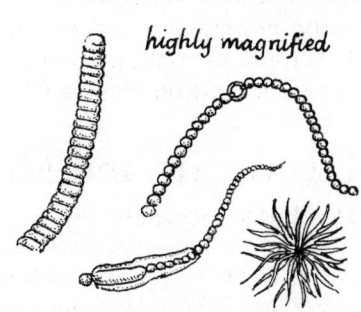

highly magnified

Blue-green Algae

The liberated oxygen also reacted with the poisonous ammonia and methane gases in the ancient air, changing them to harmless carbon dioxide, nitrogen, and water, the constituents of the modern atmosphere. Some of the atmospheric oxygen was also transformed into ozone by solar radiations. Atmospheric oxygen molecules contain two atoms of oxygen (O_2); ozone molecules contain three (O_3). Ozone is most concentrated 15 to 20 miles above the surface of the earth. This ozone layer prevents lethal amounts of solar ultraviolet rays from reaching the earth and destroying land life. Water also acts as a shield against these deadly rays and protects aquatic life.

With the establishment of an oxygen-rich atmosphere and a protective ozone screen against ultraviolet rays, new forms of life quickly evolved capable of living in and using this gas. Green algae, more advanced than their blue-green predecessors appeared and flourished in this modern atmosphere and paved the way for the emergence of plant life from water to land.

First Land Plants:
Ancient Algae

It is a scientific probability that the first land plants were descendants of green algae. Although the shores along the oceans and the shallow inland seas were teeming with life, just beyond these waters were huge tracts of uninhabited, emerging land. Here there was plenty of air, space, and sunlight, waiting for eligible occupants. Moving from water to land was a giant step in the evolution of plants. A bit of seaweed tossed up on a beach or left high and dry in a tidal zone shriveled and died in the air and sunlight. It could not make it; it was out of its depths. But step by step over hundreds of millions of years, plants that could withstand the rigors of land life evolved.

Liverworts and Mosses:
Wetland Pioneers

Among the early land pioneers were the ancestors of modern liverworts. These land invaders probably settled in swampy areas and managed to keep their heads just above the water. Primitive liverworts, like their present-day descendants, probably resembled bits of seaweed flattened on wet ground, capable of sponging up water through all parts of their bodies. On the belly side, however, liverworts developed rootlike rhizoids by which they anchored themselves to the ground so they couldn't be pushed around by wind and water. On the top side was a protective skin to prevent excessive evaporation of life-giving water. To escape dying of "sunstroke", they probably set up housekeeping in shaded spots where they live to this very day.

Liverworts and Mosses

Other early wetland settlers were the forerunners of modern mosses. Unlike their low-lying liverwort cousins, mosses are upward-striving. They are able to lift themselves by a short stem, but only a few inches above the ground. Rootlike structures, rhizoids, anchor them and also drink in soil water. This mineral water is carried up to tiny, green, leaflike structures through a thin, delicate stalk which acts like a wick in water. Since mosses do not have conducting or supporting systems, they cannot grow very tall and remain moisture-seeking, midget plants.

With these noble experiments in land living, bryophytes gained a toehold on land. But they were unable to get very far either in height, stature, or distance from their ancestral aquatic home. Like pioneers in a new land, bryophytes settled along coast lines, lake fronts, and river banks, keeping a low profile in shaded, protected places.

Terrestrial Pteridophytes:
Wet and Dry Land Lodgers

The pteridophytes were vastly more successful as land lodgers than their ancient bryophyte competitors. They seem to have been the earliest plant immigrants to come out of the sea and establish huge colonies further inland. They overshadowed and outgrew the waterlogged bryophytes who followed them on land. The secret of pteridophyte success was a vascular system for internal

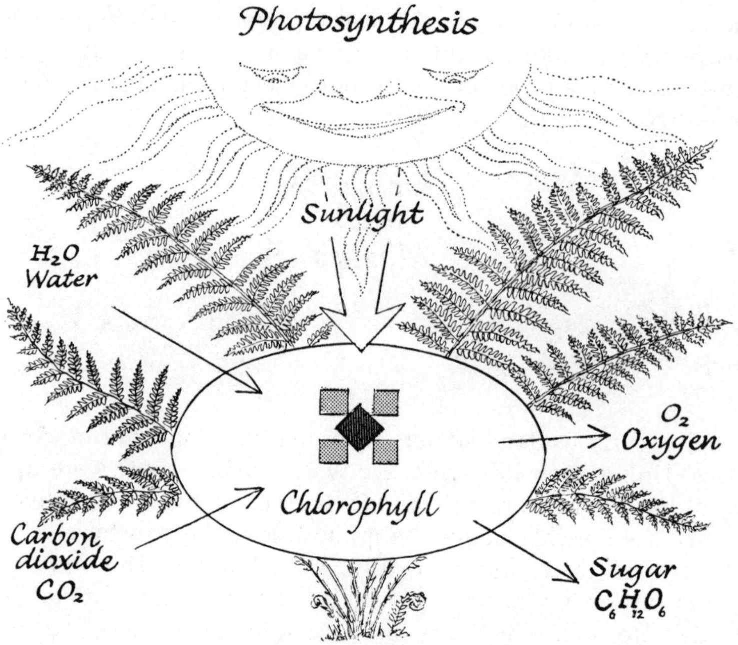

Photosynthesis

Sunlight

H_2O
Water

O_2
Oxygen

Chlorophyll

Carbon
dioxide
CO_2

Sugar
$C_6H_{12}O_6$

In photosynthesis a green plant takes in water and carbon dioxide and with chlorophyll and sunlight produces sugar and free oxygen

transportation, a structural supporting system, and the development of true roots, stems, and leaves. They were the first plants properly equipped to stand up straight and tall and conquer the land, probably resembling simple versions of present-day horsetails and clubmosses.

These newfangled devices put the pteridophytes in the driver's seat and for more than one hundred million years, the fern family was the royal dynasty that ruled the earth. During the golden age of pteridophytes, the earth enjoyed unexcelled fern growing weather. The subtropical, muggy, rainy, frost-free, stable, seasonless climate and the flat, swampy, marshy land with huge inland seas, encouraged more plant growth during this period than perhaps any other time in the history of the earth.

Fern Forests:
Giants of the Past

Immense, dense forests of tall trees covered the swampy land and dominated the landscape of a good part of the earth from pole to pole. The trees in these jungles were unlike anything we see today. Most abundant were one hundred foot trees, giant ancestors of modern midget horsetails. These towering trees were so numerous that their spores alone formed huge coal deposits. Also populating these swampy jungles were two kinds of mammoth trees, ancestors of modern midget, crawling, creeping clubmosses. One was the scale tree, *Lepidodendron* (lep-ee-dough-DEN-dron; from the Greek *lepidos:* scale and *dendron:* tree), so named because their fossils showed characteristic diamond-shaped markings arranged spirally on their trunk, indicating the position of the leaves.

The other clubmoss colossus was the seal tree, *Sigillaria* (sig-ill-LAIR-ee-ah; from the Latin *sigillum:* seal). The fossils of these trees bear seal-like leaf scar impressions in vertical rows on the trunk. *Pecopteris* (peh-COP-teh-riss; from the Greek *pekein:* comb and *pteris:* fern) describes the comblike arrangement of the fronds of this fossil, representing the modern fern families. They covered huge areas as shrubs, vines, and trees.

There were no flowering plants, birds, or mammals living in these jungles or elsewhere; they had not yet evolved. Primitive evergreens and also seed ferns, an extinct group linking the ferns and the seed plants, were in evidence.

Seed fern fossil
A link between ferns and seed plants

Coal Age Fern Forest
① *Scale Tree (Lepidodendron)* ② *Seal Tree (Sigillaria)*
③ *Horsetail Tree (Calamites)* ④ *Tree Fern (Eospermatopteris)*
⑤ *Seed Fern (Neuropteris)* ⑥ *Primitive evergreen (Cordaites)*

Flowering Flora:
Land Lords

Then came great climatic changes; the temperature dropped, glaciers covered parts of the earth, inland seas dried up, and swamps became deserts. The hothouse climate disappeared and so did the fern forests with most of their inhabitants. Those that survived are dwarf copies of their giant ancestors.

The cold, dry climate was an open invitation for the deeper penetration of the land by flowering plants. This third wave of land infiltrators came up with their own inventions to beat the weather: flowers and seeds. First appearing over 100 million years ago, flowering plants have dominated the land ever since.

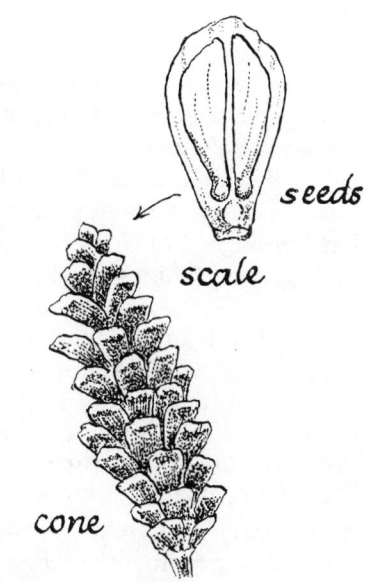

seeds

scale

cone

The conifers were the early seed producing plants

'cut-away'ovary

seeds in open pod

The flowering plant — ultimate in seed reproduction

69

Year of the Earth:
History of Plant Life

The evolution of plant life on earth is a story 4.5 billion years long. Vast stretches of time intervened between the critical steps that took place. Trying to visualize thousands of years is hard enough, but thinking in millions and billions is mind boggling. To present the most important historical stages in proper perspective and distance in time, let us reduce the age of the earth, 4.5 billion years, to one year, "the year of the earth." On this calendar one month equals 375 million years; one week, roughly 85 million years; one day, 12 million years; one hour, half a million years.

Assuming the earth was born on January 1, life first appeared in early March with approaching spring, and photosynthetic bacteria showed up later that month. Blue-green algae began the creation of the modern oxygen-rich protective atmosphere by the end of June, let's say on the fourth of July, in time to declare independence from the past and the beginning of a brave new world. It wasn't until the end of August that an oxygen-rich atmosphere with a protective ozone shield was established and the first modern green algae appeared. The floral invasion of land was launched at the end of November,

THE LADDER OF LIFE

in Earth Years

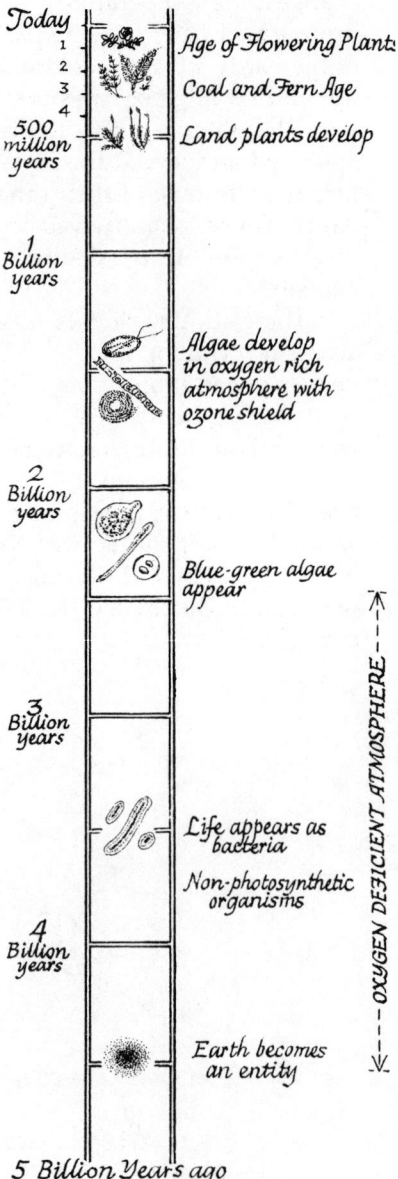

Today
1
2
3
4
500 million years

Age of Flowering Plants
Coal and Fern Age
Land plants develop

1 Billion years

Algae develop in oxygen rich atmosphere with ozone shield

2 Billion years

Blue-green algae appear

3 Billion years

Life appears as bacteria
Non-photosynthetic organisms

4 Billion years

Earth becomes an entity

5 Billion Years ago

← – – OXYGEN DEFICIENT ATMOSPHERE – – →

around Thanksgiving time, and these plants like the pilgrims gave thanks for their new home on land.

Fern forests flourished the first ten days of December, and the flowering plants took over the last ten days. *Homo sapiens,* human beings, arrived on the scene 12 minutes before New Year's Eve, and Columbus discovered America just 3 seconds before the New Year. Who knows what will happen in the closing seconds and milliseconds of this "year of the earth."

Happy New Year for all, we hope.

SUMMARY:

Looking Backward and Forward

The history of life on earth began with the creation of the solar system out of clouds of gases and dust 4.5 billion years ago. Within a billion years, living organisms, photosynthetic bacteria, had evolved in an oxygen-free environment. During the next billion years, blue-green algae arose and initiated the oxygen revolution; they displaced the more primitive photosynthetic bacteria by creating the oxygen-rich modern atmosphere and a layer of ozone to protect against deadly solar ultraviolet rays. It was only a billion and a half years ago that the ancestor of modern algae appeared. All this paved the way for the evolution of oxygen-tolerant plants, which eventually invaded the barren land.

The occupation of the land began about half a billion years ago by descendants of the green algae. Among the pioneer plants were the bryophytes which took up residence along the swampy edges of the land in the footsteps of the pteridophytes. Being nonvascular, they did not get very far either in height or in distance from water.

71

The pteridophytes, with their vascular and supporting systems were the earliest land invaders; and for over 100 million years they dominated the earth, which was then experiencing a humid, subtropical, seasonless climate. Huge fern forests grew and died continuously, filling the swamps with their partially decayed bodies, the raw material that was fossilized as coal. This golden age of ferns and coal formation was 300 million years ago during the Carboniferous period.

The earth then became cold and dry; the forest of towering pteridophytes disappeared, except for a few that managed to survive as miniature copies of their giant forebears. These sharp changes in climate were the golden opportunity for flowering plants whose hardy seeds were capable of withstanding drought and cold. They took over more than 100 million years ago and have dominated the land ever since.

Despite their reduction in size and numbers, let us not underestimate the importance of ferns as the link between water and land plants. The fabulous fern forests are long gone, but they left an immense inheritance—coal—viewed by some as black diamonds and others as black death. Regardless of how this legacy is seen, ferns of the past are once again assuming a critical position, this time as a bridge from the past to the present and the future evolution of all life on earth.

CHAPTER

VII

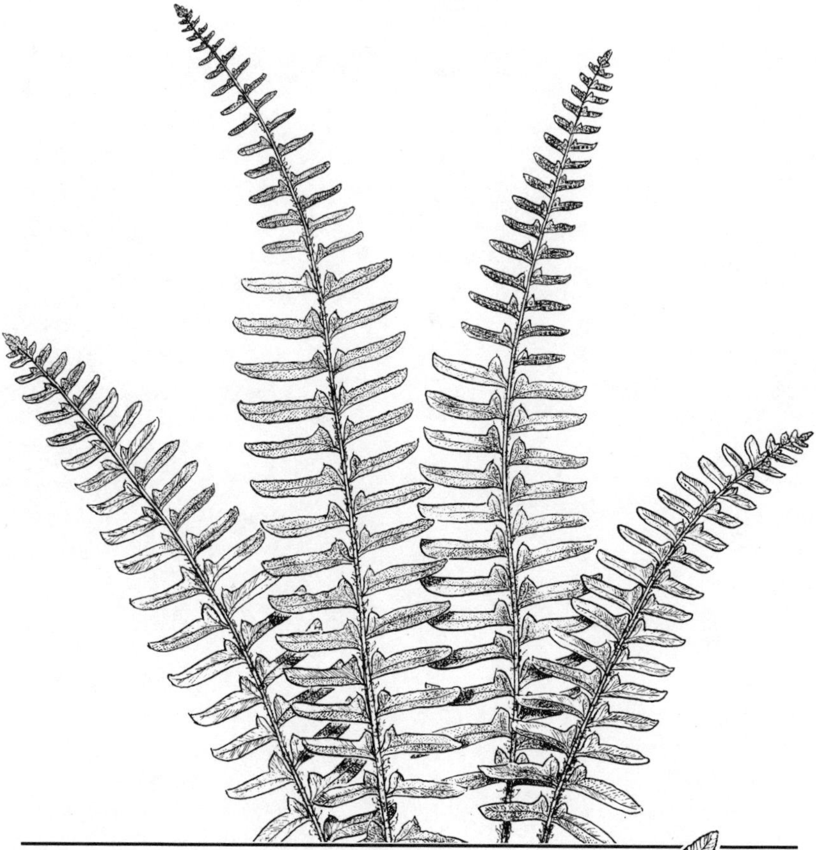

Christmas Fern

Narrowed tip of fertile frond
has spore bearing smaller
leaflets; evergreen

*eared
pinna*

*fertile
pinna*

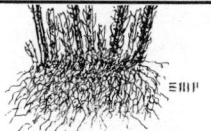

VII

Naming and Classifying Ferns

*S*ooner or later, fern foragers find their way into forest, fields and fens (swamps) looking for these modest, unpretentious plants in their native niches. Because ferns are relatively small green plants without colorful flowers, they blend into the background and become "visible" only when you seek them out. But once you find one, others begin to appear. It's like learning a "new" word which you soon discover is not new at all but appears here, there, and everywhere. At first you may know only two kinds of ferns, lady fern and "not" lady fern. Then you find others, and begin to ask, "What kind of fern is it? What is its name?" Naming is the first step in getting to know ferns, and a very important one. Once you learn its name, a line of communication is established between the fern and yourself. You also become aware of the fact that not all ferns are alike, and that if you see one fern you have *not* seen them all.

Fern Filing Systems:
Classification Schemes

Botanists faced with over a thousand kinds of ferns have created several filing systems for identifying, naming, and cataloguing these plants. If you are a stamp collector, you are familiar with catalogues in which stamps may be arranged by country, face value, market value, color, shape, date, commemoration, or any way that suits your purpose and convenience.

The current scheme of classifying living things was introduced by the Swedish botanist Carl von Linne (*Linnaeus*) in 1753. It is made up of seven basic categories, according to size, going from the largest to the smallest group:

1. **Kingdom**
2. **Phylum** (FIE-lum, singular; phyla, FIE-lah, plural)
3. **Class**
4. **Order**
5. **Family**
6. **Genus** (GEE-nus, singular; genera, GEN-er-ah, plural)
7. **Species**

All plants are grouped together in the plant kingdom. For our purposes, the plant kingdom is divided into four major groups:

1. *Thallophytes* (algae, fungi, and lichen)
2. *Bryophytes* (liverworts and mosses)
3. *Pteridophytes* (ferns and fern allies)
4. *Spermatophytes* (evergreen and flowering plants)

Each **phylum** contains several **classes.** The phylum of pteridophytes includes several classes, such as horsetails, clubmosses, quillworts, and true ferns. **Classes** in turn are divided into smaller units, **orders;** one is the order of true ferns. Each **order** is further split into still smaller units, **families;** an example is the family of common ferns. A **family** is broken down into several **genera;** one such genus is the wood fern. A **genus** is made up of **species.** The marginal shield fern is an example of one species in the wood fern genus. The family of common ferns is the largest and contains almost 200 genera divided into about 8,000 named and classified species.

The system of classification has been compared to a tree. The main stem is the kingdom; the largest limbs, the phyla; the smaller limbs, the classes; the branches, the orders; the branchlets, the families; the twigs, the genera; and the twiglets the species.

Filing Ferns by Structure and Life Style

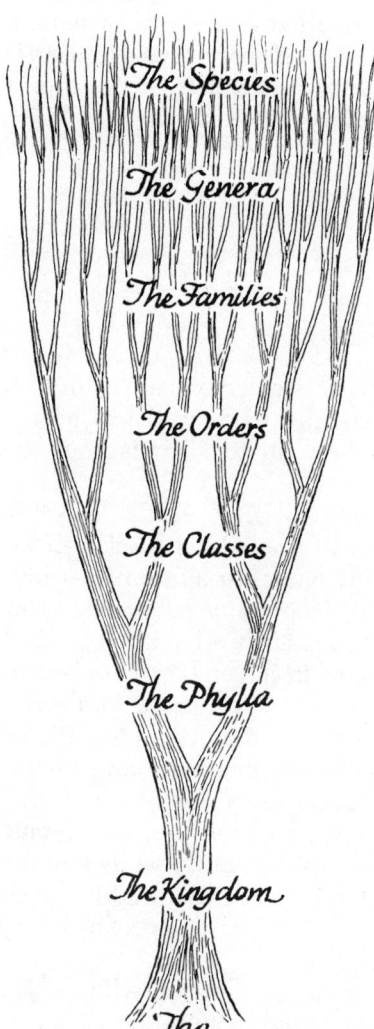

CLASSIFICATION TREE

The various divisions in a classification system are the brain children of botanists. They were created for the purpose of separating and placing plants into convenient categories on the basis of similarities and differences in structure and habitat. Plants that look alike and live alike are grouped together. Hence, vascular plants that reproduce by spores are placed in the same phylum, pteridophytes. One of the pteridophyte classes is the ferns. To qualify for membership in the fern class, the plant must have broad leaves with branching veins. Among the classes of ferns is the order of true ferns with spores located on the back of a frond, in clustered sporangia, or on separate fertile fronds. This order embraces several families, one being the common fern family of the Osmundas characterized by sporangia on fronds or parts of fronds lacking green leaf tissue. A genus may contain one or more species. The Osmunda genus for example has three common species: the royal, the cinnamon and the interrupted ferns. Each of these species is distinctly different from the others and readily recognized by the position of clusters of sporangia on the fern; the royal on top, the interrupted in the middle, and the cinnamon on separate fronds (see page 79).

The classification of ferns is far from complete. Today, plants are classified not only on physical features but also on biochemical, chromosomal, and developmental considerations. The more we know about ferns, the more accurately they can be classified and placed in their proper category. The species is recognized as the basic unit in classification and is regarded as the real or natural grouping in nature. All the other categories are considered arbitrary and contrived for the convenience of botanists, and of course are subject to change without previous notice.

Fern Names in Latin:
The Scientific Double Name

Ferns, like all other living things, have been given names. In fact, a fern has two names: one is its scientific name in Latin and the other its common name in English or in the language of the country in which it lives.

The scientific name consists of two Latin words. The first word tells you its genus and the second word, its species. *Homo sapiens*, "wise man," is the scientific name for all human beings regardless of sex, race, color, creed, income, or nationality. This two-name system was introduced in 1753 by Carl von Linne, who went so far as to Latinize his own name from von Linne to *Linnaeus* (lin-AYE-us). Before his time, a plant name consisted of a series of descriptive words in Latin, which was then the international language of scholars. Linnaeus condensed the descriptive phrase into two words, the genus name followed by the species name. It is similar to the system by which people are named. Your family name is the genus, your first name, the species. Just as you are listed in a telephone directory by family name followed by given name, so in a fern file or index the genus name is followed by the species.

For example, the royal, cinnamon, and interrupted ferns are three different species, but all belong to the same genus, *Osmunda* (Oz-MUN-dah). The scientific name of the royal fern is *Osmunda regalis;* the cinnamon fern, *Osmunda cinnamomea;* and the interrupted fern, *Osmunda claytoniana*. Linnaeus's system of classifying and naming ferns greatly simplified and standardized scientific notations and labeling. He created an international botanical language which is still being used today.

THE OSMUNDAS

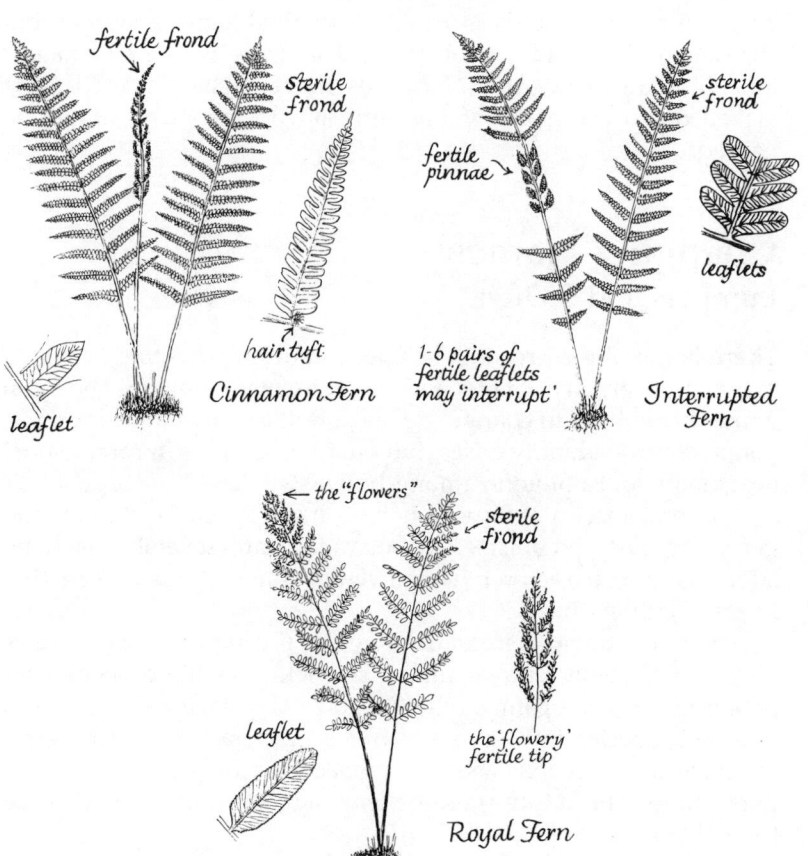

fertile frond

sterile frond

fertile pinnae

sterile frond

leaflets

hair tuft

leaflet

Cinnamon Fern

1-6 pairs of fertile leaflets may 'interrupt'

Interrupted Fern

the "flowers"

sterile frond

leaflet

the 'flowery' fertile tip

Royal Fern

Writing Scientific Names:
Genus Species

The way in which a scientific name is written follows certain rules agreed upon by botanists. The scientific name of the maidenhair fern is written as *Adiantum pedatum* L. The genus name is capitalized, followed by the species name, which is not capitalized. The name of ferns belonging to the same genus may be abbreviated, if listed consecutively, using only the first letter of the genus followed by a period, i.e., "O." for "Osmunda."

Also included in the scientific notation is the name of the botanist who first described and named the species, its godfather. Since Linneaus not only introduced the double-name system, but christened thousands of plants and animals with Latin names including the maidenhair fern, his name, abbreviated "L.", is tacked on to the name of this fern and to the many others he named.

Changing Names:
Lumpers and Splitters

There is nothing sacrosanct or fixed about the scientific names of plants; they are man-made, and therefore man unmade. The Latin names are subject to change, not as part of a conspiracy to confuse you and create identity crises, but out of differences in professional judgments and opinions among botanists.

Several species of ferns may have been placed together in one genus by early botanists, but separated into several genera by later classifiers based on new knowledge—an ongoing process that keeps classifiers busy.

Botanists do not necessarily agree on the importance of species differences; some tend to minimize them and lump species together in the same genus; others tend to maximize the differences and split species into several different genera. Those who tend to create fewer genera with more species in each are called lumpers; those who create more genera each with fewer species are the splitters.

A fern assigned to a different genus is renamed and given the name of the new genus. The species name may be retained unless there is another plant in that genus with the same species name. It is also customary to retain the name of the botanist in parentheses who first named it followed by the name of the botanist who reclassified it. The marginal shield fern is *Dryopteris marginalis* (L.) Gray. This fern was first described and named by Linnaeus, but was later reclassified by Asa Gray, the famous American botanist of the nineteenth century. Thus the names of two famous botanists are memorialized in the name of a simple, modest fern that has outlived both its classifier and reclassifier.

Another source of confusion with names of ferns goes back to the lack of agreement among botanists as to whether a fern should be regarded as a distinct species or merely a variety. A case in point is the evergreen fern, which appears both as *Dryopteris spinulosa* var. *intermedia* (Muhl.) Underw. and *Dryopteris intermedia* (Muhl. ex Willd.) A. Gray. You have the choice of either its species or variety name. Both are correct.

this pinnule not longer than the next adjacent

fertile pinnule

indusium minutely glandular

$\frac{1}{3} - \frac{1}{7} X$

Evergreen Wood-fern
(*Dryopteris intermedia*)

81

Common Fern Names:
Duplication and Confusion

To beginners, scientific names in Latin are frequently "gibberish," nonsense syllables in a foreign language which they do not understand or cannot pronounce. Common names are preferred because they are usually easier to remember and make more sense. However, name-calling in the native tongue is not always a satisfactory alternative to Latin "gibberish." The same fern may have many common names, and these may vary from country to country and from region to region within a country. Bracken (*Pteridium aquilinum*) has such folk names as brake, pasture brake, hog brake, adder's spit, erne fern, eagle fern, oak fern, umbrella fern, upland fern, eastern bracken, and turkey foot bracken. Ground pine (*Lycopodium clavatum*) has at least 20 different common names.

To add to the confusion, the same common name is given to different species of woodferns and to clubmosses. Then there are ferns that do not have common names; they are uncommon, comparatively rare, "found" only by botanists who know them and address them by their scientific names.

Common names may be very dramatic, colorful, and picturesque but may present problems in communicating with people in other countries or regions within a country. On the other hand, *Adiantum pedatum* (the maidenhair fern in the vernacular) will be properly recognized from Australia and Argentina to Zambia and Zimbabwe. There is nothing so satisfying and rewarding as meeting and greeting a fern friend by name, common, scientific, or both.

Source of Fern Names:
People, Places and Parts

A question frequently asked is "How do ferns get their names?" Ferns are born nameless; their names are human inventions. Common names are generally descriptive of some outstanding fern feature: the walking fern, the climbing fern, and the interrupted fern. The name may tell you where it lives: the marsh fern, the woodfern; or the color of some part: the silvery spleenwort; or its use: the scouring rush; or its resemblance to another plant:

ground pine, running cedar. Some common names are pure fiction and imagination, and some are of unknown origin, or local names which are often difficult for an outsider to understand. Others are translated directly from the Latin, *filix-femina*, the lady fern, for example.

Scientific names also have many sources. The genus of the hay-scented fern is *Dennstaedtia* (den-STET-ee-ah), named after the nineteenth-century German botanist August Wilhelm Dennstedt. The species name of the interrupted fern is *claytoniana* (clay-TONE-ee-ahn-ah), for the eighteenth century Anglo-American botanist John Clayton. Other names are taken directly from the ancient Greek: *Polypodium* (pol-ee-POE-dee-yum), which means "many feet," describes its many-branched rhizome. Some species names are latinized geographical locations telling where the fern was first found, such as *virginianum* (vir-gin-ee-AIN-um) for Virginia and *novaboracensis* (no-vah-BORE-ah-sen-siss) for New York. In the great majority of the cases the species name is an adjective of Latin origin describing some parts or feature of the fern: *fragilis* for fragile, *bulbifera* for bulb-bearing; or where it grows: *arvense* for field, *palustris* for swamp. A little knowledge of Latin or Greek may go a long way in translating scientific names, but do not assume that a knowledge of these languages alone will make these names easier to understand or pronounce.

Pronouncing Scientific Names:
Anglicized Latin

The pronunciation of scientific names is often difficult, confusing, and embarrassing, even if you have studied Latin and Greek. Scientific names are generally pronounced as if they were English words. However, *Adiantum*, the maidenhair fern genus, is pronounced in four syllables (ad-ee-AN-tum); *arvense*, which means fields, is pronounced in three syllables (are-VEN-see). To acquaint you with the scientific names of ferns and to make them less forbidding, most of the ferns appearing in this book are given both the common and scientific names. To help you with the scientific names, their pronunciations, translations, and meanings are presented. The bilingual approach in learning the proper pronunciation and names has some advantages; two names are better than one, and one name is better than none.

Classified Fern Directories:
Keys

To identify a fern, you probably will turn to an expert or to the pages of a classified fern directory, a key, or to both. A key consists of pairs of short, contrasting statements describing some fern features, one of which will apply to the fern you are attempting to identify and the other statement will not. You choose the correct statement and are referred to another set of contrasting statements. Step by step through a process of elimination you eventually arrive at the name of the fern. A full description follows, which may be supplemented by line drawings or photographs showing diagnostic structures or "field markings" that are helpful in making a positive identification.

The "keying out" process is the botanical version of the old-fashioned parlor game of "twenty questions." The contrasting statements are really questions to which you answer "yes" or "no." The modern version of this game is played with a computer. You feed the information into the computer, which has been programmed to name the fern. To get the correct answer, you must supply the correct data. Botanists have written computer programs for identifying plants. The yes-no format is ideal for computers.

Keying Out:
Identification Routes

"Keying out" sounds simple and straightforward, a sure-fire way to identify ferns. And it is, under certain circumstances. First, keys require a knowledge of "fernese," the botanical language found in descriptive key statements. Often these statements are written in highly technical terms describing various aspects of the vegetative parts of a fern: its leaves, stems, roots, rhizomes, fiddleheads, the pattern of the conducting tubes in the stem, the vein pattern in the fronds, and divisions of the fronds. Key statements describing various aspects of the sexual reproductive structures are also included: sori, sori coverings, sporangia, spores, and prothalli. In fact, reproductive structures are regarded as more constant, reliable and less subject to change than vegetative fern features and are therefore the basis of most technical botanical keys.

Second, your fern specimen should be normal, healthy, and have all the structures found in the key. Attempting to "key out" a fern without spores may be difficult or impossible if the key is based mainly on spore features. Then there are the nonconformist fern specimens, "fern freaks," that defy identification. They may compel the bewildered botanist to resort to several "face-saving" alternatives, such as dismissing the fern as a "horticultural variety," a "hybrid," an "illegal alien," or just another "fern freak." (Such explanations are not entirely unknown among botanists, both experienced and inexperienced.) Or the specimen, with all available information, may be taken to or sent to an "expert" for a professional opinion. The specimen may be compared with herbarium or other specimens. In this way, it may be possible to find out who or what is at fault: the key, the key operator, or the specimen. In any event, if you don't succeed at first, try, try again.

Third, to be successful in this name game you must have the right kind of key. Without it you will not be able to find and open the "door" with the correct nameplate. An exercise in futility is trying to track down the name of a fern in a technical manual written by and for experts. Unless you have the expertise, patience, and motivation don't do it. There are keys written specifically for beginners, in nontechnical language with ample illustrations, covering the common ferns in a particular area of the country. Such popular field guides are based on the premise that one picture is worth a thousand words. Matching the actual specimen against verbal and pictorial descriptions is probably the most frequently used road to the recognition and identification of ferns.

To demonstrate how an illustrated key is constructed and used, several fern families have been arranged in the typical yes-no format. You are going to play the fern family name game. The object is to place a fern specimen in its proper family. Try it with any fern or fern ally, using the illustrated key following on the next two pages.

Directions: Select one of the paired contrasting statements, 1a or 1b, which best describes the specimen. This leads to numbers 2 or 5 on the right and to another pair of statements. Again select one and repeat until you reach the name of the family to which the specimen belongs.

1a. Leaves small, needle-, grass-, or scale-like, with one unbranched vein; sporangia on stem or base of leaf or in cones; fern allies. **2.**

1b. Leaves *not* as above; broad with branching veins; sporangia on leaves or in nut-like capsules; ferns .... **5.**

2a. Stems grooved, hollow, jointed; leaves minute, scalelike, whorled; branches when present, whorled, long, green, pine-like; sporangia in terminal cones. ....
HORSETAIL FAMILY
(Equisetums)

2b. Stem not as above; leaves arranged spirally. .... **3.**

3a. Leaves long, grass-like; sporangia sunken in leaf base; grows in or near water. ....
QUILLWORT FAMILY
(Isoetes)

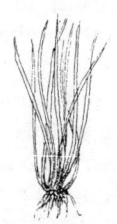

3b. Leaves *not* as above; sporangia at base of leaves or in cones; land plants. .... **4.**

4a. Cones cylindrical, terminal or at base of small leaves; spores all alike. ....
CLUBMOSS FAMILY
(Lycopods)

4b. Cones *not* as above, 4 sided; two kinds of spores. ....
SPIKEMOSS FAMILY
(Selaginellas)

5a. Fernlike in appearance; one kind of spore; lives in varied habitats. .... **6.**

FERNS AND FERN ALLIES

5b. Appearance *not* fernlike; two kinds of spores in capsules; lives in water, floating or rooted in mud. .... **8.**

6a. Stems and leaves fleshy; leaf divided into sterile and fertile parts with spike-like sporangia; leaves not coiled in bud. ....
ADDER'S TONGUE FAMILY
(Succulent Ferns)

6b. Stem and leaves *not* fleshy and not as above; plant fernlike; leaves coiled in bud. ...... **7.**

7a. Fertile leaves or parts consist of masses of sporangia; young spores green; grows in wet places. ....
ROYAL FERN FAMILY
(Osmundas)

7b. Fertile leaves and parts *not* as above; sporangia usually on back of leaves; most common. ....
TRUE FERN FAMILY
(Polypods)

8a. Plants floating; upper surface of tiny leaves covered with hairs. ....
FLOATING FERN FAMILY
(Salvinias)

8b. Plants rooted in mud; leaves divided into four equal parts, clover-like. ....
WATER CLOVER FAMILY
(Marsileas)

SUMMARY:

Naming and Filing Systems

In 1753, Carl Linneaus brought law and order into the art of naming and classifying living things. The Linnaean system adopted by biologists internationally consists of seven basic categories. Starting with the largest and all-inclusive division, the kingdom, living things are assigned into progressively smaller groups—phylum, class, order, family, genus, and species. Ferns are classified on the basis of similarity in appearance and life style. The more alike ferns are in how they look and live, the more closely related they are assumed to be, and therefore classified in the same genus or species.

Another Linnaean contribution is the system for naming living things with two Latin words. The first is the name of the genus (which is capitalized) and the second, the name of the species (lower case). The genus-species name is latinized, regardless of the language from which it came. The scientific name is followed by the abbreviated name of the botanist who first found and named the fern. If it was subsequently reclassified, the abbreviated name of the reclassifier is also added.

Ferns also have a common name. Although easier to understand and pronounce, common names have a limited local range and often cause confusion. The same fern may have many common names depending on the locality, and different ferns may have the same name.

Ferns are listed and described in classified directories, most of which are "keys" compiled by botanists to assist in the identification of these plants by name. A key usually consists of pairs of contrasting descriptive statements. By choosing the statement that correctly describes the specimen, you are referred to another set of statements. Again you choose the description that applies, and eventually this botanical game of "twenty questions" leads to the name of the fern. Line drawings and photographs supplementing a full description of the identified fern are usually provided. The "keying" process requires a knowledge of botanical terminology, a specimen that fits the key, and a key that fits the "keyer."

Bracken

Thrice-cut triangular blade
horizontal to ground; sori in
rolled over edge of leaflets

fertile pinnule

VIII

Fact and Folklore About Ferns

*F*erns, no less than other plants, have played a significant role in human history. Not only have they been a source of food and pharmaceuticals (drugs), but they have been featured prominently in fables and folklore. The Victorian era, more than a hundred years ago, was indeed the golden age of ferns, matched only by the Coal Age hundreds of millions of years earlier. A wave of fern frenzy swept through Victorian England and the United States, leaving in its wake a fabulous following of fern fanciers. Everybody who was anybody had outdoor and/or indoor ferneries in which native and foreign species were cultivated. Normal and abnormal forms were developed, and fern foragers combed the world in quest of these plants. Over a thousand varieties were recorded by Victorian fern faddists, including more than 300 forms of the common lady fern (*Athyrium filix-femina*).

It is fascinating to explore the past and discover what our ancestors knew and thought about ferns. Learning about their past history gives ferns charisma and adds another dimension to our understanding and appreciation of ferns today. A considerable amount of literature exists in which the fern–human relationship of thousands of years is described in fact and fiction, fables and folklore, song and story.

Fabulous Fern Seeds:
Myth and Mystery

Ancient and medieval fern fanciers ascribed all kinds of magical and mystical powers to ferns by simply substituting fiction for facts and superstition for science. They supposed that ferns were no different from other plants, that they had flowers and seeds which could not be seen simply because they were invisible. However, if you looked in the right place at the right time, armed with the right charms, performed the right ritual with the right magical words, you would find fern flowers and seeds, and they would give you magical powers.

In the Middle Ages, it was believed that ferns produced tiny blue flowers, but only on one day of the year, at dusk of June 24, St. John's Day. At precisely the stroke of midnight, the very moment the Saint was born, the flowers ripened into fiery, golden seeds which fell to the earth. You could acquire "wonder-working powers" by catching these saintly seeds on a white cloth. A pinch of fern seeds in your shoes or stomach could make you as invisible as the seeds themselves. They could also give you second sight, to see into the past and the future, to find lost objects and great hidden treasures. Fern seeds, they thought, could also grant you the greatest gift of all: eternal youth. What a prize if only you could capture them.

An anonymous poet of the time told this fern-seed fable:

> "But on St. John's mysterious night,
> Sacred to many a wizard spell,
> The time when first to human sight
> Confest, the mystic fern seed fell.
>
> I'll seek the shaggy, fern-clad hill,
> Where time has delved a dreary dell,
> Befitting best a hermit's cell;
> And watch 'mid murmurs muttering stern,
> The seed departing from the fern,
> Ere watchful demons can convey,
> The wonder-working charm away,
> And tempt the blows from arm unseen,
> Should thoughts unholy intervene."

"Watching the fern" was a very popular pastime in the Middle Ages. On St. John's Eve, bands of believers armed with white sheets and magic wands set forth in quest of the fabulous fern seeds. They spread the sheets under ferns, waved their magic wands over the plants, delivered up prayers, uttered magic words, entreated demons and gods, and appealed to heaven and hell. But nothing happened. They returned empty-handed after a fruitless and seedless search, but not discouraged. There was always next year, they said.

In time, these expeditions got out of hand. Sorcery, black-magic, and witchcraft were invoked; these ungodly practices became so widespread that the church in France placed a ban on fern seed foragers and forays on St. John's Day.

So popular and accepted was the belief in the magic of fern seeds that it appears in the literature of the Elizabethan period. In Shakespeare's play, Henry IV (Act II, scene I) Gadshill proposes that:

> "We steal as in a castle, cock-sure;
> we have the receipt of fern-seed—
> we walk invisible.

To which the skeptical Chamberlain answers:

> "Nay, by my faith, I think you are
> more beholding to the night than to
> the fern-seed for your walking invisible.

On the other hand, there were some Elizabethan skeptics who questioned the fern-seed fable. Henry Lyte, a sixteenth-century English botanist, took an unpopular position and exposed the fern-seed fraud in his book "A niewe Herball or History of Plantes (1578):

> "This kind of Ferne beareth neither flowers
> nore sede, except we shall take for
> sede the black spots on the backsides of the
> leaves, the whiche some do gather thinking to
> worke wonders, but to say the truth, it is nothing else
> but trumperi and superstition."

Fern Pharmaceuticals:
Harmless and Harmful

Ferns have been applied in the treatment of human ailments for thousands of years. As far back as 300 B.C., Theophrastus, the Greek botanist and physician, prescribed an oil extract of a fern to expel worms from the body. And it worked. This medicine made from the roots of the bracken fern (*Pteridium aquilinum*) and the male fern (*Dryopteris filix-mas*) was the drug of choice until very recently. But do not be misled; the Theophrastus prescription is the rare exception. Most pharmaceuticals derived from ferns are ineffective, and in some instances, harmful. The medicinal merits ascribed to a particular fern in olden times were based on a mixture of fact, fiction, fantasy, and fable, to which were added liberal amounts of fraud, fakery, and falsehood. Mysticism, necromancy, demonology, mythology, alchemy, astrology, and wortcunning (the art of using magic herbs) were blended in varying amounts with botany, medicine, pharmacy, and scientific study, in deciding the healing properties of ferns. However, the problem then as now remains the same: how to know which fern physic is effective against which disease.

The earliest attempts to assess the medical merits of ferns were by trial and error, with humans serving as guinea pigs. More often than not, the plant prescriptions were harmless, but in some instances they brought relief to the sufferer by either curing or killing the patient. Drug dispensers, doctors, herbalists, astrologers, sorcerers, shamans, and medicine men supplemented their limited knowledge with whatever means they had at their disposal—with no holds barred. They studied the characteristics of the plant with the hope that the plant itself would suggest its proper medicinal uses.

Doctrine of Signature:
The Sign of the Fern

In the sixteenth century, Theophrastus von Hohenheim *alias* Theophrastus Bombastus *alias* Paracelsus (the latter the name by which he has come down in history), fathered a medical theory, the Doctrine of Signature. This highly imaginative and ingenious theory held that every plant was "signed" by a mystical bond to a given human ailment and was under the influence of a star or planet. The signature was inscribed in the size, shape, color, aroma, texture, and habitat of the plant and its position with respect to the heavenly bodies. In this way the Creator let people know that plants with liver-shaped leaves were good for curing liver diseases and heart-shaped leaves mended broken hearts. Astrological medicine gained great popularity and was very fashionable in the sixteenth and seventeenth centuries. Despite their proven falsity and fraudulence, some of these beliefs still persist among astrologers, food faddists, and medical quacks.

Fiddleheads and Fiddlesticks

By a remarkable coincidence, both medieval Europeans and early American Indians, although widely separated in time and space, viewed rolled-up fiddleheads as curled snakes or worms and therefore used them for killing and expelling worms from the body. The Cherokee also placed great value and faith in fiddleheads of several ferns as a remedy for rheumatism. They observed how a fern frond emerges from the curled-up fiddlehead and reasoned that fiddleheads were good for straightening out the bent muscles and limbs of rheumatics.

Bracken:
A Fern that Everybody Knows

The bracken or brake fern (*Pteridium aquilinum*) is one of the best-known species, with a world-wide range and an international reputation that goes back thousands of years. It is found in almost every country of the world and grows in almost any environment, except the extreme polar regions, deserts, and deep forests. Bracken flourish where most ferns fail—in barren, sandy soil, in open fields and pastures, and in direct sunlight. This fern is tough and rugged; its deep, far-reaching, creeping rhizomes enable bracken to outgrow its competitors so completely that it becomes a weed, taking over vast stretches of open space.

Fiddleheads:
Eat, Drink, but Be Wary

People throughout the world have found many uses for bracken. Its rhizomes, for example, are rich in starch and have been a source of food in various countries. For the inhabitants of the Canary Islands, the Maori of New Zealand, the natives of the Society Islands in the South Pacific, and the aborigines of Australia, bracken has been a staple in their diet.

American Indians prefer the rhizomes of the royal fern. The fiddleheads of bracken as well as those of other ferns are consumed as a vegetable by briefly steaming them and then eating them; they taste like asparagus. Fiddleheads are considered a gourmet's delight. A note of warning to those planning to feast on ferns. There is evidence that some ferns contain cancer-causing chemicals or **carcinogens** (car-SIN-oh-gins). Cattle feeding on bracken develop stomach tumors that may be caused by the carcinogens present in that fern. The royal and ostrich ferns also contain carcinogens. The relationship between these carcinogens and cancer in humans has yet to be established. Nevertheless, add these ferns to the growing list of possible sources of human cancer. It is much safer to gaze than to graze on ferns.

In Siberia and Norway, fiddleheads were one of the traditional ingredients used in brewing beer. The rhizomes were also used to dress kid and chamois leather. The ashes of this fern found their way into the manufacture of glass, soap, lye, and fertilizer. The fronds served as feed and bedding for cattle, as packing material, thatch for roofs, and as ground cover. In New Zealand, the trunks of fern trees can be seen in the construction of fences, crude houses, and ornaments. A use for every part of bracken has been found, including a lead role in fern fables and folklore.

Tall Tales:
Told by Bracken

Bracken ferns have been the inspiration for many fascinating fern fables. Several tall tales originated from attempts to interpret the shapes and patterns of the conducting bundles present in their roots and stems. Cross sections have suggested various images to viewers. Carl Linneaus, the greatest botanist in his time, saw an eagle in the cut end of the lower part of the stem, and this prompted him to name the species *aquilinum*, the Latin name for eagle.

In medieval times, the letter "C" was seen in the cut end of the root, the initial of Christ. Bracken was therefore looked upon as protection against witches, goblins, and other servants of the devil. The Scots saw the letter "X" stamped on the cut end of the stem, the Greek initial for Christ, and used it to drive evil spirits away. But not all Scots saw the same signature in bracken. Some beheld the mark of the devil's hoof in its stem and the divine sign of Christ on its roots. This gave bracken the power to dispel devils and terrify witches and werewolves.

The stem bundles conjured up an image of the oak tree, and in some parts of England, bracken is called "King Charles in the Oak Tree." This name alludes to a story which tells how King Charles II of England and Scotland escaped his enemies by hiding in the thick foliage of an oak tree.

The Irish were more creative and imaginative; they named bracken the "Fern of God," because when the stem was cut in three places, they saw the letter "G" in the first part, "O" in the second, and "D" in the third. It may have been divine guidance that directed them to read the letters in the proper order.

Still another myth was that you could find the initial of your sweetheart in the cut end of the stem, an embarrassing situation if your girl friends happen to be Mary, Marion and Mildred.

Bracken is the supposed source of the fabulous seed ferns. It was then called the female fern and later the lady fern. According to authorities, with the change in name from female to lady, it lost its reputation as having magical powers. Apparently, medieval men thought mystique was more powerful in females than in ladies.

Bracken:
The Medical Marvel

Bracken has earned a special place in the annals of botanical medicine. It was highly regarded as a **vermifuge** (worm-expeller) for more than two thousand years and was slowly phased out by modern medical practices. In the seventeenth century, Nicholas Culpeper, an astrological herbalist and disciple of Paracelsus, cited several medical merits for this fern in the famous "Culpeper's Complete Herbal," published in 1653:

> The roots being bruised and boiled in mead and honeyed water, and drunk, kills both the broad and long worms in the body, and abates the swelling and hardness of the spleen.

In addition he writes that the leaves when eaten:

> purge the belly and expel choleric and waterish humours that trouble the stomach.

An ointment made from the root boiled in oil or hog grease "heals wounds and ulcers." Bracken fern smoke was also recommended as an insect and snake repellent.

John Gerard, also a seventeenth-century astrological herbalist and Paracelsian partisan, in his book "The Herbal or General History of Plants," published in 1633, found an additional bracken benefit and recommended that the roots be placed in wine to keep it from turning sour. His suggested treatment for thigh aches (sciatica), was to "smoke the leg thoroughly with Fern Bracken." It would appear that this treatment is worse than the disease.

The beauty of bracken was not lost on the popular nineteenth-century Scottish writer, Sir Walter Scott, who in his narrative poem, "Lady of the Lake," refers to it:

> The heath this night must be my bed
> The bracken curtain for my head.

Spleenworts:
For Sickly Spleens

The spleenwort ferns (*Asplenium*) with their spleen-shaped fronds, occupied a special place in medieval medicine. Unique curative properties were attributed to these ferns, which were dispensed for treating disorders of the spleen because of the shape of the fronds. Unfortunately, the "signature" of spleenworts proved to be a forgery and its fronds a fake in curing sick spleens.

Wall-Rue:
The Spleenwort for All Seasons and Reasons

Several species of spleenworts have been known since antiquity. Wall-rue (*Asplenium ruta-muraria*) is a tiny, delicate, evergreen fern with fan-shaped leaflets that thrives in the cracks and crannies of limestone outcrops, and especially on old walls. According to its patrons, wall-rue was virtually a one-fern pharmacy, capable of curing ailments from head to toe. Culpeper extolled its medical marvels:

> [Wall-rue] helps those that are troubled with shortness of breath, yellow jaundice, disease of the spleen, stopping of urine, and helps break up stones in the kidney. And it cleans the lungs and by rectifying the blood causes good color to the whole body. The herb when boiled in oil of camomile dissolves knots, allays swellings and dries up moist ulcers. The lye made from it is singularly good to cleanse the head from scurf (dandruff) and from dry and running sores.

The wonders of wall-rue do not end here. Culpeper also heralded it as a hair-raising panacea and gave the following instruction for compounding this nostrum:

> [Wall-rue] stays the shedding or falling of the hair and causes it to grow thick, fair and well colored, for which purpose boil it in wine, putting some smallage (wild celery) seed thereto and afterwards some oil.

The 300-year-old formula for Culpeper's Wall Rue Hair Restorer leaves little to the imagination and adds less to bald pates.

Maidenhair Fern:
Magic Medicine

Maidenhair fern (*Adiantum pedatum*) is widely distributed in North America and grows abundantly in rich, moist woods. Its fragile, fan-shaped leaflets are supported by thin, black, shiny stems. It has had a long and distinguished medical history. Dioscorides (die-us-co-RYE-dees), the father of medical botany who was a physician in the Roman army of the infamous Emperor Nero, prescribed the maidenhair fern for chest ailments.

John Gerard went one step further and in "The Herbal" wrote the following about maidenhair:

> It [maidenhair] consumeth and wasteth away the
> King's evil [scrofula, swellings in the neck caused by
> tuberculosis of the lumph glands] and other hard
> swellings, and it maketh the haire of the head and
> beard to grow that is fallen or pulled out.

The myth of maidenhair as a hair restorer somehow persisted. Two hundred years ago, elixirs of maidenhair ferns were the "thing" for European bald pates. More recently, a hair restorer and scalp tonic was concocted consisting of the ashes of maidenhair ferns mixed with olive oil and herb vinegar. Baldness can now be treated unsuccessfully with Culpeper's Wall-Rue Hair Restorer or Gerard's Maidenhair Scalp Tonic or a modern maidenhair restorer–scalp tonic combination. Take your choice.

Culpeper added these words about the medical marvels of maidenhair:

> This and all other Maiden Hairs is a good remedy for
> coughs, asthmas, pleuracy and the like and on account
> of its being a gentle diuretic also in jaundice, gravel,
> and other impurities of the kidneys.

He warns, however, that "All the Maiden Hairs should be used green and in conjunction with other ingredients because their virtues are weak." This fern's preference for a wet habitat was the signature that made it an effective agent "in febrile diseases and intermittent fever and as an expectorant in catarrhal conditions and bronchial congestion."

American Indians prepared an ointment from this fern to treat inflammations of the skin. For the Cherokees, maidenhair was the specific for expelling worms from the body and for breaking fevers.

The maidenhair fern was believed to have the curative properties of a wide-spectrum antibiotic capable of healing every ailment from A (alopecia, i.e., baldness) to Z (zooparasitism, i.e., worm infestations). As a fern, maidenhair has great beauty and charm, but as a precursor of penicillin, it is powerless.

The Male and Female Ferns:
Sex Symbols

The male fern (*Dryopteris filix-mas*), rare in this country but common in Europe, was granted the same medicinal powers as bracken plus a few additional attributes. An ointment made from its roots was considered excellent for healing wounds; the powdered roots were the supposed remedy for rickets in children.

Gerard, the authority on astrological medicine wrote this very detailed prescription for "driving forth" worms:

> The roots of the Male Fern, being taken in the weight of half an ounce, driveth forth long flat worms, as Dioscorides writeth, being drunk in mede or honied water, and more effectually, if it be given with two scruples [units of the apothecaries' weight] or two thirds part of a dram [another unit of the apothecaries' weight] of scammonie [a plant whose roots yield medicinal resins], or of black hellabore [another plant]; they that will use it, must first eat garlicke.

Although male fern roots were an ancient remedy for curing worms and were described as such in the works of Greek and Roman physicians, it was not until 1775 that its virtues as a vermifuge became generally known. A Madame Nouffer, the widow of a Swiss surgeon, sold a secret remedy for curing worms to King Louis XV of France. This proved to be nothing less than the powdered roots of the male fern. Modern medicine casts serious doubt on the value of this preparation as a "dewormer." Physicians using it have obtained contradictory results. One of the chief constituents of the male fern, aspidium, causes paralysis of the voluntary muscles. It is also a violent poison, but its use does not always lead to serious illness and death because the body absorbs very little of it. It does, however, poison and paralyze parasitic worms that live in the intestines.

At one time the male fern also had a reputation as an aphrodisiac (a stimulant of sexual desire, named after the Greek goddess of love, Aphrodite). It was the secret ingredient of love-potions, particularly those concocted by witches, who apparently were experts in the art of bewitching. The rhizome of this fern was also prized as a good luck charm when it was fashioned to resemble the fingers of the hand and then dried over the smoke of a midsummer bonfire. It also had some other more practical uses; infusions of the roots and stem of the fern were substituted for hops in brewing beer.

The lady fern (*Athyrium filix-femina*) is also called the female fern. Its Latin name was originally applied to bracken, but Linnaeus transferred the name to the lady fern for two possible reasons. First, the lady fern is more delicate and finely cut than the male fern. Second, it appears in a perplexing number of forms. This inconsistency, Linnaeus thought, was more characteristic of the female than the male of the species. The lady fern was assigned the same medicinal properties as its male counterpart, but was considered less powerful (another case of medical male chauvinism).

However, what the lady fern lacked in medicinal might, it made up for in literary recognition and stature. Sir Walter Scott, the nineteenth-century Scottish poet and novelist, paid his respects to the lady fern in the following lines:

> Where the copse woods is the greenest,
> Where the fountain glistens sheenest,
> Where the morning dew lies longest
> There the Lady Fern grows strongest.

Edwin Lees, a nineteenth-century poet–botanist also paid tribute to the lady fern in a poem published in his book "Botanical Looker-Out," (1851) a portion of which is given here:

> When in splendour and beauty all nature is crown'd,
> The fern is seen curling half hid in the ground,
> But of all the green brackens that lie by the burn,
> Commend me alone to the sweet Lady Fern.

> Filix-mas in a circle lifts up his green fronds,
> And the Heath Fern delights by the bog and the pond

Through their shadowy tufts though with pleasure I turn,
The palm must still rest with the fair Lady Fern.

Common Polypody:
Uncommon Medicine

Common polypody (*Polypodium virginianum*), the rock-sitting fern, was promoted as a remedy for "chasing away the blues" and for preventing "fearsome and troublesome dreams and nightmares." The ancients found its roots to be a mild laxative, and considered them a tonic for dyspepsia and a treatment for skin diseases. A draft of boiled polypody leaves, they insisted, cured whooping cough in children; relieved liver complaints, coughs, and catarrh conditions; helped in early stages of consumption; and was successful in ridding the body of some kinds of worms. The roots were also credited with relieving rheumatic swellings, jaundice, dropsy, scurvy, hardness of the spleen, and colic.

William Cole, the seventeenth-century English herbalist and advocate of the Doctrine of Signature, in his "Adam in Eden" (1657) declared:

> The rough spots that are on the underside of the leaves of Polypody as also the nags [knots] or excrescences on each side of the roots, is a sign that it is good for the lungs and the exulcerations thereof.

Few ferns were thought capable of performing as many pharmaceutical feats as many-footed polypody.

Royal Fern:
Royal Remedy

The royal fern (*Osmunda regalis*) is one of our most dignified and regal species. It thrives in swamps and bogs and grows gracefully in water "up to its knees." This fern was highly prized by Victorian fern fanciers. The British countryside was almost picked clean of the royal fern. It found its way into English gardens and conservatories where it became a middle-class status symbol. Fortunately, the royal fern frenzy has died down and this fern is making a comeback.

103

The fern has been known for a long time under different names. Among its many aliases are "flowering ferns," because it displays handsome terminal fertile leaflets that resemble spikes of flowers; "water fern" and "ditch fern," since it seems happy wallowing in water and mud; and "snake brake," explained in the following ancient superstition:

> Brake the first brake you see,
> Kill the first snake you see
> And you will conquer every enemy.

The Latin name *Osmunda* has several possible origins. It may be derived from the Saxon word *osmund* (*os:* house and *mund:* peace), which means domestic peace. It has also been traced to Osmunder, the Saxon counterpart of the Norse god, Thor. Another source traces it to a legend about Osmund, a waterman on Loch Tyne, who saved his wife and young daughter from invading Danes by hiding them among these ferns. Years later, the daughter named these tall ferns Osmunder after her father.

The nineteenth-century English poet, William Wordsworth, expressed his own ideas about the origin of the name in the following lines:

> . . . Many such there are
> Fair ferns and flowers, and chiefly that tall fern
> So stately, of the Queen Osmunda named.

Osmunda has also been traced to a Latin origin describing its medical use to clean bones (*os:* bone and *mundare:* to clean).

The therapeutic values of the royal fern lie in its roots, which were prescribed to cure jaundice (if applied in the early stages of this affliction), to remove obstacles from the intestines, and to treat lumbago.

Culpeper praised the royal fern and wrote:

> It is accounted singularly good against bruises and bones broken or out of joint, and gives much ease to the colic and speletic diseases; as also for ruptures and burstings.

Another old world belief was that biting the first royal fern frond seen in the spring was assurance against toothaches for the rest of the year, a royal remedy for tooth decay with ferns instead of fluorides.

Adder's Tongue:
For Snake Bites

The fronds of adder's tongue fern (*Ophioglossum vulgatum*) resemble a snake's tongue from which its name (*Ophio:* snake and *glossus:* tongue) and reputation are derived. This strange fern which is 3" to 12" tall grows in grassy fields and moist meadows, making it as difficult to find as a green snake in the grass.

As you have no doubt surmised, at one time its fronds were prescribed as the antidote for snake bites. William Coles, again in his "Adam in Eden" published in 1657, wrote:

> This plant is called adder's tongue because out of every leaf it sendith forth a kind of pestal like an adder's tongue; it cureth the bite of serpents.

Its reputation as a wound healer goes back to Gerard, who in his book "The Herbal" wrote:

> The leaves of adder's tongue stamped in stone mortar, and boiled in olive oil unto the consumption of the juice, and until the herbs be dried and parched and then strained, will yield most excellent greene oil or rather a balsame for greene wounds comparable to oil of St. John's-wort (a plant) if it does not far surpasse it.

Adder's Spear Ointment, also known as Green Oil of Charity, made from the fresh fronds of this fern, is said to be in demand as a remedy for wounds to this day. The juice of the fronds was also extracted to treat internal wounds and bruises, vomiting, bleeding at the mouth or nose, and sore eyes.

Michael Drayton, the Elizabethan poet and botanist in his book "*Theatrum Botanicum*" (1640), extolled the virtues of adder's tongue for snake bites in the following lines:

> For them that are with newts or snakes or adders stung
> He seeketh out a herb that's called adder's tongue,
> As Nature it ordained its own like hurts to cure,
> And sporative, did herself to niceties inure.

Despite these paeans of praise, victims of snake bites generally prefer the distillates of John Barleycorn (hard liquor) to the soft licks of adder's tongue.

Moonwort Ferns:
The Magic of Moonlight

The moonwort fern (*Botrychium lunaria*) is an unusual and uncommon fern, with half-moon or fan-shaped fronds. It appears more often in fables and folklore than in fields and meadows where it lives. This fern was looked upon with great respect and awe because of the many magical attributes it was reputed to possess.

Drayton was also familiar with moonwort but called it lunary:

> Then sprinkled she the juice of rue
> With nine drops of the midnight dew
> From Lunary distilling.

One of the most popular moonwort myths was its talent to open locks and unshoe horses that stepped on it, from which this fern earned the names "blasting root" and "spring wurzel."

Culpeper made the following very cautious appraisal of moonwort magic:

> Moonwort is an herb which they say will open locks
> and unshoe such horses as tread upon it; these some
> laugh to scorn, and these no fools neither, but
> country folks that I know, call it Unshoe the horse.

Cole reiterates the myth with similar caution:

> It is said, yea, and believed by many, Moonwort
> will open locks wherewith dwellings are made fast,
> if it be put into the keyholes; as also it will
> loosen shoes from those horses that go on the places
> where it grows.

George Withers, seventeenth-century English lyricist, also alluded to the magic of moonwort:

> There is an herb, some say, whose virtue's such
> It in the pasture, only with a touch
> Unshoes the new-shod steed.

Guillaume du Bartas, in his book "Divine Weeks and Works" (1641) described this fern as one of the wonders of creation because of its magical might:

Horses that feeding on grassy hills,
Tread upon Moonwort with their hollow heels,
Though lately shod, at night goe barefoot home,
Their master musing where their shoes be gone,
O Moonwort, tell us where thou hid'st the smith,
Hammer and Pincer, thou unshoest them with,
Alas, what lock and iron engine is't,
That can thy subtile secret strength resist,
Sith the best Farrier cannot set a shoe,
So sure, but thou so shortly cans't undoe.

Not everybody came under the spell cast by moonwort. John Parkinson, the king's herbalist in the sixteenth century denounced the moonstruck lunatic fringe of that day:

It hath been formerly related by imposters and false knaves, and is yet believed by many, that it will loosen lockes, fetter and shoes from those horses feete that goe places where it groweth; and have been so audacious to contest with those who have contradicted them, that they have known and seene it to do so; but what observation so ever such persons doe make, it is all false suggestions and mere lyes.

The shape of the moonwort pinna, according to the Doctrine of Signature, placed it under the influence of the moon. Therefore moonwort was good for all diseases of a periodic nature and the sine qua non for curing lunacy, which was attributed to the moon. Moonwort had to be gathered by the light of the full moon to be efficacious:

Then rapidly with foot as light
As the young musk roe's, out she flew
To cull each shining leaf that grew
Beneath the moonlight's hallowing beams.

Moonwort was also said to hold the same healing powers as adder's tongue. Witches, sorcerers, exorcists, necromancers, and black magic devotees resorted to moonwort for their incantations. Alchemists prized this fern, it was said, because it had the ability to change quicksilver into real silver. Moonwort has the distinction of failing to live up to its reputation, even in the light of a full moon.

107

SUMMARY:

Fern Fables and Folklore

As a source of food and drugs, ferns have been part of human history. Lacking seeds and flowers, ferns generated many fables and are featured in folklore. Fanciful fables are told about "invisible" fern seeds which could make the finder not only invisible but the possessor of magical and supernatural powers.

Ferns have been prescribed for the treatment of all kinds of human ailments and conditions. The Doctrine of Signature, a medieval medical myth, strongly influenced the use of ferns in the treatment of diseases and finally fell of its own dead weight.

Several ferns are famous in folklore, such as the ubiquitous bracken, for its many uses as food and fables; the spleenworts and maidenhair ferns for their failure to prevent baldness; the male and female fern, more successful as vermifuges than as aphrodisiacs; the royal fern, as a source of innumerable fables; adder's tongue, as a useless antidote for snake bites; moonworts, as the possessor of many magical powers bordering on lunacy; and common polypody as an antidepressant.

Bulblet Bladder Fern

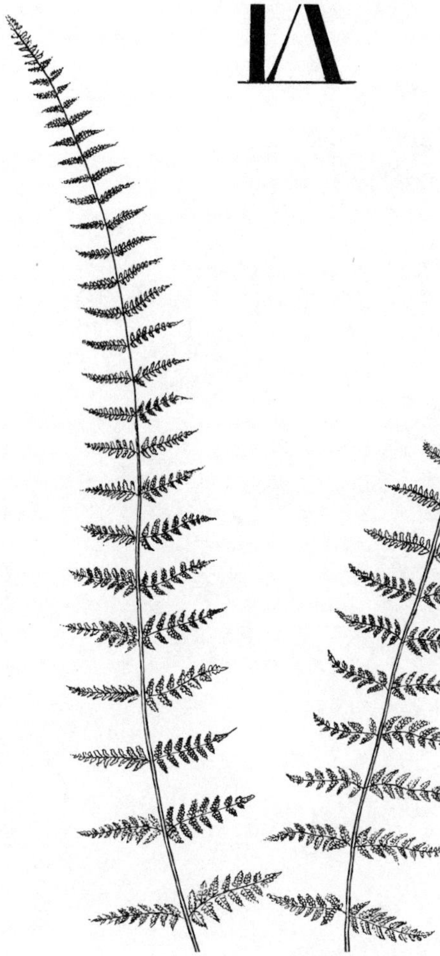

Thrice-cut narrow frond
Bulblets on underside of rachis

Bulblet on fertile pinna

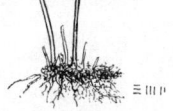

IX

Sowing Spores and Reaping Ferns

Of all the things you can do with ferns, the most productive and constructive is spore culture. This hobby has attracted many followers, because fern spores can be cultured any time of the year, in almost any place. They require a minimum of space, equipment, training, and money, but lots of time and patience.

From a conservationist's viewpoint, spore sowers are mid-wives helping to deliver more fernlets than would ordinarily survive in a world of shrinking forests, fields, and green space. Although almost all pteridophytes are protected by law against pickers and plunderers, fern felons are rarely if ever apprehended. The future of the world's fern population, especially the rare, threatened, and endangered species, may well be in the hands of spore farmers who become fern protectors and propagators. A compelling reason for encouraging spore culture is that a small piece of a fertile frond goes a long way in propagating hundreds of offspring without destroying or damaging parent plants.

Spore Search:
Seeking and Finding Spores

The best source of spores is living ferns. You will recall that spores are packed in spore cases bunched together as sori; they appear either as visible brown spots or streaks on the underside of the fern fronds, or crowded on fertile pinnae, or on separate fertile fronds. For most wild ferns, summer time is "sporing" time. Domesticated, home-grown ferns may be in spore any time of the year. Organize your spore safari accordingly.

You want spores that are not too young, not too old, but just ripe. You can tell when spores are ready to be harvested by the color of the sori. White or green sori are too young; their spores are immature. Shriveled, frayed, tan sori are too old; their spore cases are empty, the spores having been discharged. Dark-brown, shiny, plump sori are just right, full of ripe spores ready to be

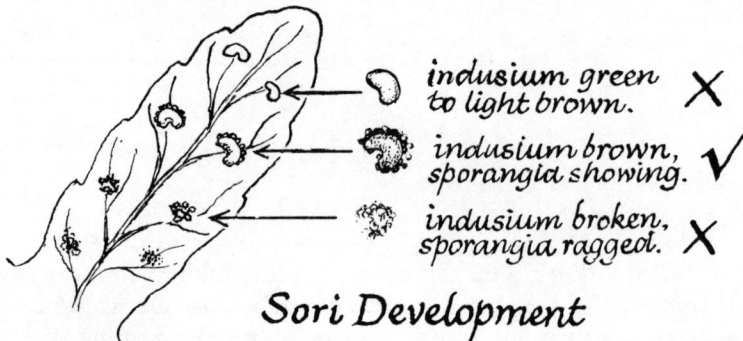

indusium green to light brown. **X**

indusium brown, sporangia showing. **√**

indusium broken, sporangia ragged. **X**

Sori Development

harvested. Spore maturity may be verified by a magnifying glass, a highly recommended procedure since a frond may hold spores at various stages of development. Generally, plump, brown sporangia with intact indusia (spore case coverings) are the pick of the spore crop.

Salvaging Spores:
Collecting, Cleaning and Storing

Once you find the spore source, remove a piece of the frond invested with ripened spores. Place it in an envelope for storage or face down on a piece of clean, smooth, white paper. Cover the frond with a blotter or newspaper to prevent the spores from blowing away and also to hasten their release by absorbing moisture from the specimen. After a day or so, carefully remove the covering sheet in a sheltered place away from drafts; spores are very light and easily blown away.

Place fronds, sori side down, on a sheet of paper; cover and add weight. Let stand for 24 hours.

Collecting Spores

*Remove upper
sheet slowly,
lift frond(s), tap
gently; crease
lower sheet
carefully so
spores do not
blow away and
tap lightly into a
vial or envelope —
LABEL*

The white paper will be sprinkled with a fine brown dust which may also be green, yellow, black, or some other colors, depending on the species. The dust is a mixture of spores, fragments of sporangia, indusia, and frond bits. Thinking ahead, it is desirable at this point to get rid of nonsporing debris; this will help to reduce contaminating algae, fungi, and mosses in the spore gardens. To remove unwanted rubbish, tilt and tap the side of the paper on which the spores are collected. The debris will "dance" off the edge of the paper while the spores will stick. Fold the paper in half and gently tap its side to collect the spores in the crease. To store spores, hold one end of the crease over the mouth of a container—an envelope or a sterile vial. Guide the spores into the container by tapping the sides of the paper. Label with the name of the fern, where and when collected, and store in a cool, dark place until you are ready to use them. A refrigerator is fine and extends the life of some spores.

Life Span of Spores:
From Days to Decades

The life span of fern spores varies from days to years. Green spores characteristic of the *Osmunda* ferns (royal, cinnamon, and interrupted) are short-lived and should be sown within a day or two after collection. Refrigeration prolongs their lives, but fresh, green spores germinate in greater numbers and faster than stale ones. An exception is the green spores of the ostrich and sensitive ferns, which live for a year or more without losing their vitality.

Nongreen spores are long-livers, tough and rugged; most are viable for months, some for years. Spores one hundred years old that germinated when planted have been reported but not confirmed. The life span of these spores also is increased by refrigeration.

Because of their longevity, dried fern specimens should not be overlooked as a spore source, providing excessive heat was not used to preserve them. An excellent source of spores are the spore banks of plant nurseries and fern societies. The American Fern Society maintains one of the largest spore banks and exchanges containing over 800 kinds of spores from rare and common ferns, donated regularly by its members and pteridophiles around the world. These can be purchased by American Fern Society members at a very nominal fee. Investing in a spore bank yields fantastic "fernancial" returns.

Spore Gardens:
"Sporariums"

Having collected spores, the next step is to sow them. Any container of glass or plastic with an airtight cover for retaining moisture and creating a high humidity ambiance is suitable as a "sporarium." Wide-mouth, screw-top, flat jars or plastic refrigerator containers do very well. For the more adventurous and ambitious spore sowers, plastic shoe boxes are ideal. They hold exactly sixteen 2 1/2-inch square plastic flowerpots. Different spores may be planted in each of the flowerpots and the shoebox becomes the "sporarium." Most important, in fact imperative, is that these containers be sterile. Unless this precaution is taken, alien algae, foreign fungi, and marauding mosses which grow like weeds will take over, and the sporelings will never have a chance to see the light of day. Glass containers and covers may be sterilized by boiling them in hot water or by soaking them overnight in a 10 percent solution of Clorox.

Spore Soil:
Growing Medium

There is no one "best" medium for growing spores. Most spore sowers have a favorite medium and special recipe for cultivating spores and swear by it. Among these "best" mediums are sterile water, sphagnum or peat moss, sand, vermiculite, blotters, soil, tiny pieces of clay flower pots, and various combinations of these "goodies." Regardless of the medium used, it too, must be sterile. Soil and soil mixtures may be sterilized by baking them in an oven for 2 to 3 hours at 300°F (150°C) or steaming in a pressure cooker.

Soil sterilized by baking must be kept moist and in a closed container, otherwise it will dry out and burn. Commercial pre-sterilized packaged soil, such as African Violet mixture, will also serve your purpose and eliminate the chore of choosing and cooking spore soil.

Sterile spore soil is spread in a thin layer, about 1/2-inch thick, in each sterile container and moistened with sterile water. Avoid unboiled tap water; it may contain the spores of algae, fungi, and mosses, which can crowd out and strangle fern sporelings. Also, the chemicals in tap water are sometimes toxic to germinating gametophytes and young struggling sporophytes. To create a high humidity environment, moisten the spore bed, but drain off excess water. Too much water, indicated by soggy soil or standing water, will suffocate spores.

Sowing and Growing Spores:
"Sporing"

Once the sterile soil is in a closed sterile container and moistened with sterile water, the garden is ready to be "spored." Remove the container cover and quickly spread the spores thinly and evenly over the soil surface by gently tapping the side of the receptacle holding the spores. Re-place the container cover imme-diately to minimize exposure of the spore soil to the surround-ing air, loaded with unwanted spores. Be sure to label the spored container with the name of the fern and the seeding date. Place the "sporarium" on a windowsill with a northern exposure or on an open shelf, but not in the direct sunlight. The surest way to prepare sun-stewed spores is to place the "sporarium" in sunshine where a greenhouse becomes

Tap gently to disperse spores

Sterile Soil Mix

With spores sown, add water and cover pan with glass

a hothouse. If you do not have access to indirect natural light, artificial illumination will do just as well, if not better, according to some spore growers. They see advantages in being able to control the strength and duration of exposure using light bulbs.

Exposure to a single fluorescent fixture about one foot above the spore garden about 14 hours a day yields excellent results. Whether you use natural or artificial light, spores need light to start growing and to keep going. Room temperatures between 65°F and 75°F (18°C and 24°C) favor healthy spore growth.

Sprouting Spores:
Sporelings

Another Method
1. *Fill clay pot with wet moss*
2. *Invert in a saucer of water*
3. *Sow spores on outside of pot*

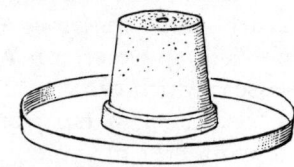

You are now on the threshold of the most difficult and perhaps the most frustrating stage of spore farming, waiting for the spores to show signs of life. Spores take their own sweet time in sprouting. It may be

4. Cover pot with glass jar

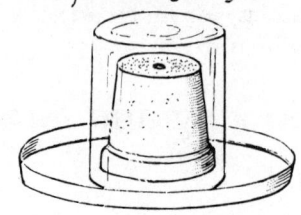

5. Wait, keeping water in saucer at all times

months before you see any evidence that all your labors have not been in vain. Fussing and fuming are futile. Opening and closing the containers helps even less. It is an open invitation for uninvited spores to enter and for precious water to leave. The best approach is to sit back and wait; spores thrive on planned neglect.

The first sign of sporeling life is a slight greening on the surface of the soil. Very fine, green, algaelike threads emerge from the sprouting spores and broaden into tiny, green, heart-shaped prothalli. These are big enough to be visible. Soon you have wall-to-wall green carpeting of growing gametophytes. To reach this stage usually takes about three months, give or take a month. Some spores, like those of the staghorns, are slow-growers; it might take a year before baby staghorns appear.

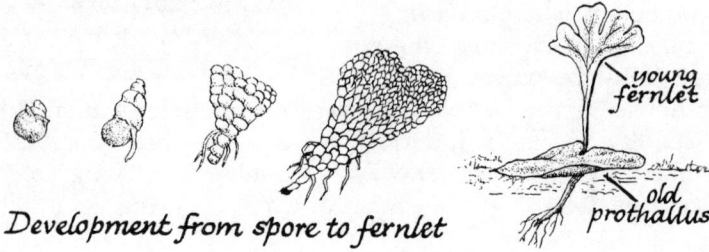

young fernlet

old prothallus

Development from spore to fernlet

At this point, water is crucial. Without it sperms cannot swim to the egg, fertilize it, and sire fernlets. A few drops, like the gentle rain from heaven, may be a message of mercy, twice blessed by the giver and taker—no water, no sex, no fernlets.

Fernlets:
Growing Up

Prothalli that have satisfied their sex drive display tiny sporophytes growing out of the notch. Only one fernlet is "mothered" by each prothallus. If this does not happen, try a few drops of distilled water or cooled, boiled tap water as a sex stimulant. Should this fail, try again and again; you have nothing to lose but your patience and spores. At worst, you are back to square one, ready to start "sporing" from scratch.

When the fernlet has developed a few fronds and roots and the prothallus withers, it is ready to be moved to larger quarters. Do not attempt to pick out individual fernlets. Select a small group and transplant to a 2-inch clay or plastic pot, giving it the same conditions that it enjoyed as a sporeling. Fernlets about one inch should be transplanted individually to 2-inch pots. Spore-sired fernlets are extremely delicate and very sensitive to changes in humidity and habitat. With each transplant, take care not to injure the hairlike roots or to expose them excessively to the air. Baby ferns need the protection of a high humidity incubator or nursery.

Fernlets may be transplanted on the tip of a knife

Fern Nurseries:
Ferneries

A large glass or plastic container with a removable cover makes an ideal fern nursery. Lining the bottom of the container with gravel covered by moist peat moss creates a high humidity home so crucial for these frail fernlets. Partially uncovering this miniature tropical fern forest, slowly conditions and hardens these ferns to live with others in the real world. Growing ferns is like raising children; they need tender, loving care.

A Fernery

Line bottom of container with gravel and moist peat moss for high humidity.

Fernlet Foes:
Molds and Algae

To the spore sower, algae, and mosses are the enemy. The spores of these fernlet foes are everywhere, in air, water, and soil. Just as a gardener must wage a constant war against weeds, so the spore sower must be mobilized against molds. The first line of defense is sterile "sporarium" conditions, maintained by minimum exposure to air. Despite the best-laid plans, molds often manage to get into the sporarium and slaughter the sporelings. Chemical warfare is the second line of defense. Very dilute solutions of copper sulfate or potassium permanganate are fairly effective mold killers. Also recommended is a DuPont product, Semesan.

Once algae are established in a culture, they are difficult to eliminate. One defense is applying Algex, one of several algae-killing chemicals. Another approach is to hope and pray that the sporelings and prothalli live long enough to produce fernlets which can be rescued and moved to new sterile quarters.

SUMMARY:

Ferns from Spores

To successfully sow spores and reap ferns, observe the following ten commandments:

1. Thou shalt sow only ripe spores.
2. Thou shalt sterilize the house of the spores.
3. Thou shalt plant spores in sterile soil.
4. Thou shalt moisten spores only with sterile water.
5. Thou shalt grow spores in a house of high humidity.
6. Thou shalt keep the house of spores neither too hot nor too cold.
7. Thou shalt give spores the light but not the heat of the sun.
8. Thou shalt patiently await the greening of the sporelings.
9. Thou shalt treat fernlets with tender, loving care.
10. Thou shalt smite their foes so that the fernlets may beget more spores.

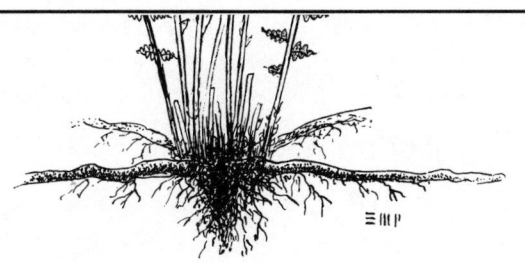

CHAPTER X

Ostrich Fern

Thrice-cut leathery fronds; pinnae
tapering to base; separate fertile
club-shaped fronds

*fertile
pinna*

X

Vegetative Propagation

A simple, fast, and inexpensive way to propagate ferns is to raise them from bits and pieces of other ferns. This method of growing ferns is called **vegetative propagation** or cloning (rhymes with moaning), because only the vegetative parts of a plant are used—roots, rhizomes, fronds, and buds—not spores or sex cells. A vegetative fern fragment has the potential for growing into a complete fertile fern by itself. The trials and tribulations of sexual reproduction with its spores, prothalli, sex organs, sex cells, and dependent fernlets are completely bypassed and life goes on without sex. Practically all ferns reproduce by vegetative means—natural cloning—and have been doing so for hundreds of millions of years. Vegetatively propagated offspring are clones, carbon copies of the single parent plant.

The methods of vegetative propagation are not innovations but rather imitations of what ferns do naturally. The formula for success in this enterprise is to follow the vegetative footsteps of ferns and the ways of Mother Nature.

Rooting Rhizomes:
Above and Below the Ground

A common and simple natural method of vegetative reproduction is by branching rhizomes. These stems, which may grow on or near the surface of the soil, not only produce roots that dig down, fronds that reach up, but also buds that sprout out. In this way, ostrich ferns fill fens, bracken conquer clearings, and hay-scented ferns pack pastures.

A generally successful and satisfactory method of vegetative reproduction is to grow clones from rhizomes. By cutting off end pieces of the rhizomes with growing tips and buds and planting them separately, you can, with a single stroke of a sharp knife, preserve the parent and produce clones for an "instant" garden.

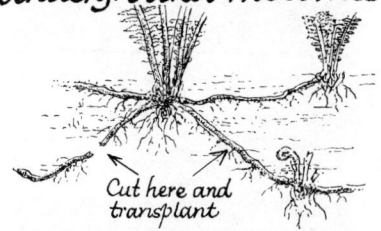

Underground rhizomes

Cut here and transplant

The underground rhizome system of the Ostrich fern simplifies propagation

Replant the rhizome sections in their former position in the soil; remove old, broken, or withered fronds; and keep the growing green fronds. Given proper soil, water, light, temperature, and humidity, these fern fragments will continue to grow in their new setting as well as they did in nature.

Ferns with bunched, tangled roots and rhizomes, such as the cinnamon, the interrupted, and the spleenwort ferns, require special handling. The entire plant must be dug up and the younger ferns growing from the base carefully cut away and planted separately in pots or gardens.

Ferns with "Feet":
Growing Footed Ferns

Ferns with exposed rhizomes, such as the many-footed wild common polypody and the cultivated "footed" ferns are relatively easy to propagate. By cutting off the ends of the "feet" of polypody and rooting them on the surface of soil, half-buried, you can increase the number of "walkers." Unless these fern fragments have roots, anchor the amputated "feet" to the soil to about half their thickness with bent pieces of wire; be careful not to bury the growing tip. Keep the rhizome sections moist but not soggy or under water. Submerged fern feet cannot walk on or under water.

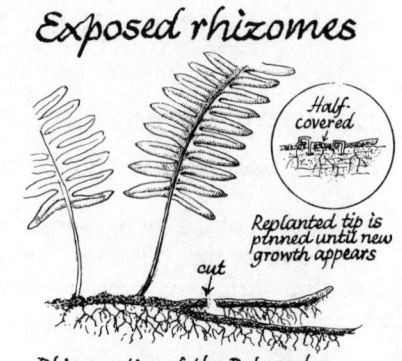

Exposed rhizomes

Half-covered

Replanted tip is pinned until new growth appears

cut

Rhizome tips of the Polypody may be cut off and replanted

The same propagation procedures apply to the "fuzzy footed" ferns, of which there are several attractive and colorful species. The "feet" are exposed rhizomes covered with colored scales, giving them the appearance of animal feet and such names as bear's foot, bear's paw, rabbit's foot, squirrel's foot, and the like.

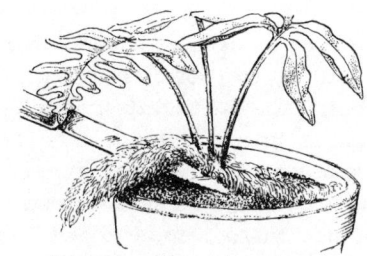

'Feet' can be cut away and pinned down until rooted.

The growth of rhizome roots can be hastened in these ferns by the air-layering technique. Tie moist sphagnum moss wrapped in plastic sheeting around the rhizome a few inches from the tip. Rooting is rapid; after roots appear, cut the rooted ends from the parent plant, dispose of the wrappings, and plant in congenial quarters.

Ferns from Buds:
Boston Runners

Ferns also propagate new plants naturally from buds, bits of growth tissue on stolons, fronds, and roots. The Boston fern, probably the best-known and best-loved household plant, sprouts long, leafless, stringlike stems among its green fronds. These threads are runners or **stolons** (rhymes with roll-ons), which bear tiny buds along their entire length. These buds take root where they touch the soil and produce fernlets. By pinning these runners to the growing medium, you can clone a string of Boston baby ferns. When the fernlets show a few fronds, cut the "umbilical cord" and deliver the babies, which will grow up and produce more runners for a Boston fern marathon.

Stolons (runners)

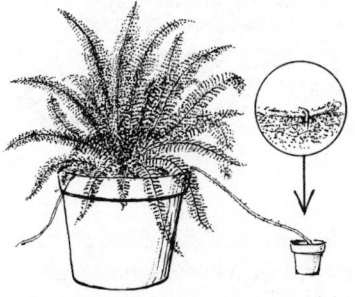

Pin tip of stolon in another pot until rooted, then cut apart.

Ferns from Root Buds:
Staghorn Style

A fern that grows fernlets from
buds on its roots is the staghorn, a name that describes its
antler-shaped fertile fronds. The
roots of this tree trunk hugger
are covered by shield-shaped
sterile fronds, under which the
young staghorns breed. When
their "antlers" are a few inches
long, the "pups," as they are
called, can be cut away from the
parent plant with some of the
basal rooted portion and set free
to raise their own "herds" (see page 159).

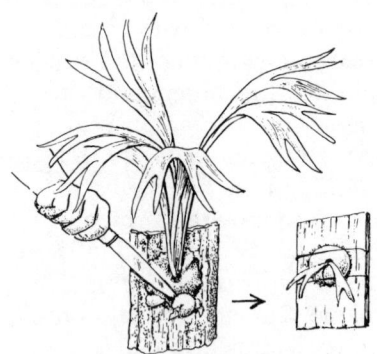

*'Pups' may be cut off staghorn
ferns and mounted separately*

Ferns from Frond Buds:
Toddlers, Bulblets, and Fernlets

Let us not forget the way in which the walking fern gets around.
The tapering tip of its simple arching frond bears a bud, and
where it touches the ground, a "toddler" appears. By carefully
cutting the frond connection, the "toddler" is set free to do its
own walking, and you qualify as an "F.D.," fern doctor.

*Snip off the tip
and transplant*

Another vegetative variation is bud-cloning from bulblets. The
bulblet bladder fern develops large, round buds resembling peas
on the underside of the frond, in addition to spores. At maturity, these bulblets fall off naturally and germinate into little baby

126

bulblet bladder ferns. By gathering and sowing these "drop-offs," you can raise a family of bulblet ferns. Such buds should be buried halfway in well-draining growth medium, watered, and covered to maintain humidity. Bulblets grow very slowly, and it may take two or three years before they look like their "mother."

Mother ferns have baby ferns sprout from the axils; cut them away and plant.

Still another asexual avenue of reproduction is seen in ferns that grow fernlets on the upper surface or edges of the fronds. Such self-cloning ferns are called "live bearers" or "mother ferns." The entire upper surface of the frond may be covered with fernlets. Some drop off or are pushed off and root themselves under the mother plant. By gathering and planting these "castoffs," you can do more for them than their "mother": you can give them room to grow. Other babies remain attached to the "mother" frond and are not free until the frond decays. You can help yourself and these "mother-bound" babies by removing the frond and pinning it to the surface of moist soil. This will encourage rooting and independence.

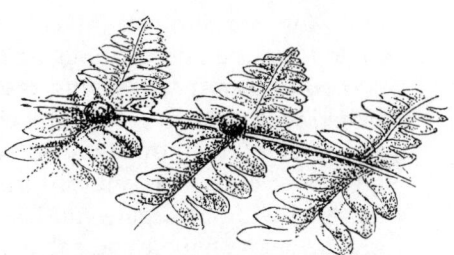

Bulblet ferns develop buds (bulblets) along the rachis

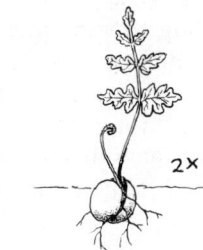

2×

Collect and sow bulblets

Tissue and Cell Culture:
Fern Cloning Under Glass

Botanists are developing new and exciting tissue and cell culture techniques for raising ferns vegetatively. Instead of planting fern fragments, such as roots, rhizomes, stolons, and buds, microscopic bits of fern tissue from any growing part and individual cells are being cultivated in test tubes to produce whole plants.

Bits of growth tissue are removed from the fern, sterilized, and grown under sterile conditions in test tubes containing nutrient agar, a jellylike material containing plant foods. Within a week, the bits of tissue grow roots. They are then transplanted into other test tubes containing agar enriched with growth-promoting chemicals. After several weeks, many plants are produced; these are separated and raised on soil as individual ferns. By this method of raising and cloning, a tiny bit of growing fern tissue produces many complete identical plants within a few months.

More startling are the cell culture techniques by which complete ferns are raised from single cells. Basically, the same culture procedures are used; young root cells, after growing on agar enriched with growth-promoting chemicals, are transferred to sterile water. Here the growing mass separates into individual and small groups of cells. The cells are then "plated out" on sterile growth material without sugar, and they develop into prothalli, the tiny, green, heart-shaped body that produces gametes. If the cells are grown on media containing 2 percent sucrose (table sugar), sporophytes develop; these are the large, green, spore-producing ferns with which you are familiar. On 0.5 percent sucrose media, single cells go through all the stages and eventually become sporophytes. What is so striking about these experiments is that by controlling the amount of sugar in the growth medium, you can control the stage in the life history of the fern.

Of course, tissue and cell culture methods are very complicated, requiring special training and special equipment. Nevertheless, they indicate at least one line of research with ferns which may revolutionize methods of vegetative propagation.

SUMMARY:

Whole Ferns from Bits and Pieces

Ferns reproduce asexually by natural cloning from fragments of their vegetative parts: roots, rhizomes, and growing tips or buds. Vegetative reproduction techniques are based on what ferns have done naturally and successfully for hundreds of millions of years.

Pieces of underground and above-ground rhizomes are easily rooted and quickly propagated and grow into complete ferns identical with the parent plant. Buds, which are points of growing tissues, are present on roots, rhizomes, runners, and fronds and have the capacity to grow into fernlets. The buds on the runners of Boston ferns produce Boston fernlets when grounded; buds on the roots of the staghorn fern grow "pups"; from the bud on the frond tip of the walking fern, "toddlers" appear; bulblets on the underside of the bulblet bladder fern drop off and develop into baby ferns; and several lesser-known ferns grow fernlets on the upper surface and edges of the frond which eventually leave the "mother" plant, grow roots, and start an independent life.

Tissue and cell culture techniques are successfully producing whole ferns from microscopic bits of tissues and individual cells. These procedures require special training and equipment and have the potential of changing our present methods of vegetative reproduction.

CHAPTER VI

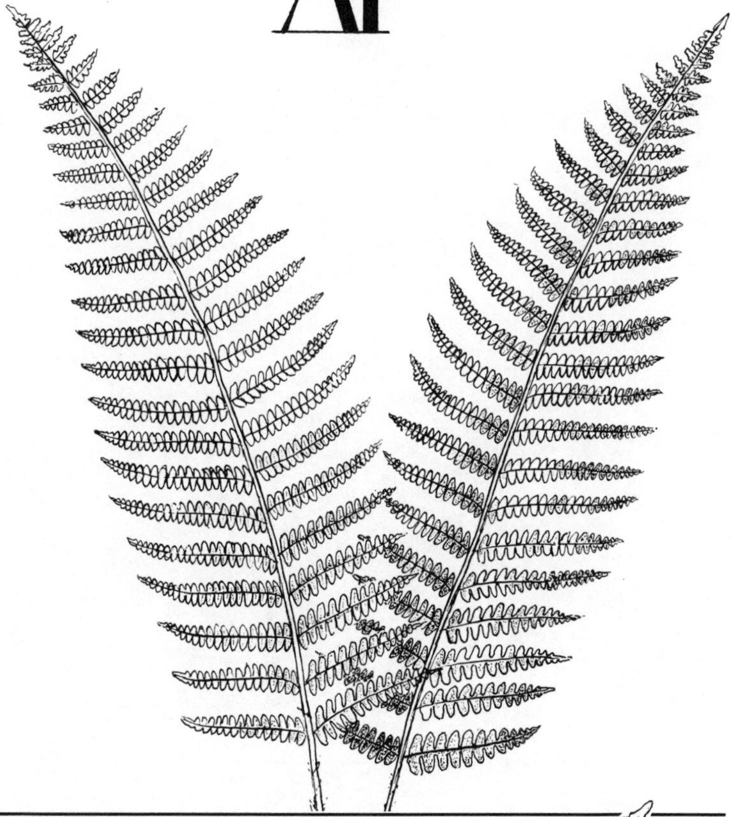

Marginal Shield Fern

Twice-cut leathery fronds; stipes scaly at stubbly base; sori along margins of pinnules; evergreen

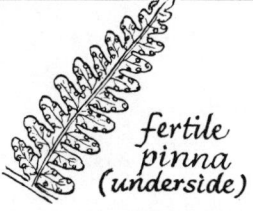

fertile
pinna
(underside)

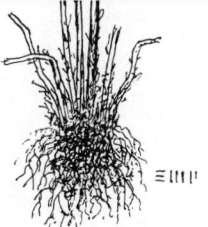

XI

Outdoor Ferneries

$\mathcal{A}$ n outdoor garden need not be without ferns. Although ferns lack brightly colored flowers and fruits, with their finely cut, delicate green fronds and stately stature they may be just the plants to fill ugly bare spots in your garden where nothing seems to grow.

To the gardener who wants the greatest return in greenery for the smallest investment, ferns have several selling points. First, ferns frequently flourish in shady places where other plants fail. Second, most are perennials; once properly planted they are self-sustaining and carry on pretty much by themselves. Third, several species are evergreens and can be enjoyed year round in the driest and coldest weather. Fourth, but not least, ferns are relatively free from parasites and predators; they beam good health. What more can a gardener ask of a plant?

Once you find a spot in your heart for ferns, you will find a spot in your garden for them. And you will begin to ask of yourself, fellow fern farmers, nursery people, and anybody who will listen, questions such as:

What kinds of ferns should be planted in an outdoor garden?

What conditions do such ferns need?

What kinds of ferns are available for outdoor gardens?

How should ferns be planted and cared for?

What are some of the problems in outdoor fern farming and how should they be handled?

Locating a Fernery:
Light and Shade

In planning your fernery, keep in mind that ferns have lived successfully for hundreds of millions of years in tropical rain forests, and most still thrive on moist humus in shady haunts. Simply stated, ferns favor shade, moisture, and spongy soil.

When it comes to light, ferns follow the middle road. They can't stand too little or too much light; "in darkness they die and in sunlight ferns fry." Most enjoy soft, subdued light, mixed with a few hours of early morning and late afternoon slanted sunlight or sunlight filtered through the leaves of forest trees and shrubs. The preferred places of shade-loving ferns are under spreading shade trees; on the shady side of buildings, hedges, and walls; in shadowy spaces between buildings; in shady woods; and along the edges of clearings.

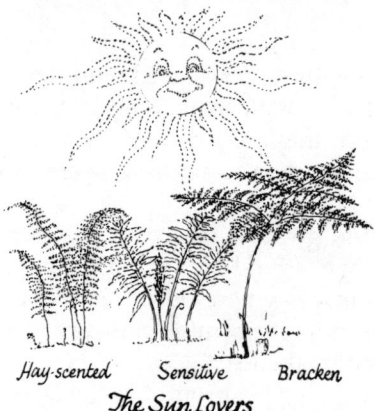

Hay-scented   Sensitive   Bracken
The Sun Lovers

There are of course a few "freak" ferns that live in open, sunny stretches; like mad dogs and Englishmen, they grow out in the midday sun. These include the hay-scented, sensitive, and bracken ferns. There is a fern for every place in your garden and a place for every fern.

Earth for Ferns:
Spongy Soil

Ferns are not very demanding, but they insist upon one earthy condition: rich, spongy soil with good drainage. Again, ferns are great compromisers. Most of them like it neither too dry nor too wet, but somewhere in-between—moderately moist. In too much water they drown, in too little, ferns dry and die.

Ferns are not too finicky about soil as long as it is porous, allowing air and water to circulate around its roots and rhizomes, which usually grow on or near the surface of the soil. Most soils, whether they are heavy clay or dry sand, can be enriched and made porous for fern farming by mixing with such leavening agents as humus, peat moss, compost, wood chips, vermiculite, or perlite.

Founding a Fern Garden:
Planning and Planting

Planning and planting a fernery go hand in hand. Before you turn the turf or stir a stone, consider the physical features of the garden-to-be: its size, soil, surroundings, exposure to sun and wind, slope, terrain, streams, swamps, stone walls, and ledges. These are some of the factors that will determine the number, kinds, and placement of ferns. Explore the habitat and habits of native ferns; they provide leads as to placement, spacing, and survival of transplants. Make your fern garden their home away from home.

Tall ferns, such as the ostrich, interrupted, cinnamon, and royal, need plenty of room vertically and horizontally to display their height, breadth, and shape. They should be set about a yard (one meter) apart in moist shaded places. Middle-size ferns—lady, shield, Christmas, maidenhairs—can use two feet of clearance in shady wooded areas. Most small ferns find a comfortable home in rocky niches and in humus-filled crevices of man-made rock gardens. Some, such as the walking, bulblet bladder, and cliff brake, have a distinct preference for weathered limestone ledges and crevices. Others, like the ebony spleenworts, fragile, and polypody ferns, make their bed in any kind of rock.

Open, sunny spots in your garden are inviting to sun-loving ferns, such as the hay-scented, sensitive, and bracken ferns. Be warned, however, that these sun-seekers have an aggressive, pushy life style which must be curbed, otherwise they will take over. These wild and weedy ferns can be tamed, trained, and contained. Once domesticated, they make excellent ground cover and can be a welcome addition to your garden.

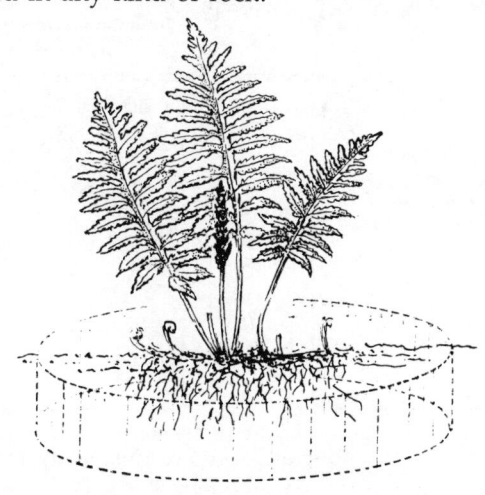

Before planting any of the Sunny Trio sink a retaining wall of plastic or metal to inhibit trespassing.

135

Suggested Fern Plantings for a Home Garden

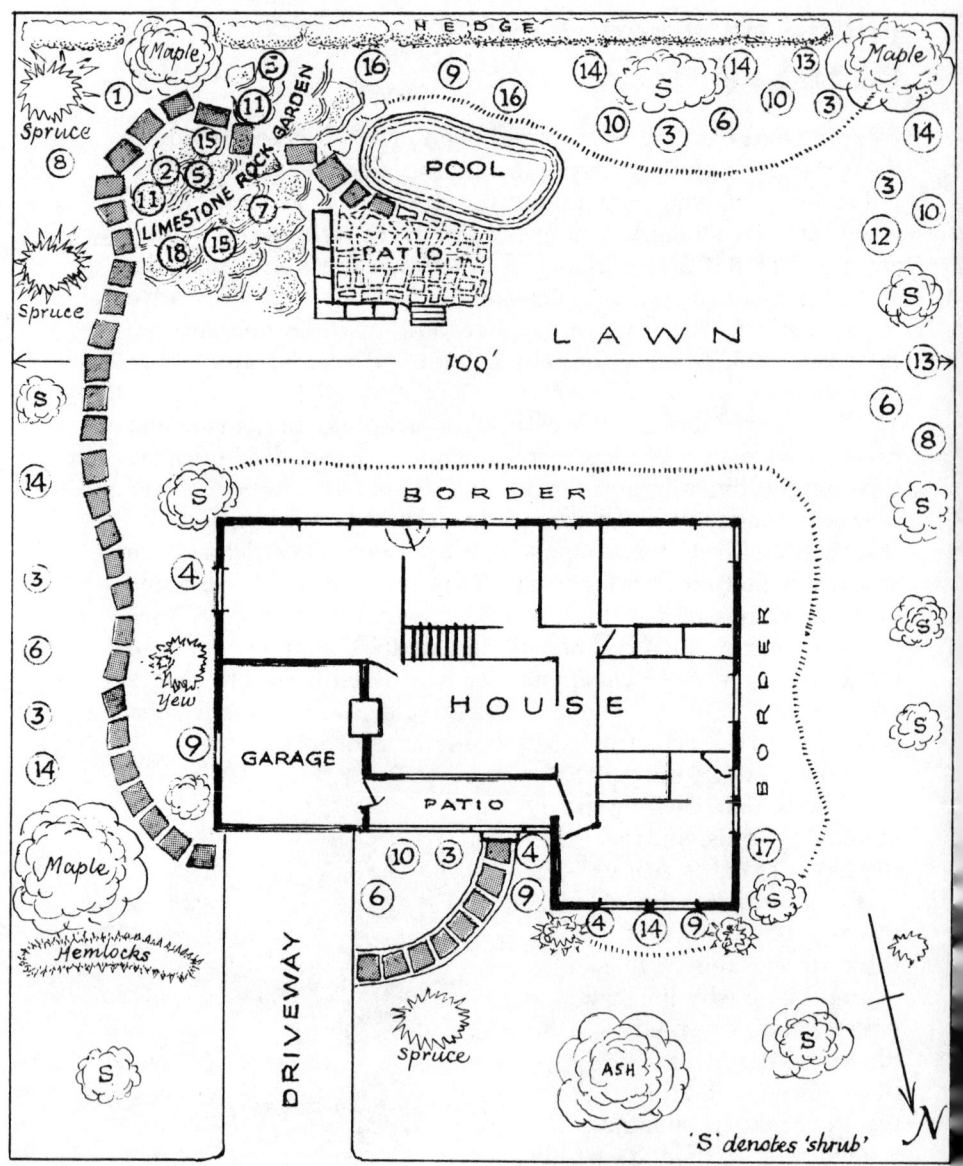

The following species are common hardy ferns that should grow well in a home garden in a temperate climate:

1. Bracken
2. Bulblet Fern
3. Christmas Fern
4. Cinnamon Fern
5. Ebony Spleenwort
6. Evergreen Wood Fern
7. Fragile Fern
8. Hayscented Fern
9. Interrupted Fern
10. Lady Fern
11. Maidenhair Fern
12. Marginal Fern
13. Chain Fern
14. Ostrich Fern
15. Polypody
16. Royal Fern
17. Sensitive Fern
18. Walking Fern

Filling the Fernery:
Placing and Caring

Transplanting ferns requires good timing and gentle handling of the transportees. The new garden home should be so much like the natural habitat that the fern will hardly "know" the difference and will not suffer from "culture shock" or "jet lag."

In freeing a fern from the soil for transplanting, dig out the entire plant, rootstock and all, with a substantial earth ball around its delicate roots to protect them from injury and desiccation. Put the fern in a plastic bag until you are ready to move it into its new quarters. Dig a hole a little larger than the root ball and line it with peat moss, compost, and a sprinkling of bone meal. Place the fern with its root ball into the hole, with the rhizome in the natural position. Do not bury surface or near-surface rhizomes; keep fiddleheads and growing points slightly above the ground level. Fill in around the transplant with porous peat moss or compost. Add soil and stones to firm up the new occupant. Cut away broken, injured, and withered parts, water liberally daily, and continue watering until the fern is well on its way. The new tenant may require extra water during a drought period.

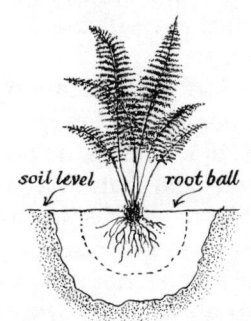

soil level *root ball*

Attention in the early spring and late fall in the form of additional compost, a bit of bone meal, and the removal of debris by hand will go a long way to keep ferns healthy and happy. **A word of caution:** Never rake fern gardens in the early spring when fiddleheads are pushing their heads through last year's dead leaves. Raking beheads fiddleheads, and a fern without a head is a fern without a future.

*Water, water, every day
Until your fern is on its way.*

137

Ferns for a Fernery:
Native and Foreign

The fern population in an outdoor garden depends principally on geography—where you live. In warm, wet, tropical and subtropical climates without winter freezes, practically any greenhouse fern can be cultivated outdoors. In warm, dry climates, water is the limiting factor. Further north with freezing winters—you are restricted to hardy ferns, of which there are at least two or three dozen common species including evergreens. Hardy ferns do no better in the Southeast than their subtropical counterparts do up north.

To find out which kinds of ferns will grow in your garden, in addition to exploring local natural preserves, visit local fern gardens in nurseries, botanical gardens, and in the neighborhood. The more you learn about ferns, the more likely are you to be successful in establishing and maintaining your own fernery. You don't have to be "fernetic" to grow ferns, but it helps.

Do not overlook hardy foreign ferns, especially those that come from countries with climates similar to yours. Several European and Asiatic species that are commercially available adapt themselves very well to the American climate and quickly become naturalized as have other plant and animal immigrants in the past.

SUMMARY:

Fern Gardens in the Great Outdoors

Ferns are ideal outdoor garden plants. Most are perennial that live in shady places and are relatively free from parasites and predators. Porous moist soil and shade favor their growth. A few thrive in open sunny spots and unless controlled they may become weeds. In planning a fernery, the physical facilities of the garden provide the guide lines for picking, spacing and placing "successful" ferns.

Transplanting should be carried out with a minimum of disturbance to roots and rhizomes. The new setting should be similar to the old natural habitats. The outdoor fern garden population is a matter of geography: the hot humid climate of the southeast favors greenhouse ferns: hot dry locales of the southwest support drought resisters while the north and the northeast with their freezing winters sustain hardy ferns. To choose the ferns best suited for your garden, stop, look and listen to people and places where ferns thrive.

Oak Fern

Thrice-cut broadly triangular
horizontal blade; sori few.
A delicate miniature bracken

fertile
pinna

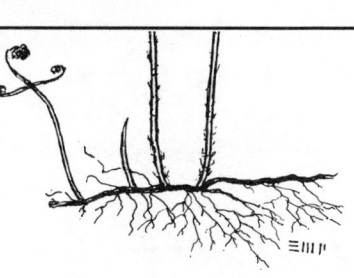

XII

Indoor Fern Gardening

$\mathcal{F}$erns, indoors and outdoors, are beholden to four natural elements for their health and your happiness: light, air, soil, and water. The first three are not too difficult to supply indoors. The fourth, the amount of water in the air or humidity, has driven many would-be indoor fern fanciers up and over a wall wailing. To provide ferns indoors with the high humidity to which they are accustomed outdoors is especially troublesome in heated homes during the long winter months. The humidity of this air is extremely low and approaches desert conditions, a climate for cacti. Ferns moved indoors to keep them from freezing to death frequently wind up "drying" to death.

Fern fanciers who want ferns around during freezing or drought periods can have their heart's desire without building a greenhouse or converting their home into a glass house. Two solutions are suggested. One is to increase the humidity in the fern farming section of the house, a condition that will benefit both ferns and farmers. The second is to find ferns that can live at the humidity you can provide.

Heightening Humidity:
Pebble Tray Humidifiers

The simplest, least expensive, and generally most satisfactory way to increase the humidity for a group of your favorite ferns is with a homemade humidifier—a pebble tray. A shallow, waterproof, rustproof tray lined with pebbles and filled with water to just

143

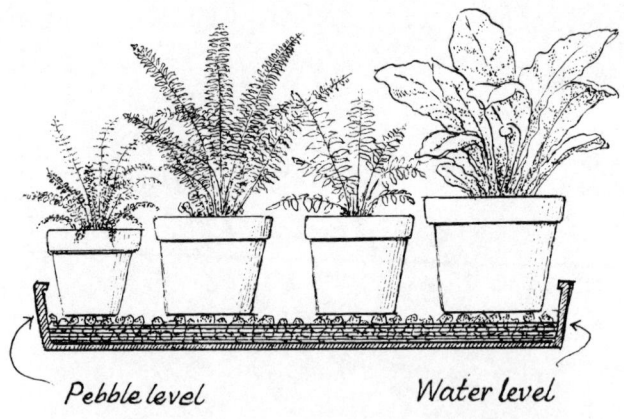

Pebble level   Water level

A simple home humidifier

below the level of the pebbles is all you need. You can purchase grooved plastic trays in nurseries made for just this type of fern culture. Potted plants are set down in the tray with their bottoms resting on the pebbles just above the water level. As long as this water mark is maintained, the humidity generated by the evaporation of the tray water is sufficiently high for most potted house plants to cope.

Additional water vapor is added to the air by the plants themselves, which are continuously transpiring, giving off water as vapor through thousands of tiny pores in their fronds. Bunched together in the tray, the ferns increase the humidity of the air around them. For the more affluent, commercial humidifiers can be installed. The more ambitious fern farmers can construct a mini-greenhouse from plastics.

Potting Soil:
Good Earth

The foundation of good gardening is good earth. And good earth is not just dirt. Soil is a complex mixture of mineral particles (disintegrated rocks), humus (the remains of decayed plants and animals and their products) and microbes (mostly soil bacteria, fungi, and their products). Soil is poor when it lacks one or more of these components. Soil is good when it contains all these ingredients. Two additional substances in the soil are vital to ferns: air and water. Spongy soil enables these essential materials to circulate, allowing the roots of the fern to breathe, drink, and keep merry.

For the beginner and the apartment agriculturist, selecting good earth may be a perplexing problem. Picking the brains of "experts" or trying to follow the advice of gardening books, magazines, or commercial ads may become an exercise in futility, since they frequently yield such contradictory information that one is left in complete confusion. Soil mixes are like cooking or baking recipes. There are as many "bests" as there are "experts," and as many good earth mixes as there are mixers.

A mix that can do much good and little harm consists of equal parts of the three S's: sand, sphagnum (moss), and soil. It is simple, safe, and sound, a satisfactory mix for most ferns. If you are not an expert or committed to a particular soil mix, try a commercial blend. It is easier, quicker, and less trouble than trying to find the "mix" to top all mixes.

Fern Containers:
Miniature Gardens

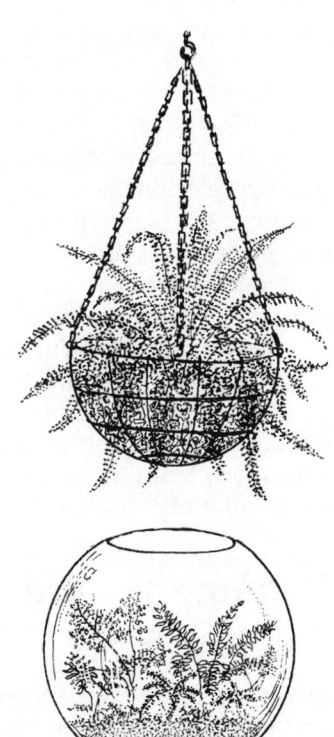

An indoor garden consists of plants set into containers in a handful of earth. Although the contents are more important than the container, the latter merits careful consideration if you wish to enjoy both. Ferns find their way into a bewildering variety of receptacles, including pots and vases, enclosed jars, hanging baskets, and wall plaques.

A container chosen purely for its artistic or esthetic merits may not display the fern to its best advantage. First, some thought should be given to the size of the container. A little fern in a big pot looks lost and lonely. A big fern in a little pot appears equally out of place and slowly dies of suffocation. A pot whose diameter is about one-third the height of the fern is about right.

Containers may vary from glass bowls to hanging baskets.

145

Fern Pots:
Clay and Plastic

Ferns can do equally well in clay or plastic containers, provided you remember that clay is porous and plastic is not. The porous walls of the common red flower pot allow water to seep through and evaporate. Clay containers also permit air to pass into the soil to the roots and rhizomes. Therefore, ferns in clay pots require more water, but those in plastic pots need coarser, more porous soil. Another suggestion is to avoid ceramic containers without drain holes. If you feel compelled to use such closed containers,

Ceramic containers holding potted ferns require the water-pebble treatment.

place extra drainage material at the bottom of the receptacle before planting. Or plant the fern in a clay container with drain holes and place it in your favorite closed-bottom container. By adding pebbles or gravel the potted fern sits above the level of accumulated water.

New kinds of plant pots are constantly appearing and are very appealing and attractive. Regardless of what claims are made by the manufacturer, the general consensus among plant "pros" is that ferns flourish in low, shallow, clay or plastic containers with drain holes at the bottom. The pot does not make the fern, but it certainly can help.

Potting the Fern:
Proper Planting

In potting the plant, remember that drainage of water and the circulation of air are as important as the soil and the light. To insure proper drainage, line the bottom of the container with pieces of broken pottery or pebbles. In this way, excess water drains out through the holes, but the soil is retained. The drainage holes in small pots, 2 1/2 inches in diameter, need not be covered; very large pots, 10 inches or more, should be lined with a layer

146

of drainage material. Fill the pot halfway with the moistened soil mix. Place the fern on top of the mix with its rhizome in the natural growing position. Pack soil around the plant, keeping the rhizome at or slightly below the ground level. Do not bury growing points or fiddleheads; keep them above the ground level. Pack the soil down and around the fern to give it firm footing; then water liberally. If the excess water drains off within a few minutes, the plant's plumbing system is working properly. Set the potted fern in a shady, cool, humid spot for a few days. Covering it with a plastic bag helps it through the difficult days of adjustment to new surroundings by providing a see-through, high humidity chamber. Now sit back and feel fairly confident that you can ignore Murphy's law which says, "Anything that can go wrong, will."

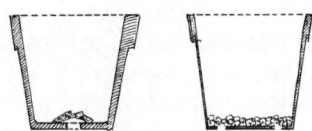

Pottery pieces or pebbles hold soil and permit drainage.

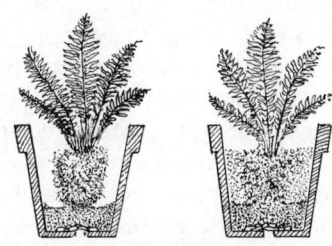

Potting Procedures
(a) *Add soil at bottom of pot*
(b) *Hold soil ball centrally with crown 1"-2" below rim of pot*
(c) *Add soil all around*

Ferns in a Basket:
Hanging Gardens

Not all ferns prosper in a pot; some do much better in a hanging wall plaque or a basket. Many of the ferns that prefer life in a basket live on the trunks and branches of trees that grow in moist tropical forests. Such airborne ferns are called **epiphytes** (EPP-ih-fights; from the Greek *epi:* upon and *phytes:* plants). Although epiphytic ferns live on trees, they are not parasites. Lacking contact with the ground, they absorb minerals and moisture from the host tree trunk and from dead and decaying vegetation (humus) that accumulates on its branches and in crotches. Being able to survive periods of drought and low humidity, several fern epiphytes are grown in a hanging basket especially fitted for the dryness of indoor life. Other basket-dwellers are some of the ground-rooted ferns, those with long, drooping fronds; and the "footed" ferns, with brightly colored, exposed, creeping rhizomes.

Fern baskets are made from wood, wire, cork, coconut, fern fibers, or ceramics. To plant a fern in a basket, first line the container with several inches of moist, coarse, uncut moss or fern fibers. Place the fern in position; set in sphagnum moss or potting soil rich in humus if it is an epiphyte, and regular potting soil if it is a ground-rooted fern. Press the potting material around the fern and cover the soil with lining material to prevent water from washing away the soil. Water your newly acquired hanging garden with a gentle spray or dunk it in a tub for a few minutes. Properly planted and monitored, hanging ferns live for years.

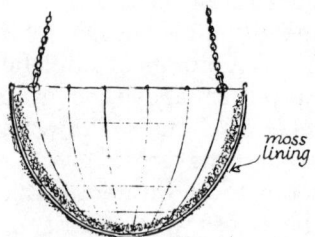

Wire baskets require a lining of sphagnum moss

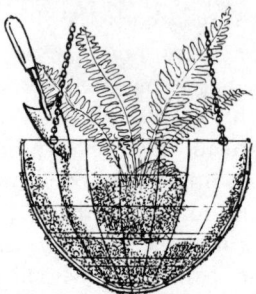

With soil ball 2-3" below rim of basket add soil all around.

Illumination:
Light and Lively

Ferns are light lovers but not sun worshippers. In direct, strong, midday sun ferns fry and die. It is equally "fernicidal" (fern-killing) to put them in dark, dingy recesses where they can hardly see or be seen. In poorly lit corners, ferns reach for light, growing paler and thinner until they collapse and expire—but not without a struggle.

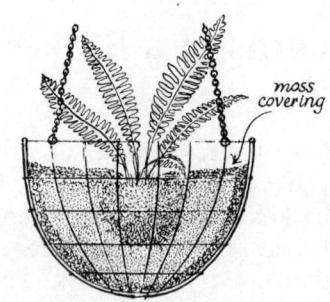

Cover potting soil and 'ball' with a layer of moss; water slowly but well—plug leaks.

The favored place for ferns indoors is near a window where they can "see" the sunrise in the east and the sunset in the

west for a few hours during the daytime and the North star at night. A sunny southern exposure is too much; bright sunlight sears ferns and dark shadows starve them. When the light is right ferns have a healthy green complexion.

Artificial Light:
Incandescent and Fluorescent

The lack of windows or proper exposure is no reason for not growing ferns indoors. By substituting artificial light for sunlight an indoor fernery can be set up anytime, anywhere, in the most unlikely and previously forbidden places: dark hallways, alleys, cellars, on book shelves, and in windowless rooms. With a flick of a switch, you can change night into day and gloom into a garden.

By exposing your ferns to cool white fluorescent lights, 12–14 hours a day, about a foot away, you can cultivate and enjoy a fern garden in the middle of the night in the coldest or driest winter. Fluorescent lamps have several advantages over incandescent bulbs for illumination. Fluorescents are less costly to operate and give off less heat than ordinary light bulbs. However, either can be used to light the way to indoor fern farming.

Water:
The Liquid of Life or Death

A perennial and perplexing problem for indoor fern farmers is watering: how much and how often. There are no reliable rules of thumb or watering schedules. You may be haunted by the specter of seeing your ferns victims of a deluge or a drought. Be advised that fern fatalities occur more often by drowning than by drying.

The thirst of a fern depends upon such variables as the size and nature of the container (porous or nonporous, with or without drainage holes); the nature of the soil (porous or nonporous); the size and spread of the plant; and especially, the humidity of the surrounding air.

Over- and Underwatering:
Fern Signals

The answer to the watering issue is to be found in the ferns themselves. They tell you whether or not they are "thirsty."

149

Start by watering your ferns every other day, giving them enough water to soak through the entire plant. Discard the water that collects below. If your ferns sit on a pebble tray, check the water level to be sure that the containers are sitting on but not in the water. Never permit ferns to wallow in water. If you are overwatering, the soil remains soggy for some time, growth slows down, no new fiddleheads appear, the fronds discolor, and the roots rot. These are the fern's SOS: Stop Oversoaking. Your fern is telling you that it is waterlogged and drowning. As soon as you "read" the fern's SOS, start emergency first aid treatment. Dump the excess water and check its plumbing system. You may be able to revive the foundering fern by repotting it in properly draining soil providing root rot has not gone too far. Dry it out and give it a chance to breathe.

At the other end of the water table are ferns on the verge of death by dehydration. They proclaim their plight by wilting, withering, browning and eventually dropping dead. First aid for these drought victims is to immerse them, pot and all, in water for several hours. Let them drink to their roots' content. If any life is left, the ferns will perk up. However, it may take several days before the baptism gives them a new lease on life.

A time-honored watering test is the "Jack Horner" method. Instead of putting your thumb into a plum pie, stick it into the soil. "If it comes up dirty, dry, 'Give me water' is the cry; if it comes up muddy, mired, no more water is desired." The point of the lesson is to water ferns on "demand," not when you think they need it. Daily watering of every fern may be as death-dealing as giving them a bath once a month, whether or not they need it. Water is the stream of life: don't make it their river of death.

Fern Food:
Fertilizers

Ferns eat, drink, and breathe through their roots, subsisting on a liquid diet. Their food is mineral water, which they absorb from the soil through millions of very delicate microscopic structures growing out of the roots in all directions. Water carries dissolved minerals from the soil to the ferns and to all parts within the fern. As long as the fern is rooted in moist, spongy soil, there is a constant circulating supply of minerals and water.

Indoor gardeners, like parents, worry that their plant pets are not getting enough minerals and vitamins and will develop all kinds of deficiency diseases. For this reason they feed ferns natural fertilizer, such as decayed parts and products of plants and animals, or artificial fertilizer, such as commercial plant foods and growth-promoters.

Ferns raised in rich soil generally do not need fertilizers or supplements. Their fronds are luxuriant with a healthy green color. Ferns that need fertilizer show off-color fronds that are smaller and slower growing than their well fed fern friends. Adding natural fertilizer in modest amounts does give a fern a "lift" improving its complexion. However, ferns are sensitive to the kinds and amounts of fertilizers applied. Therefore, it is important to know which ones to use and how to use them.

Almost any commercial house plant fertilizer, liquid or powder, can be used with ferns. To be on the safe side, use them at half the strength recommended by the manufacturer and add them each month to the water schedule. Liquid fish oil and bone meal are highly recommended. In spite of your good intentions, the growth stimulants contained in commercial fertilizers may do more harm than good, particularly when ferns are in their resting periods. Ferns sleep during dry and cold periods and respond poorly to prodding. Let sleeping ferns sleep. Beware of plant pep pills; these are quick-acting fertilizers that may be as dangerous and destructive to ferns as pep pills are to human pill poppers. Above all, it does not follow that if a little fertilizer is good, a lot is better.

A Fertilizing Guide for North Temperate climates

Temperate Temperatures:
Indoor Climate

In keeping with their middle-of-the-road posture with respect to water and light, ferns generally prefer temperate temperatures, neither too hot nor too cold. They grow best in room temperatures between 60°F and 70°F (15°C and 20°C) in the daytime and about

151

10°F (−8°C) lower at night. However, the temperature tolerance of ferns varies. Based on the lowest temperatures at which they can survive, ferns are divided into tender and hardy ferns. Tender ferns are generally native to tropical and subtropical climates and are rarely able to survive a sustained cold snap. Hardy ferns live in temperate and colder temperature zones and can withstand short periods of freezing and near-freezing weather. Night temperatures no lower than 50°F (10°C) best suit these tender ones. A few ferns native to cool tropical upland areas, as well as tree ferns and epiphytes, do better with cooler nights. Knowing the natural habitat of a fern, its "roots," is very helpful in picking its proper indoor climate.

Frozen Ferns: Frostbite

Ferns, even the delicate and tender ones, can weather surprisingly low temperatures, down to 40°F (5°C), without freezing to death or "catching a cold." This should relieve you of worry about ferns on a cold winter night when the thermostat is turned down. But don't push them too far down the thermometer; below 40°F they usually shrivel and freeze.

Thoroughly chilled ferns turn yellow and slowly wither away. Before giving them up for dead or moving them into warmer quarters to revive them, find out if the ferns are dormant or dead. During their rest period the fronds of many ferns drop off or turn yellow; there is little growth and they appear lifeless. However, if they are just resting, arousing them from sleep usually does more damage than just letting them slumber.

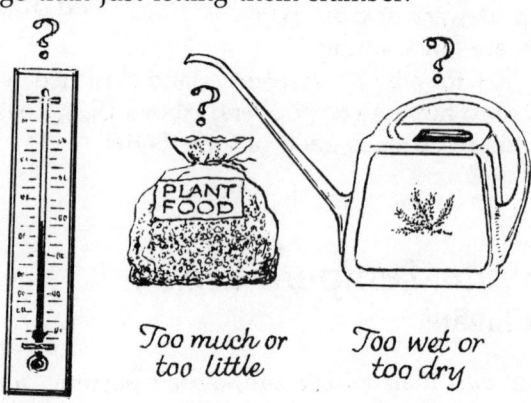

Too much or too little

Too wet or too dry

Too hot or too cold

The Human Triple Threat

Frozen or frostbitten ferns wilt, and their fronds turn black. Less severely frost-damaged fronds have a scorched or burned appearance. Those with frozen fronds but intact rhizomes recover, but gradually.

Injury from high temperature is difficult to distinguish from low humidity damage. Excessive heat causes wilting and scorching of the fronds. If they do not recover from heat burn, the fronds turn brown and brittle and drop off.

Temperature and Humidity: Fern Thirst

Room temperature also affects the amount of watering ferns require. Like humans, ferns "perspire" more in warm weather than in cold. Hence, they are thirstier and drink more in summer than in winter. The relative humidity of the air is also a factor. More water evaporates into the air at lower humidity than at higher humidity. Ferns in a cool room need much less watering than in a hot area. However, since the air in a heated room in winter is relatively dry, indoor plants may require as much watering in the winter as in the summer. Watch the ferns, not the calendar or the thermometer, to keep them happy and well watered.

Fern Foes: Pests and Problems

Being indoors is no protection against plant pests. Outdoors, insects and other pests generally avoid ferns. The same ferns indoors are fair game for indoor plant pests that do not discriminate but attack all plants with equal gusto.

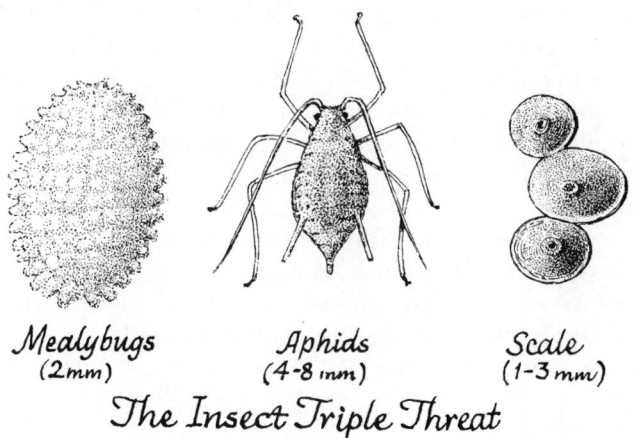

| *Mealybugs* | *Aphids* | *Scale* |
| (2mm) | (4-8 mm) | (1-3 mm) |

The Insect Triple Threat

153

Scale Insects:
Sap-Suckers

The most ferocious of the fern foes are scale insects. In Dracula-like fashion, they suck the life sap of plants. If unchecked, scales drink their victims to death. Scale insects appear on the veins and stems of fern fronds. The most common is the brown scale, identified by the brown spots on its back. Young brown scales are very small and spend most of their time crawling around in search of food. Later, they settle down under a turtle-like shell, where they are safe and sound sucking fern sap.

Two strategies are suggested in scale warfare. One is hand-to-scale combat, picking or scratching scales off their victims. The other is a chemical counteroffensive using water soluble insecticides such as Malathion or Sevin mixed to half the prescribed concentration. Applying these chemicals either by spraying or washing may defeat the enemy. Badly infected ferns may be beyond help; these should be destroyed quickly before they become the base for raising another army of scale soldiers against other fern victims.

Aphids and Mealybugs:
Other Sap-Suckers

Aphids are other fern foes that are also sap-suckers. These tiny tyrants, also called plant lice, are soft-bodied insects. Aphids that prefer ferns are black with white legs. They attack in armies like the scale insects, swarming over and chewing up growing points, the youngest and tenderest parts of a fern. To halt the assault of aphid armies, wash them away with soap and water. Failing this, resort to chemical warfare, using the same insecticides as with scale insects.

Mealybugs, white cottony sap-sucking insects, also feast on ferns, particularly the young tender parts. The wash-and-spray offensive may be effective against them. Continue to watch carefully for surviving stragglers that may continue to wage guerrilla warfare for several weeks.

Flies, Slugs and Snails:
More Fern Foes

This does not end the list of fern foes. White flies, red mites, millipedes, snails, and slugs are among pests with a ferocious appetite for ferns. Plant pests usually seek out and feed on your prize plants; somehow they know which are your most precious plants, and these become their gastronomic delight. Against each kind of fern feaster, there is some kind of defense to curb its appetite. Some defenses are strange indeed. Slugs and snails, for example, which enjoy ferns as a midnight snack, like to wash down their meal with a bit of beer. To trap these midnight marauders, set out a saucer of beer next to your ferns. The morning after, you are likely to find soused slugs and snails in the beer, dead drunk. For the skeptics, invest in a few drops of beer.

To keep your ferns from the ravages of plant pests requires eternal vigilance and the constant application of plant pesticides, of which there are many kinds. You don't know how effective they are until you try them repeatedly. Don't stop fighting fern foes, but know when the battle is lost, and when to retreat strategically. Above all, do not expose new plants to older house residents, since the new arrivals may be carriers of pests or may be very susceptible to existing ones. Quarantine new plants for a few weeks before admitting them to your fern family.

Ferns that Flourish Indoors:
Cultivated and Wild

A question frequently asked by beginning fern fanciers is "What kinds of ferns make good indoor plants?" The most successful and best known are not local species; most are tropical rain forest epiphytes that thrive at a lower humidity than ground rooted ferns and survive periods of drought and irregular watering. Such characteristics qualify these ferns to live in low humidity heated houses and in the hands of forgetful fern fanciers. You have a choice of naturalized and completely housebroken ferns from the groups described on the following pages.

155

Boston Ferns:
The Most Beloved Basket Fern

The leading citizens of the indoor fern population are the Boston ferns and the amazing number of their hybrids. Their ancestors are not Backbay Bostonians who came from England on the May-flower, but descendants from good American stock. The grand-daddy of the Boston fern is the wild sword fern, a native of Florida, where it lives as an epiphyte on tree trunks. The Boston

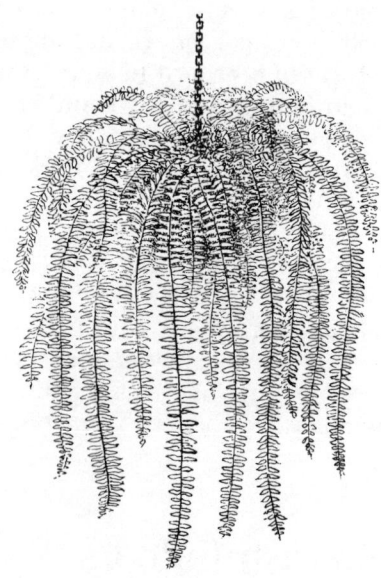

Boston Fern

fern was named for one of the offspring of a stowaway found in 1894 in a cargo of sword ferns being shipped from the West Indies to Boston. Until then, the Boston fern was a run-of-the-mill species which you could take or leave. This Boston-bound fern was a "freak" with long, lacy, feathery fronds quite different from its staid, stiff forebears. Plant propagators saw its beauty, fell in love with it, and began to cultivate it without restraint. The Boston beauty was an instant success and quickly became the fern of the year, a status it has maintained ever since.

There are several varieties of Boston ferns. Some have ten-foot frond tresses which can be displayed to advantage in a hanging garden. Others grow short, upright, feathery fronds that look best in pots at eye level. They are all "cuts" from the sword fern.

Boston ferns grow new fronds around the outside of the root ball. The inner ones turn brown and dry, giving the plant a shabby appearance. When this occurs the plant is telling you that it is getting too big for its "breeches" and needs to be divided and repotted.

These ferns have another attractive feature that is sometimes misunderstood and neglected, its backup reproductive system. Boston ferns generally do not reproduce sexually by spores. In addition to growing bright-green, feathery fronds, Boston ferns sprout long, thin, leafless threads. These are runners (stolons) that take root where they touch soil and beget Boston babies. Such fernlets, when they have a few fronds, can be cut off and planted separately. When cultivated in a hanging basket, the runners grow through the soil and sprout fernlets around the outside of the basket making an unusually attractive display. Given bright indirect light, moderate temperature, moist soil and a bath or shower once a week, Boston ferns can live a decade and even longer.

Fuzzy-Footed Ferns:
Basket Dwellers

Another group that can endure the rigors of indoor life are the "fuzzy-footed" ferns. These are so named because they have prominently exposed rhizomes covered with colored scales that make them look like the fur-covered feet of animals. Hence they are named deer's foot, rabbit's foot, and the like. Planted in pots, these popular and easy-to-grow footed ferns sprawl over the surface of the container, sending up new green fronds as they crawl over and down the sides. The rabbit's foot fern, for example, with its brown "feet," makes an ideal wire basket-dweller. Its rhizomes grow over, under, and around, pushing its feet through the open sides of the hanging basket to form an attractive fern display. No indoor collection is complete without one of these friendly fuzzy-footed ferns wandering around a hanging basket.

157

Rabbit's-foot Fern

Staghorns:
Wall Ferns

If you have a space near or between windows and would like an unusual living wall decoration, try a staghorn fern. It is prized for the striking appearance of its fronds, of which there are two kinds: sterile and fertile. The large, forking, leathery, gray-green, antler-shaped fronds are the fertile ones. They grow out of the center of several layers of shield-shaped, smaller sterile fronds that hug the tree trunk and give the plant a firm base. Water and dead, decaying vegetation accumulate in these pocket-shaped sterile fronds, supplying the fern with the moist humus on which it lives.

Staghorns are easily mounted as a wall display on pieces of tree bark, slabs of redwood or cedar, or any other kind of wood

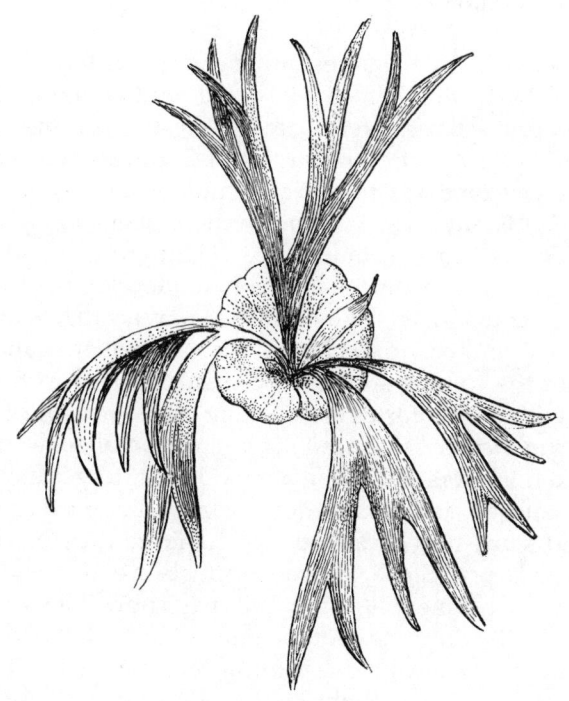

Staghorn Fern

that does not decay when wet. To mount a staghorn, place a nest
of soil mixture surrounded by sphagnum moss in the middle of
the piece of wood. Position the roots of the fern in the center of
the nest. Tie the entire assembly together with nylon fishing line
or some other colorless, rot-resistant string. Water thoroughly and
hang on a wall near a window. Staghorns require watering about
once or twice a week, which can be done by soaking in a bathtub
for a few minutes.

Given proper care and attention, a staghorn will produce a
family of "pups" at the base of the plant. When the "pups" are
big enough they can be cut loose and will provide a source of
staghorns for you and your friends. Before long you can display
your wall trophies and tell stories about your safari stalking wild
staghorns.

Other Indoor Ferns:
Exotic and Native

There are many other interesting and unusual ferns from which to choose. Bird's nest, green cliff brake, button brake, silverback, goldback, and climbing ferns are among the favorite indoor exotics. Each one has its own distinct personality and charm and may be a welcome addition to your indoor fern family.

Strange to say, we know much more about foreign than domestic ferns as domestic indoor pets. Plant growers and nurseries have not given too much attention to developing local native species as house plants. One reason may be that many of our wild ferns lose their fronds in dry and cold weather and retire to rest up for the coming spring. It seems that a fern without fronds is a fern without friends or has only fair-weather friends. But there is some evidence that this need not be so. Several domestic species, when taken indoors and given a good home, forget their outdoor behavior and act as if winter never comes. Local evergreens may be a good start, providing you can duplicate their outdoor environment in a pot. Small, delicate annuals are also worth trying; such ferns that come out of the cold may show their appreciation by keeping their fronds. Adopt one or two of the local ferns. Befriending them may be a very rewarding experience. The Christmas fern, for example, might be very sociable and happy in your home year round.

SUMMARY:

Indoor Fern Farming

In addition to the culturing concerns of outdoor fern gardening—soil, light, air, and water—indoor gardeners are confronted with special problems of humidity and pest control. To increase the humidity of dry heated household air, to make it favorable for ferns, the simplest and most effective method is to crowd ferns into a pebble tray filled with water just below the bottom of the plant pots. Installing humidifiers and building mini-greenhouses are not discouraged, however.

Ferns prosper in clay or plastic pots planted in porous soil mixtures kept moist but not soggy. Epiphytic ferns prefer hanging baskets; footed ferns and those with long, flowing fronds look better hanging than sitting in containers. Almost all ferns thrive in the indirect light of a northern exposure or in controlled artificial light.

Fertilizer, water, light, and temperature requirements of ferns are modest and moderate. Extremes of these necessary factors are damaging and death-dealing.

Among the indoor fern foes are scale insects, aphids, mealybugs, white flies, slugs, and snails. To control their appetites for ferns, specific physical treatments and pesticides are recommended. By quarantining new entrants and disposing of old, badly infected ferns, infestation by plant pests can further be kept under control.

Among the most popular and well-adjusted indoor ferns are Boston, fuzzy-footed, and staghorns, but these are not the only ones.

VIII
CHAPTER
XIII

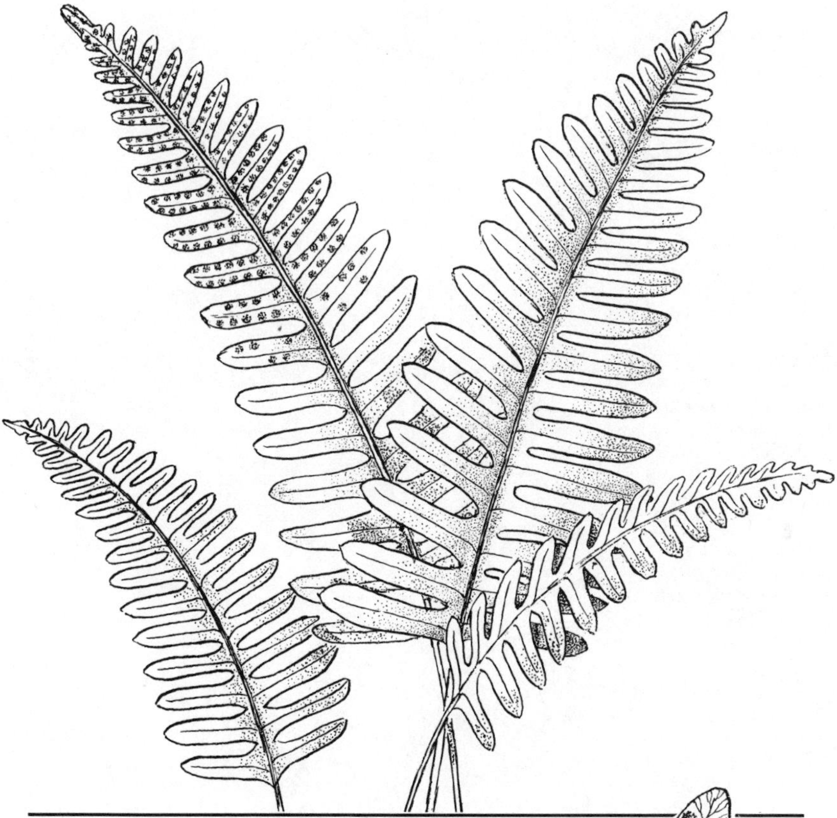

Common Polypody

Sterile fronds, leathery, evergreen
lobes alternate with rounded tips;
sori large, underside of lobes

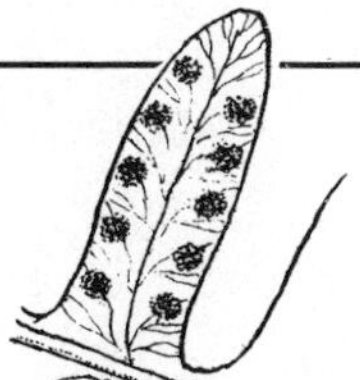

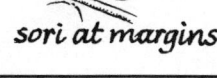

sori at margins

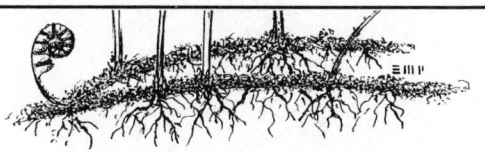

XIII

Terrariums

$\mathcal{F}$ern gardens under glass are becoming increasingly popular and appealing, and for very good reasons. They are relatively inexpensive, easy to construct, and, when properly maintained, glass gardens are not only attractive but take care of themselves for years. In addition, you can farm ferns in glass houses any time of the year, anywhere; and the garden can be as large or as small as you choose. All that is required is a clear glass or plastic container, soil, small-growing ferns, and the ability to follow directions.

A glass or plastic container enclosing a garden of plants is called a **terrarium** (te-RARE-ee-um), which means "a place of earth." It is also called a bottle garden or a Wardian case. Botanical license allows you to call it a "fernarium," and to spell terrarium as "pterrarium" (with a silent *p*). Fern terrariums are mini-greenhouses, chambers with the constant high humidity of the tropical rain forests where many of these plants flourish.

Terrariums look deceptively simple, and the uninitiated may rush in where ferns fail to follow. Before you invest time, money, and energy in "ferning" under glass, it seems proper to brief you on terrariums: their history, the types of containers used, growing mediums, ferns best suited for life in terrariums, setting up and caring for gardens in glass houses. If your intentions toward ferns are serious, read the material that follows and enjoy the fruit of your labor: a beautiful, self-contained and self-sufficient fern garden under glass.

Although the idea of raising ferns in a glass container seems ridiculously simple, the terrarium was not discovered until 1829, and then quite by accident. The story of its discovery and discoverer is worth telling to illustrate how an unanticipated event revolutionized the cultivation and transportation of plants, especially rare, delicate, exotic species—a fine example of serendipity.

The Tale of the Terrarium:
Dr. Ward's Wonder Case

Once upon a time, there lived in London, England, a physician whose name was Nathaniel Bagshaw Ward. From the time he was a little boy, Nathaniel was deeply interested in nature, particularly the plants and animals that grew around his London home. As a physician, he divided his time between his patients and his plants, with the lion's share going to plants.

In 1832, Ward published a paper entitled "On the Imitation of the Natural Conditions of Plants in Closely Glazed Cases." In it he described an incident that took place in the summer of 1829, when he was 38 years old. In his explorations he had come across a moth pupa (the resting stage between the caterpillar and the adult moth) and decided to watch it emerge as an adult moth. He picked it up and buried it "in some moist mould (soil) in a wide-mouthed glass bottle covered with a lid," a perfectly normal and natural thing for a naturalist to do with an insect. Watching the bottle day by day, he recounted that "moisture which during the heat of the day arose from the mould, became condensed on the internal surface of the glass, and returned whence it came, thus keeping the mould in the same degree of humidity."

A week before the adult moth was scheduled to emerge, the unexpected happened, an event that could have very easily been overlooked or dismissed as unimportant ". . . a seedling fern and a grass had made their appearance

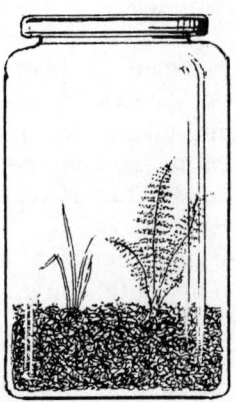

In Ward's wide mouth jar, a fern and a grass appeared

on the surface of the mould." Ward was so struck by this observation that in his excitement he forgot all about the moth and became interested in the plants growing in his closed container. For years he had tried, in vain, to grow mosses and ferns on an old wall near his home. The smoke, soot, and dirt in the polluted air of nineteenth-century industrial London had killed off all his plants. However, inside the covered container the plants thrived. He went on to say, "I placed the bottle outside the window of my study—a room facing north—and to my great delight the plants continued to grow well . . . They required no attention . . . and here they remained for nearly four years . . . At the end of this time, they accidentally perished during my absence from home, in consequence of the rusting of the lid and the admission of rain water." But this is only the beginning of the Ward case.

The Open and Shut Wardian Case:
The Birth of the Terrarium

Ward was so fascinated by this discovery that he began to experiment with all kinds of plants, particularly ferns. The results were unbelievable; the plants that could not survive in the poisonous, polluted air, flourished inside a glass container without care or watering. His proudest achievement was a bottle of ferns and mosses which grew for 18 years without being watered, a record not equaled by camels or cacti.

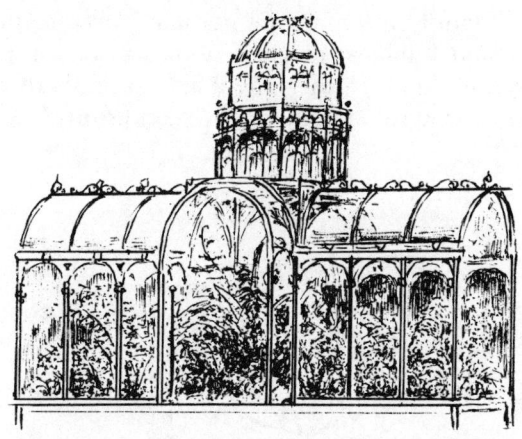

Not a cathedral, - just a six foot Victorian 'Wardian Case' terrarium
(1851)

167

Before long, "Wardian cases" as they were now called became all the rage in England. Ornate, elaborate terrariums became a standard part of the early Victorian household decor. By coincidence, these cases became popular just about the time that the fern frenzy swept England and the United States. Fern farming under glass was the "in" thing, and fern-filled terrariums became the middle-class status symbol.

Wardian cases also proved to be a boon to plant hunters whose forays carried them all over the world in search of rare and exotic plants to satisfy the insatiable appetite of "fernatics" to fill their gardens and terrariums with ferns. For the first time, plants were successfully transported over thousands of miles on long sea voyages in glass cases modeled after Ward's original bottle. Ward's fortunate discovery is as exciting to fern fanciers today as it was to Ward and his followers in the nineteenth century.

Containers for Terrariums:
Bottles and Bowls

Once you begin to think terrariums you become container conscious. Clear glass or plastic receptacles, regardless of what they held originally, become possible "fernariums." Fish tanks, gallon jars and bottles, plastic shoe boxes and containers, cookie jars, candy jars, chemist's flasks, distilled water bottles, carafes, wine bottles, and peanut butter jars are not just jars or bottles for long. Glass bowls and bubbles, or glass domes fitted with flat dishes are visualized as full of ferns. There are no limits to the sizes or shapes of see-through containers as "pterrariums."

Terrariums come in all shapes and sizes

Wide-mouth containers with screw-top covers (or their equivalent) and at least a three-inch opening are easily planted by hand. Narrow-necked flasks, small-mouth jugs with openings just large enough to ease through small, slender ferns offer the same challenge as slipping ship models into bottles. Here is a golden opportunity to exercise ingenuity, originality, and artistry in selecting containers and contents as bottle gardens. All containers intended as fern gardens must be scrupulously clean, otherwise your ferns will have a dirty, moldy end.

Water for Terrariums:
Repeating Rain

The hallmark of a successful terrarium is constant high humidity attained by continuously recycling water through evaporation and condensation. The basic principle is the same in all terrariums; water vapor which is produced by the evaporation of moisture in the soil and by the transpiration of plants, condenses on the cool walls of the container and drips back into the soil. The cycle is repeated as long as there is water and heat. Light supplies the heat, the pumping power that circulates the water. Recycling it also requires a porous soil with good drainage, an ingredient sometimes overlooked with fatal consequences.

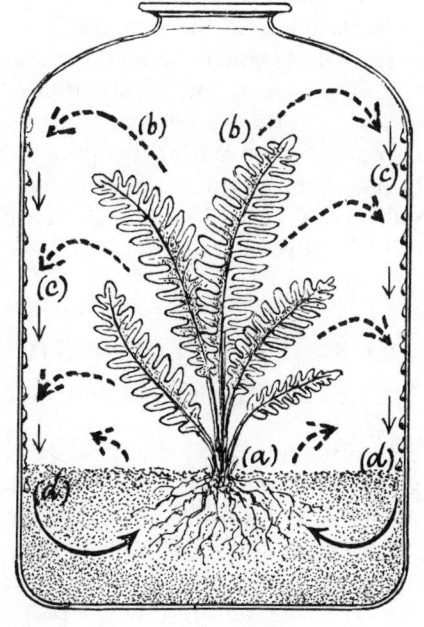

Water Circulation in a Terrarium

(a) *Fern roots absorb water*
(b) *Fronds give off water vapor*
(c) *Water vapor condenses*
(d) *Water runs back into soil*

169

Terra for Terrariums:
Plant Potpourri

To create a mini-tropical rain forest in a container, first line the bottom with an inch of gravel or marble chips, or any other drainage material. Add a sprinkling of charcoal to absorb the gases formed by the natural decay of vegetation under warm, moist conditions; this upsets the chemistry of the soil and the growth of the ferns. Top with a 2-inch layer of porous, sterile soil for good drainage and also to allow the roots of the fern to breathe. Sterile soil reduces the number and kinds of plant predators that like nothing better than to feast on ferns.

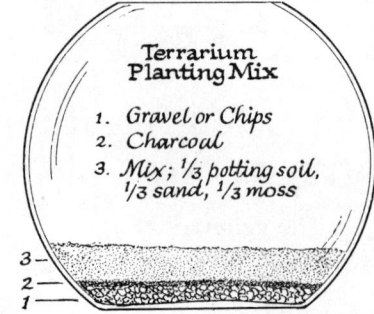

Terrarium Planting Mix
1. Gravel or Chips
2. Charcoal
3. Mix; 1/3 potting soil, 1/3 sand, 1/3 moss

The soil mixture is a matter of personal taste and experience, about which there is usually little agreement. A mixture of one part potting soil, one part peat moss, and one part sand, vermiculite, or perlite is quite satisfactory. Packaged sterilized house plant mixtures are commercially available in nurseries and will save you the fuss and bother of mixing your own unless you are a confirmed "do-it-yourselfer."

Tenants for Terrariums:
Mini Ferns for Mini Fern Gardens

Selecting terrarium tenants is not as difficult as it may seem. Small, slow growers, ferns that are small to begin with and remain small, are ideal. A fern that normally grows to be four feet tall will have its life style cramped in a one-foot container.

Several delicate, dainty, native woodland ferns almost impossible to keep alive when potted and transplanted do well in high-humidity terrariums. Among such ferns well-suited to life in a "fernarium" are the spleenwort, walking fern, fragile fern, rock fern, and woodsia. Not only do these thrive in a container climate, but they usually do not grow to more than six inches in height. For ground cover, spikemoss, a fern ally, is a good choice; this makes an all-pteridophyte terrarium, a "pteridarium."

Planting the Terrarium:
Bottle Gardens

A terrarium is ready to receive tenants when the container is sparkling clean and the sterile soil has been moistened with sterile water. To prevent ferns from wilting until they are planted, keep them in a plastic bag. Handle them with tender loving care, especially the roots, which are easily damaged. Wash away soil particles adhering to the roots and examine the entire plant for insects.

"Ferning" in wide-mouth containers is done easily and quickly by hand and presents no particular problems. The real challenge comes in planting narrow-necked containers, bottle gardens. However, with special tools, patience and gentleness, ferns can be ferried through these narrow-necked bottles and safely anchored in the soil.

Bottle Gardening

  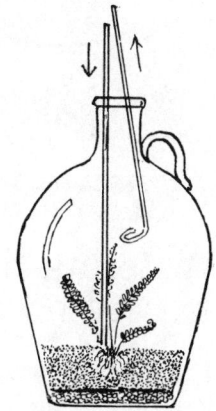

Use a rolled paper to direct the mix. Tamp down. *Lower fern in loop to position inside bottle* *Hold fern with dowel, lift out loop and tamp down*

The beds in bottle gardens also consist of three tiers of materials: an inch of gravel for drainage at the bottom, a sprinkling of charcoal to absorb gases that "sour" and spoil the soil, and a few inches of sterile soil on top. With a funnel or rolled paper tube pour each of these materials into the container and spread them out evenly by swirling and tapping the sides of the container. With a long rod, poke holes in the bottle bed to position the ferns.

Slip the fern into a "fern fork" or "pick-up" tool. A "fern fork" can be made from a coathanger by straightening it and bending one end into a one-inch loop with a gap. A "pick up" tool (available in hardware stores) is a two-feet long metal tube with a claw at one end and a plunger at the other for opening and closing the claw. With the fern carrying tool, gently lower the plant into the bottle and place it in the previously prepared hole. Cover the roots with about one-half-inch of soil and pack this down firmly with the end of a dowel rod or a piece of square wood molding. Remove the tools, and water.

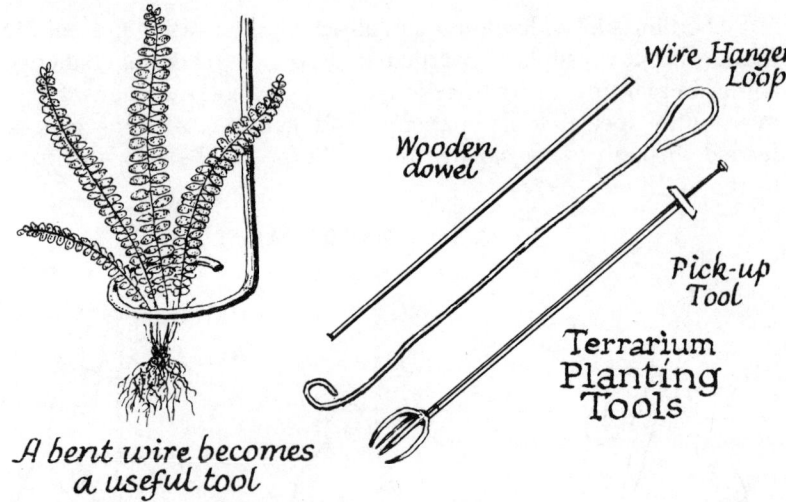

Wire Hanger Loop

Wooden dowel

Pick-up Tool

Terrarium Planting Tools

A bent wire becomes a useful tool

Watering the Terrarium:
Too Wet, Too Dry

There does not appear to be any one correct way of watering a terrarium. Watering techniques and schedules are highly individual and are determined by what works best with your terrarium. After the initial moistening (which is crucial) you can arrive at a watering schedule by observing certain signals in the terrarium: the color of the soil, and the amount of condensation on the walls of the container. A light mist and medium-dark soil are signs of sufficient water; no mist, even at night, indicates a lack of water; a heavy mist and very dark soil mean too much water. Excess water can be removed by inserting long strips of absorbent paper. Of course, the best indicator is the appearance of the ferns in the container. If the ferns look hale and hearty, what you are doing waterwise is right.

Airing the Terrarium:
Open or Closed

To cover or not to cover terrariums, particularly wide-mouth containers, is an unresolved problem. A common practice with wide-mouth terrariums is to cover but not to close them. Opening them a crack allows air to circulate and excess moisture to leave; this helps to reduce decay and mold growth. Bottle gardens with narrow necks lose very little water by evaporation and can remain uncapped and unwatered for long periods of time, even years. A perfectly balanced terrarium can be sealed and requires no additional air or water, also, for years.

Light and Temperature for Terrariums:
Too Much, Too Little

Ferns in terrariums need light, both to make food and to circulate water; the problem is how much. Too much light is as deadly as too little. A fern terrarium in direct sunlight for more than an hour becomes a crematorium. In dark recesses and dimly lit rooms, ferns gradually turn yellow, then fade away and die. The choice location is a northerly exposed window; this affords maximum indirect light without any direct sunlight.

In the opinion of many experienced indoor fern fanciers, artificial light will do just as well and has some advantages over natural light. It can be controlled and regulated with respect to the intensity and duration of exposure. Illumination by two cool-white 40 watt fluorescent tubes for about 14 hours a day, that sit about a foot above the terrarium works very well. However, it is wise to experiment with the distance from and the length of exposure to light sources, natural and artificial.

Temperatures around 68°F (20°C) are fine for terrariums. Air is an excellent insulator and the air inside the terrarium protects the plants against rapid changes in room temperature. The best authority on optimum light and temperature is the terrarium itself. If you use natural light, move the terrarium around the room to find out where the light and temperature are best for your glass garden. Experiment with artificial light, do not take fern illumination too lightly.

173

SUMMARY:

Terrariums in Review

Terrariums provide protected high-humidity habitats in which ferns can be grown anywhere, anytime, and by anybody who so desires. Success in this endeavor depends upon:

1. A clean, clear container which may be of plastic or glass; the size and shape are a matter of personal preference and taste.

2. Sterile growth mixtures consisting of successive layers of gravel for drainage, charcoal for absorption of the noxious gases of decay, and soil for anchorage and food.

3. Ferns selected as slow growers, and chosen for shape, personality, and suitability for life in a terrarium.

4. Cultivation by providing moderate amounts of water, air, light, and temperature as determined by the continuing good health of the terrarium tenants.

CHAPTER XLV

Marsh Fern

Sterile frond with blunt tipped
pinnules; fertile frond taller
with rolled over pinna margin

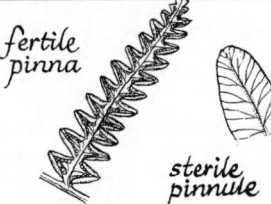

*fertile
pinna*

*sterile
pinnule*

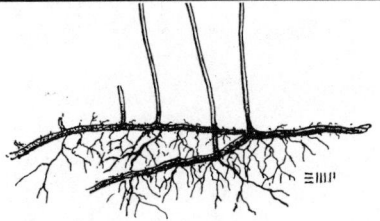

XIV

Herbariums

*H*uman beings are extremely susceptible to a highly contagious and almost incurable disease called "collectivitis." The chief symptom of this affliction is an uncontrollable urge to collect anything and everything, from arrowheads to zithers, for pleasure or profit. Ferns are not immune to the ravages of this malady. Fern foragers are constantly plundering the earth in search of foreign and native species for private and public gardens, homes and herbariums (her-BEAR-ee-yums). A herbarium is a classified collection of dead, dried, pressed, mounted, and labeled plant specimens. It is a record or voucher of the flora found in a particular locale at a particular time. Fern folios are part of the libraries of botanical gardens and societies, colleges and universities, and individual *pteridophiles* (fern-lovers).

Although living ferns in their natural settings or in gardens are far more attractive than dead ferns glued to paper, fern folios have some advantages. The specimens are usually typical, complete, carefully selected representatives of the species; they last indefinitely, requiring less space and care than their living counterparts; and they are available when you want them for study and research. Such practical considerations compensate for their lifelessness.

177

Forbidden Ferns:
Do Not Pick

The best way to learn about ferns is to study living ones in their natural habitats. However, the urge to collect and possess ferns cannot be disregarded. Before setting out on a fern foray, arm yourself with knowledge of the existing laws for protecting plants, including ferns. In most states, all ferns and fern allies are protected by law, except for the weedy and widespread hay-scented, sensitive, and bracken ferns, which flourish where most ferns fail. Lists of rare, endangered, and threatened plant species have been published by environmental protection agencies on the federal, state, county, and local levels. Picking or uprooting such plants on public land is forbidden, and punishable under the law by fines and by your conscience.

If pick you must, only select plants that grow in profusion; do not "liberate" rare, threatened, or endangered species, no matter what your intentions are. When in doubt, spare the fern or carefully remove a single fertile pinna as a source of spores for propagation. Since most ferns are perennials, carefully removing a single pinna or frond will not permanently injure or destroy the fern. Do not be carried away and carry away more than you need for preparing a herbarium specimen. "Let it not be said to your shame, that ferns grew here before you came."

Collecting Ferns:
With Care and Caution

Ferns collected as herbarium specimens should include the entire plant: roots, rhizomes, sterile fronds, and fertile fronds. You may have to use a pick and shovel to dig up the fern. Soil clinging to the roots should be removed by shaking and washing. Not only is this soil unnecessary and a nuisance in preparing a herbarium specimen, but it may contain the eggs, larvae, seeds or spores of plant pests that can damage and destroy dried specimens and contaminate other plants in the collection. Unless you are ready to press your ferns, to prevent wilting and wrinkling, place them in a plastic bag and store them in a refrigerator, where they will keep for a few days.

There are those who would rather photograph than collect ferns, a commendable and highly recommended method. Ferns are very photogenic, and a folio of photographs of ferns in their natural settings is an excellent way of recording information about your specimens in a "fern photarium."

Flattening Ferns:
Drying and Pressing

Living ferns are preserved as herbarium specimens by drying them between sheets of newspaper and flattening them under pressure. Unfold a sheet of a newspaper and place the fern on it. Arrange the specimen to avoid any overlap of parts, showing the upper and lower surfaces of the fronds. Include fertile and sterile fronds; spores are essential in identification. Fronds longer than the newspaper should be folded with a minimum of overlap (see page 181). Cover the laid-out specimen by folding the newspaper over it. Identification data may be written on the edge of the newspaper, including the date, location, and the like. Place a sheet of cardboard or blotting paper over the folded specimen.

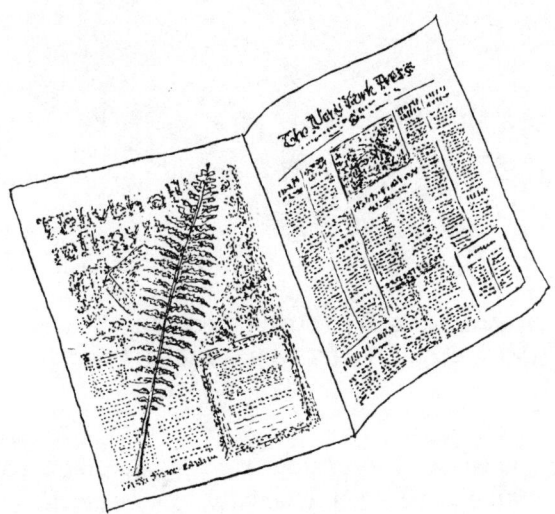

Place specimens in folded newspaper

Repeat the above procedure with each of your specimens. Place the pile of alternating layers of cardboard and newspaper under a heavy weight or in a plant press. Ferns that are quickly dried and flattened retain much of their original shape and color. A plant press may be purchased or constructed. It consists of strips of wood two inches wide that are nailed, glued, or screwed together to make two 12-inch-by-18-inch frames as supports. This is slightly larger than the size of a folded sheet of newspaper. A pair of one-inch straps about 4 feet long, or nylon cord tightened around the pile of specimens provide the pressure to flatten without creasing or breaking the ferns.

A Plant Press

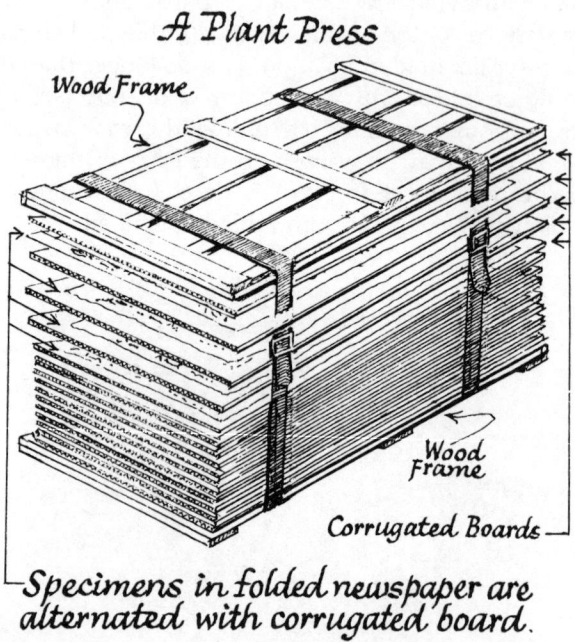

Wood Frame

Wood Frame

Corrugated Boards

Specimens in folded newspaper are alternated with corrugated board.

A very satisfactory substitute for a plant press, particularly for small specimens, is a telephone book or a magazine with pages of uncoated paper which are very absorbent. Slip the specimens between the pages and write identifying information on the edges. Pile other books or weights on top to supply pressure. The drying and pressing process usually takes about a week. The specimens are then removed and are ready for mounting. "Old telephone books need never die, between their pages ferns may lie and dry."

Framing Ferns:
Herbarium Specimens

Ferns earmarked for herbarium collections are mounted on standard size herbarium paper (11½ inches by 16 inches) which can be obtained from a biological supply company. The usual adhesives are Elmer's glue, a special mounting plastic, or narrow, gummed linen strips. Cellulose tape is discouraged as an adhesive since it dries, cracks, discolors, and eventually peels off.

Fern specimens are mounted to show all parts of the plant. Both sides of a frond can be displayed by bending and turning over part of a long frond or by mounting two short fronds, one showing the top and the other the bottom side. Spore cases are as important in identifying ferns as flowers are in recognizing flowering plants.

Information describing the specimen is written on special herbarium labels, which are placed in the lower right-hand corner of the sheet. The label gives the scientific name of the fern, the place where it was collected, the date, habitat, and the name of the collector.

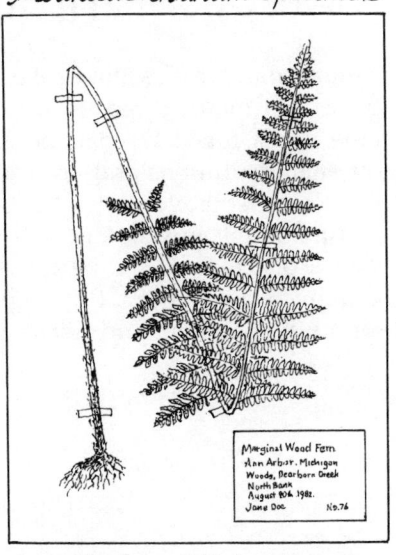

Mounted Herbarium Specimen

Large fronds are folded and 'taped' to the herbarium sheet then labeled with all collecting information.

For personal use, specimens may be mounted in notebooks with cellulose tape, or on index cards with the specimen on one side and the identifying data on the reverse. These cards can be stored in a file box and are very convenient for study, reference and display.

SUMMARY:

Herbariums

Herbariums are classified collections of dried, pressed, mounted plant specimens, a record of the flora of a given area at a given time. Such folios are part of the libraries of botanical and educational institutions and are used for study and storage.

Representative fern specimens are collected, pressed, dried, and mounted on standard size herbarium paper with identifying data. Collectors should be aware of existing laws protecting ferns in a given community. Private personal herbariums are suggested for study, teaching and demonstration.

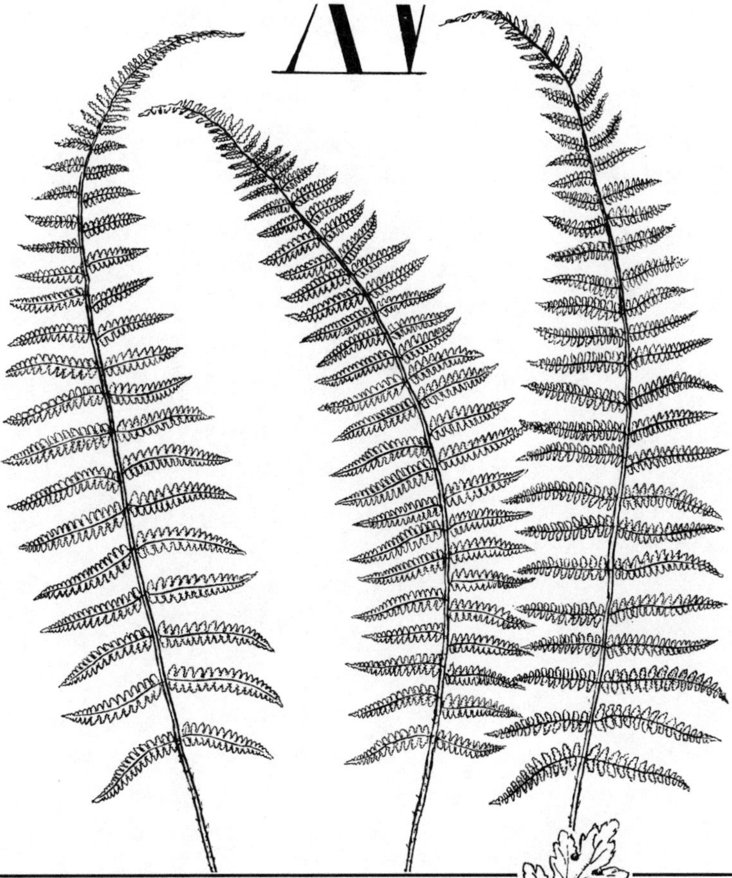

Hay-Scented Fern

Lacy, delicate, velvety touch;
sori, open cups in crotch margin
between lobes of pinnules

fertile
pinnule

sorus

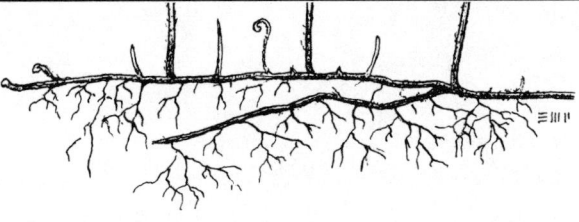

XV

Ferncrafts

In addition to gardening and collecting, there are many other ways to have fun with ferns. Several "do-it-yourself" projects are presented here which will appeal to nongardeners and noncollectors who would rather play than plant ferns. Some may be old, some new, but all are lots of fun for frolicking with ferns.

Fern Mountings:
Card Making

If you have ever made or seen a fern herbarium you probably were impressed by the delicacy and the beauty of many species. It seems a pity to consign such "beauties" to a herbarium where they are seen only occasionally by a very limited audience and usually viewed as scientific specimens. There is no reason why ferns cannot be mounted artistically on any one of several kinds of materials and displayed for the enjoyment of all.

The mounting materials may be paper in various textures and colors, canvas, cardboard, masonite, wood, or plastics. To preserve these mountings, they can be sprayed with shellac or transparent plastic. Mounted on letter-size paper, they can be folded into greeting or birthday cards. By covering the mountings with transparent contact paper, the ferns can be protected and preserved. What is more appropriate than sending a Christmas fern card on that joyous holiday, or a lady fern card to your "lady," or a rattlesnake fern card to "you know whom"?

Fern Photos:
Positive and Negative Pictures

If you can't take a photo in focus, you can still get both negative and positive pictures of ferns in color, without a camera. Positive pictures are made by coating the surface of the fern frond with paint and making a print of it on paper, wood, or some other material. A negative picture is created by placing the fern on paper, cloth, or wood and spraying or rolling paint over it, leaving an outline or silhouette. Fern silhouettes can also be recorded with blueprint or ozalid paper.

Fern Forms:
Blueprints

The delicate outlines or silhouettes of ferns can be captured and recorded by the blueprint paper technique. The materials required are blueprint paper (available in drafting supply stores); a pane of glass; a piece of cardboard cut to the size of the glass; wide masking tape to hinge the glass to the cardboard, or hinged clothespins. In a dark room, cut the blueprint paper into sheets of the desired size and place them in an envelope until they are ready to be used. Keep the coated light sensitive side, gray-blue in color, away from light. When these materials are assembled, proceed as follows:

1. Place the pane of glass on a flat surface.
2. Arrange the fern frond on the glass.
3. Cover the fern with a sheet of cut blueprint paper, keeping the coated side face down.
4. Put the cardboard on top of the blueprint paper.
5. Using either masking tape, or two hinged clothespins, clamp the entire assembly together.
6. Turn over the assembly and expose it to either artificial light or sunlight until the blueprint paper turns blue.
7. Remove the exposed blueprint paper and wash it in running tap water for about ten minutes.
8. Dry with a sponge.

You now have a white fern silhouette against a blue background. Several ferns of the same or different species maybe silhouetted on the same sheet of blueprint paper.

To keep the blueprint from fading, place it in a weak solution of potassium dichromate (available from chemical supply houses) for five minutes before washing in tap water. This solution is made by dissolving a few crystals of the chemical, enough to cover a dime, in a glass of water.

Fern Forms:
Ozalid Color Prints

A variation of the white silhouette on a blue background theme is possible with ozalid prints. With ozalid paper, the silhouettes are colored and the background is white, the reverse of blueprint pictures. The steps in preparing ozalid prints are essentially the same as those for blueprints, with two differences. First, ozalid paper replaces blueprint paper. This paper may be obtained in many colors and is available in art supply shops. Second, instead of washing in tap water, exposed ozalid sheets are washed in a weak solution of ammonia water. A collection of blueprints and ozalid prints of ferns make a very colorful display.

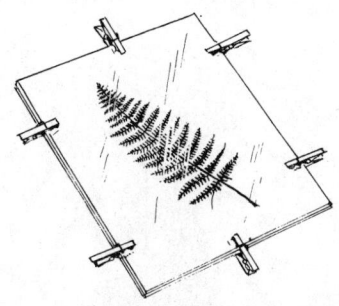

Silhouette fern prints may be made with picture glass, clip clothes pins and light sensitive paper

Fern Silhouettes:
Spatter and Spray Prints

Making spatter prints is one of the old standbys for paint putterers. It can be a bit messy, but with practice the spatter can be confined to the target and reduced to small spatters. To spatter, provide yourself with old newspapers, paper on which the spatter print is to be made, the pigment to be spattered, a piece of fine wire screening, and an old toothbrush. Then

1. Cover with newspaper the flat working surface on which the operation is to be performed.

2. Lay the sheet of paper on the newspaper and place the fern on the paper. Pin down any parts of the fern that do not lie absolutely flat, otherwise the spatter will spread and produce a fuzzy silhouette.

A Negative Spatter Print

3. Dip the toothbrush in a bit of the pigment (water-soluble paint, ink, or black printing ink). Make a test spatter to determine the required pressure of the toothbrush. Hold the screening about a foot above the fern.

4. When the paint is dry, carefully remove the fern.

Considering the various places and purposes to which spray paints have been applied and misapplied, it would be unforgivable not to include its use in making fern spray prints. Spray prints are made the same way as spatter prints and with equally pleasing results. For best prints, fasten the fern to the paper with rubber cement, otherwise the spray paint will get under the specimen and give poor results. When the print is dry, simply remove the frond.

Fern Prints:
Paint Pictures

Positive prints are produced by painting the fern frond and making a print of it on a variety of materials shaped and colored according to your taste. Japanese rice paper (available at most art supply shops) yields fine, delicate details and makes very beautiful prints. In addition to the paper, black printing ink, a paint brush with stiff bristles, and newspaper are needed. The printing process is as follows:

1. On newspaper, flatten the fern frond underside up. (You may find it artistically and scientifically advantageous to place another fern frond of the same species next to it topside-up.)

2. Brush paint on the frond, or ink with a rubber roller using printer's ink.

3. Move the inked frond to a fresh piece of newspaper.

4. Place a sheet of paper (or other material) on top of the inked fern and gently press down and rub to bring out the details and complete outline.

5. Gently lift the paper off the fern; avoid smearing the print.

189

Fern prints make unusual greeting cards and wall hangings.

Fern Place Mats:
Do-It-Yourself

Fern fronds have found their place in place mats, which with the proper materials are not too difficult to make. In addition to dried, pressed ferns, two matting materials are needed: a linenlike, nontransparent backing material called Chartex, and a mylar laminating film called Seal-Lamin. Both these materials may be purchased at art supply or camera stores. After you have rounded up these supplies proceed as follows:

1. Cut the Chartex backing material to the desired size and shape.

2. Arrange the dried fern fronds on the Chartex in a pleasing arrangement.

3. Cut two pieces of clear Seal-Lamin a half-inch larger on all sides than the Chartex.

4. Place the ferns and the Chartex between the two sheets of Seal-Lamin.

5. If you have a dry mount press, follow the instructions for sealing. If not, a hot iron may be substituted, but first make

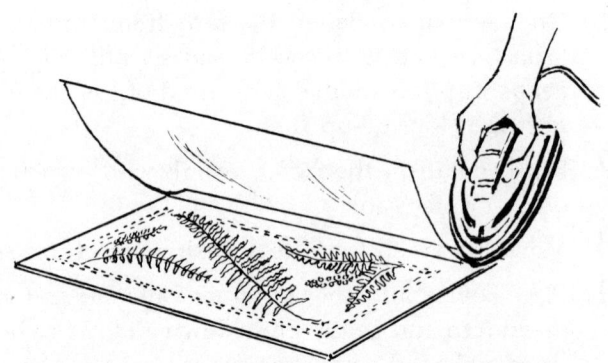

With a hot iron, anchor the film along one edge before sealing.

Courtesy of Virginia Otto, Westboro, MA.

a few test runs on some scrap Seal-Lamin to determine how hot the iron should be and how long to press it. Seal the corners and edges first before making the overall seal. After the materials are cooled, trim off the edges of the transparent Seal-Lamin.

The end result will be a permanent place of honor for ferns and a tribute to your creative talents.

Ferns in Plaster:
Plaques

Another way to preserve fern forms is in plaster of Paris plaques, which make decorative hangings.

1. Start by preparing a mold of the desired size and shape, either of cardboard or wood, about 6 inches by 8 inches and 1¼ inches deep; then grease it.

2. Mix plaster of Paris as directed on the package. It may be purchased in a paint or art supply store.

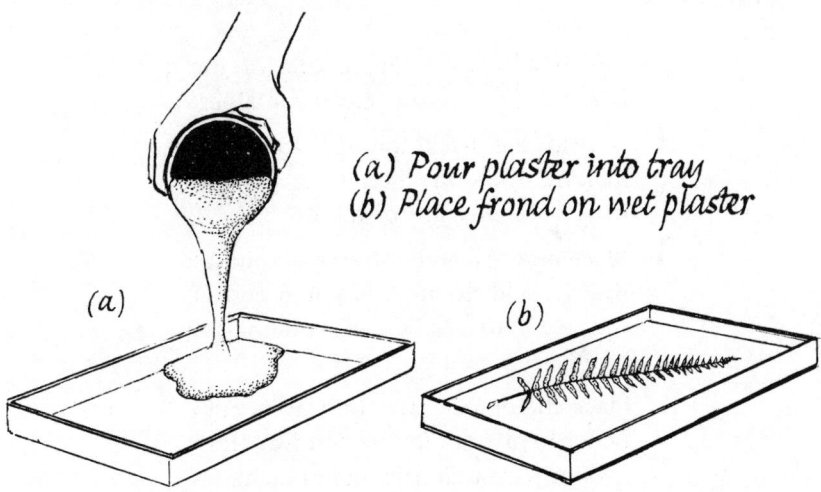

(a) Pour plaster into tray
(b) Place frond on wet plaster

(a)

(b)

3. Pour the plaster into the mold to a depth of one inch.

4. Place fern fronds on the wet plaster, insuring contact on all surfaces.

5. Allow the plaster to dry, and then remove the fronds with a stiff brush.

6. Color with paint and spray with clear acrylic (which can be purchased in an art supply store).

You have now preserved a fern in a plaster plaque, ready to be hung.

Ferns in Wax:
Candle-Making

Candlestick-makers may be a dying breed, but the art of candle-making still flickers. Amateur candle-makers may find that adding fern fronds to their molds is a new and exciting twist of the candle wick. To fabricate fern candles, supply yourself with the following materials: a container to serve as a casting mold, a thick wick, clear wax, pieces of colored wax, and a supply of pressed ferns. The wax and wick may be purchased in hobby shops. Once you have assembled these materials, you are ready to commence candle-making.

1. Punch a hole in the middle of the bottom of the empty, clean container.

2. Thread the wick through the hole, making a knot at the end to prevent it from pulling out of the can.

3. Place a pencil across the open end of the can and tie the unknotted end of the wick to the pencil, pulling as tightly as possible.

4. Place the empty can in a tray of cold water to prevent the melted wax from leaking through the opening at its

base. Seal the outside of the opening with clay to prevent wax seepage.

5. Spray the inside of the container with a mold release or water.

6. Fill another container with clear wax and place it in a saucepan of boiling water. Keep it in this hot water bath until the wax melts.

7. Carefully pour about two inches of the melted wax into the mold.

8. Insert the dried fern fronds into the mold using clothespins to hold them against the sides of the container.

9. Fill the container with pieces of colored wax; these will also help to keep the fronds in place.

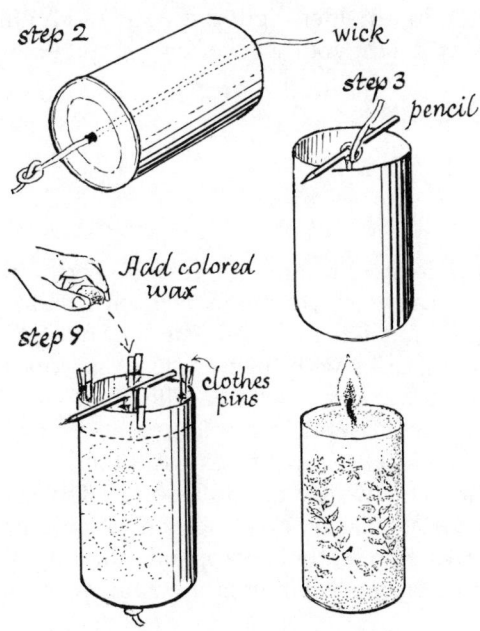

Steps in decorating candles
Courtesy, Chas. Anderson, Mahwah, N.J.

10. Now pour melted wax into the mold as it begins to cool, that is, just as it begins to form a skin. If the melted wax is too hot, the individual colored cubes will melt.

11. Cool the mold and its contents in a container of cold water deep enough to reach its rim. After a few minutes, add more melted wax to fill the container.

12. Permit the mold to cool for 12 hours. Cut the knot at the bottom and pull the candle out of the mold. If there is resistance, place the mold into boiling water for a few minutes to melt the wax holding it to the container. Even out the bottom of the candle.

Place the candle in a holder, light the wick and admire your first fern candle. May it light your way for bigger and better fern candle power.

Fern Play:
More Ideas

Once you fall in love with ferns, there is no end to the ways and means you can carry on your romance with them. For shutter bugs, photographing ferns can become a way of life, especially close-ups of living ferns with their endless patterns of sporangia, frond forms, and leaf arrangements. The artist will discover that ferns are ideal models and interesting subjects for canvas, silk screen, printing blocks, and the like. Another way to have fun with ferns is the creation of fern accessories. The construction of planters from metal, plastic, or wood; log cabin hanging baskets; propagating trays; mini-greenhouses; and indoor light gardens are among the projects that will enrich your life with ferns.

SUMMARY:

Fern Frolics

In addition to collecting, classifying, and growing ferns, these plants lend themselves to a wide range of creative artistic activities. Their beauty is enjoyed by mounting them on a variety of materials for display or as greeting and birthday cards. Fern forms may be captured and recorded on blueprint and ozalid paper, as well as by spatter and paint prints. They make attractive and unusual placemats, plaster plaques, and candles. For the construction-minded hobbyist, planters, mini-greenhouses, hanging baskets, and indoor light gardens may be added to a list of "things to do with ferns."

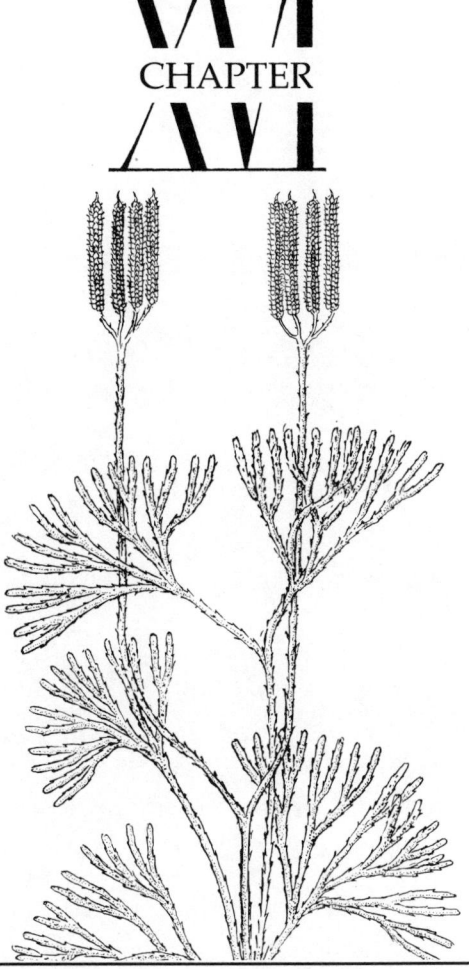

Running Cedar

Branches flattened, fan-shaped,
evergreen; four club-shaped cones
in candelabra

*fertile
cone 'leaf'*

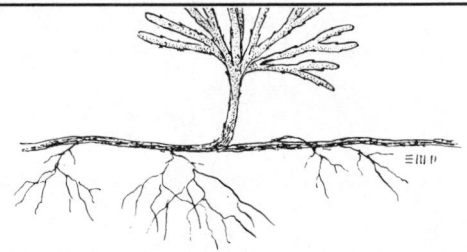

XVI

Ferns, Fossils, and Coal

T he story of ferns would not be complete without considering the impact of their past history on the present energy crisis and on the future of life on this planet. Coal is a fossil fuel derived mostly from the fern family. As an energy source, it is the center of a bitter battle generating considerably more heat than light. Power, profits, politics and people meet head on in this coal controversy. The fern forests of the distant past are linked to the feuding fossil fuels of the present.

From Ferns to Fossil Fuel:
Coal Formation

Let us back up in time and return to the fantastic fern forests of yesteryear. Only a handful of the dwarf descendants of these giants of antiquity have survived. However, the story of their past glory and splendor is indelibly imprinted in the earth as coal.

The formation of coal began half a billion years ago soon after plants invaded land; it was at its greatest height during the Carboniferous (car-bow-NIF-err-us) period, the Coal Age, 350 million years ago. For more than 100 million years, successive generations of ferns and their relatives flourished and died, absorbing and storing solar energy in their bodies.

Billions of tons of ferns and their spores piled up in swamps and bogs around the world, forming layers of partially decayed vegetation called peat. Fern fallout piled up so quickly and in such quantities that the lower 2 percent of the peat layers were quickly buried and escaped complete decay. The sheer weight of accumulated vegetation probably depressed the land, allowing nearby

Hundreds of millions of years ago the earth abounded in swamps and forests of ferns and fern allies

As the ferns and plants died they filled the swamps with layers of partially decayed vegetation known as peat

inland seas to flood the swamps and peat bogs. Layers of sand, silt, mud, and lime were deposited by the waters of the invading seas. These sediments not only sealed the peat but compressed it further, squeezing out moisture and gases. Under this pressure the peat was "coalified", compressed first into brown coal (lignite), then into soft coal (bituminous), and finally into hard coal (anthracite).

The continuous pressure squeezed more and more moisture and gases out of the compacted vegetation, increasing its carbon

3

New plants grew upon old; water and sand mixed with them sealing and compressing layers of peat

4

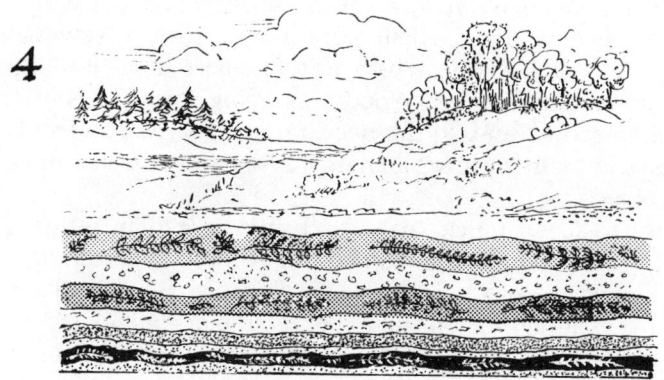

Increased pressure and heat further compressed the peat, first into brown coal, then into soft coal, and finally into hard coal

content from 60 per cent (as peat) up to 95 per cent (as hard coal). Heat is also needed to turn peat into coal. This heat was supplied by the earth itself. The deeper the vegetation was buried, the hotter it was, since the temperature of the earth increases 1°C with every 55 feet of depth. Additional heat and pressure came from the folding and buckling of the crust of the earth during mountain-making movements and from molten lava flows near coal deposits. Further heat and compression can transform coal into graphite and diamonds, both of which are pure carbon.

201

The amount of coal buried in the earth is enormous. It is estimated that over 16 trillion tons were laid down (a trillion is 1,000,000,000,000, a million million), half in North America. About 5 percent of the total has been mined to date. It is estimated that at the present rate of coal consumption, the earth's supply will last several hundred years.

The Rise of King Coal I:
Coal Comes of Age

Although coal has been known for thousands of years, it was not until the invention of the steam engine in the eighteenth century that coal revolutionized industry and society. For a long time it was the poor man's fuel, a substitute for wood. As early as the twelfth century, the English were mining coal in Newcastle and shipping it to London, which was fast becoming the largest industrial city in Europe. Wood was being burned faster than it could be grown and so the need for coal increased. The English were faced with a growing energy crisis, and coal became a hate-love object.

By 1300, so much coal was being burned in industrialized London that people complained about the city becoming "dirty, smelly, and unhealthy" from the coal smoke. Six years later, King Edward I banned the burning of coal "in that smoggy, sooty city". But this did not stop the use of this "dirty, smelly, unhealthy" fuel. Faced with waning wood but copious coal supplies, the shift from wood to coal was inevitable, and indispensable for England's industrial growth. By the nineteenth century, Britain was the great world power, the empire on which the sun never set, the master of the emerging coal age, and home of the "famous" London fog.

Coal did not become king in the United States until the beginning of the twentieth century. It remained the principal fuel until the 1940's, when it was pushed into second place by two other fossil fuels, oil and natural gas. Today, coal supplies about one-fifth of our total energy needs; about three-quarters of the coal mined in this country is burned in power plants to produce electricity. The shift from coal to oil and gas was not a matter of necessity, as was the previous shift from wood to coal. Gas and oil are preferred fuels, because they burn cleaner, are more easily transported, and are more efficient than coal. However, in the past decade, the dream of unlimited supplies of inexpensive gas and oil has been shattered forever. The current energy crunch is compelling us to take a second look at coal as the chief energy source. Can we, should we, or must we go back to coal, to the reign of King Coal II?

The Coal Controversy:
Black Diamonds or Black Death?

What is the price we must pay for burning more coal? The most powerful argument against increasing the use of coal is that it is the "dirtiest" and most detested of the fossil fuels, a prime polluter of air, soil, water, life, the source of innumerable and growing environmental problems. Underground coal mining is at best dangerous, dirty work with the dubious distinction of having the highest rate of occupational injury. Black lung disease, caused by the constant inhalation of coal dust, has killed or crippled more miners than we know. The federal government is paying about $1 billion a year as compensation to the victims of black lung or their survivors.

Underground mining is also responsible for cave-ins of surface land that have disastrous environmental consequences. Runoff of acid water from coal mines is another major environmental problem. The sulfur-bearing minerals in coal, when dug up and exposed to air and water, form sulfuric acid, which is carried to rivers and streams by water draining through coal mines. This strong acid contaminates the waterways, injuring and poisoning water plants and animals. Surface coal mining—strip mining—has turned millions of acres of beautiful landscapes into barren moonscapes. Some of this land is being reclaimed, but most—abandoned years ago—is denuded and badly eroded.

The pollution of the air by coal smoke is nothing new. Over 300 years ago, John Evelyn, seventeenth-century diarist, described the quality of the air in the coal-burning city of London as "corrupting" and "befouling" everything exposed to this sooty, suffocating smog. Air pollution is still a major problem in many large metropolitan areas. When fossil fuels, particularly coal, are burned, several pollutants are discharged into the air, some cause illness and several are suspected of causing cancer. The three major pollutants present in fossil fuel fumes are unburned particles (ash), the oxides of sulfur, and the oxides of nitrogen. More than half of these pollutants come from coal-burning power stations that generate electricity.

Fossil Fuel Fumes:
Acid Rain and Snow

"It droppeth as . . . gentle rain from heaven upon the place beneath . . ." alluded to by Shakespeare in the "Merchant of Venice"
is rapidly becoming an acid rain, without mercy and unblessed.
Measurements have shown that in the past 200 years, the rains
and snows falling on parts of the northeastern United States and
western Europe are becoming more and more acidic. Many atmospheric scientists and ecologists believe that the increasing acidity of precipitation constitutes one of the most serious world-wide
environmental problems we face in the immediate future.

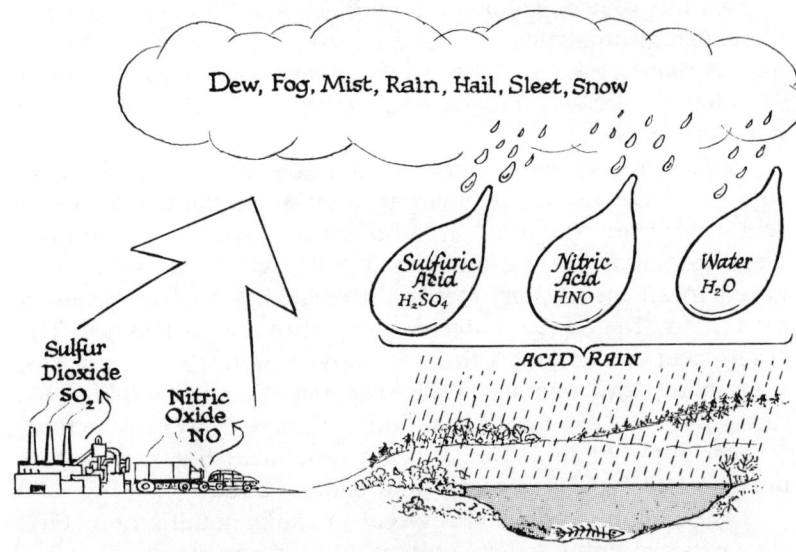

ACID RAIN UPSETS THE ECOLOGICAL BALANCE

The source of these acids are the oxides of sulfur and nitrogen
released when fossil fuels are burned. The sulfur oxides come
mainly from coal-burning and oil-burning power plants, steel
mills, factories, and smelters that burn sulfur-bearing ores. The
nitrogen oxides are spewed out largely by automobile exhausts.
These toxic oxide fumes combine with water vapor in the atmosphere and form tiny droplets of acids. The oxides of sulfur become

sulfuric acid, the oxides of nitrogen, nitric acid—both very strong, corrosive chemicals. Air currents carry these deadly droplets sometimes hundreds or thousands of miles from their place of origin, across state lines and national boundaries. Eventually, they fall to the earth as acid rain or snow. Acid fallout can kill and cripple fish, damage and destroy plants, erode and crumble buildings and statues, reduce soil fertility, and undermine health.

Rain as sour as vinegar (acetic acid) was recorded in Scotland in 1974. The most acidic rains and snows in this country fall mainly in the Northeast. Some 5,000 lakes in the Adirondacks and Canada have become so acidic that their fish population has declined or disappeared. The complete destruction of all life in almost 200 Adirondack lakes is attributed to acid fallout. The acid fallout fouling up plant and animal life in the Adirondacks originates several hundred miles away in midwestern (American) industrial areas, where large amounts of "dirty" coal is burned in power plants. It also is blown across the United States' border from Canadian smokestacks to the north. Likewise, Canadian life is being destroyed by U.S. emissions carried north. Acid rain and snow know no political borders.

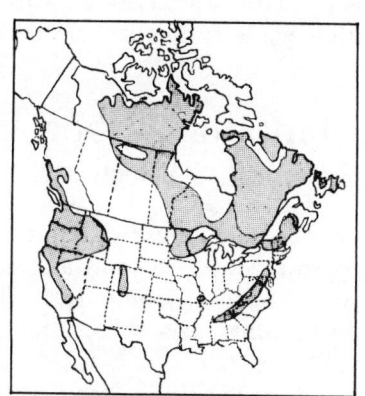

There seems to be no single simple solution. The most obvious and most difficult solution is to limit the amount of acid-forming gases being released into the air. Shifting to low-sulfur coal and oil, removing the sulfur oxides from smokestack gases, conserving energy, and using cleaner energy

Shaded portions denote areas where acid rain creates ecological problems.

alternatives may be too little and too late. The gains made by these measures are easily offset by growing demands for energy especially from increased coal consumption. As a consequence, we face still another international environmental problem which we cannot wish or blow away, namely increased carbon dioxide emissions from the combustion of fossil fuels, which have possible devastating effects on the world's climate.

Carbon Dioxide and Climate:
Coal, the Culprit

Mark Twain once remarked that everybody talks about the weather but nobody does anything about it. Not true—we are doing something, but we are not entirely aware of what we are doing nor how it will affect the weather. Many scientists believe that the increased burning of tremendous quantities of fossil fuels, especially coal, will add excessive amounts of carbon dioxide to the atmosphere that could dramatically change world climate.

Carbon dioxide (CO_2) is a colorless, odorless gas naturally present in the atmosphere in very small amounts, 0.03 per cent or 3 parts of CO_2 per 10,000 parts of air. Despite its presence in only trace quantities, billions of tons of this gas are constantly entering and leaving the atmosphere. Carbon dioxide comes as a natural byproduct from decay of dead organisms, the respiration of living ones, and the combustion of fossil fuels. Coal, in particular, throws off about twice as much CO_2 as oil, and synthetic fuels made from coal release twice as much CO_2 as natural coal.

Climbing Carbon Dioxide Content:
Greenhouse Effect

Careful scientific measurements of atmospheric carbon dioxide beginning in 1958 show a steady increase in concentrations of this gas in the atmosphere. But only about half the amount discharged by burning fuels during this period is present in the air. Where is the rest?

A good part is absorbed by the oceans of the world. The CO_2 exchange between the atmosphere and the oceans is extremely slow, which may account for its current accumulation in the air. CO_2 is also taken up by green plants for photosynthesis. In this food-making process, solar energy captured by chlorophyll splits water molecules into hydrogen and oxygen. The hydrogen is joined to carbon dioxide to produce carbohydrates, sugars, and starches, the substances out of which plants are made, and the ultimate source of food for all life. The oxygen is used to burn some of the carbohydrates, releasing energy and also carbon dioxide and water, the two original building blocks. Thus, sour carbonated water (carbon dioxide and water) becomes a sweet oxygenated beverage (sugar and oxygen), the nectar of life.

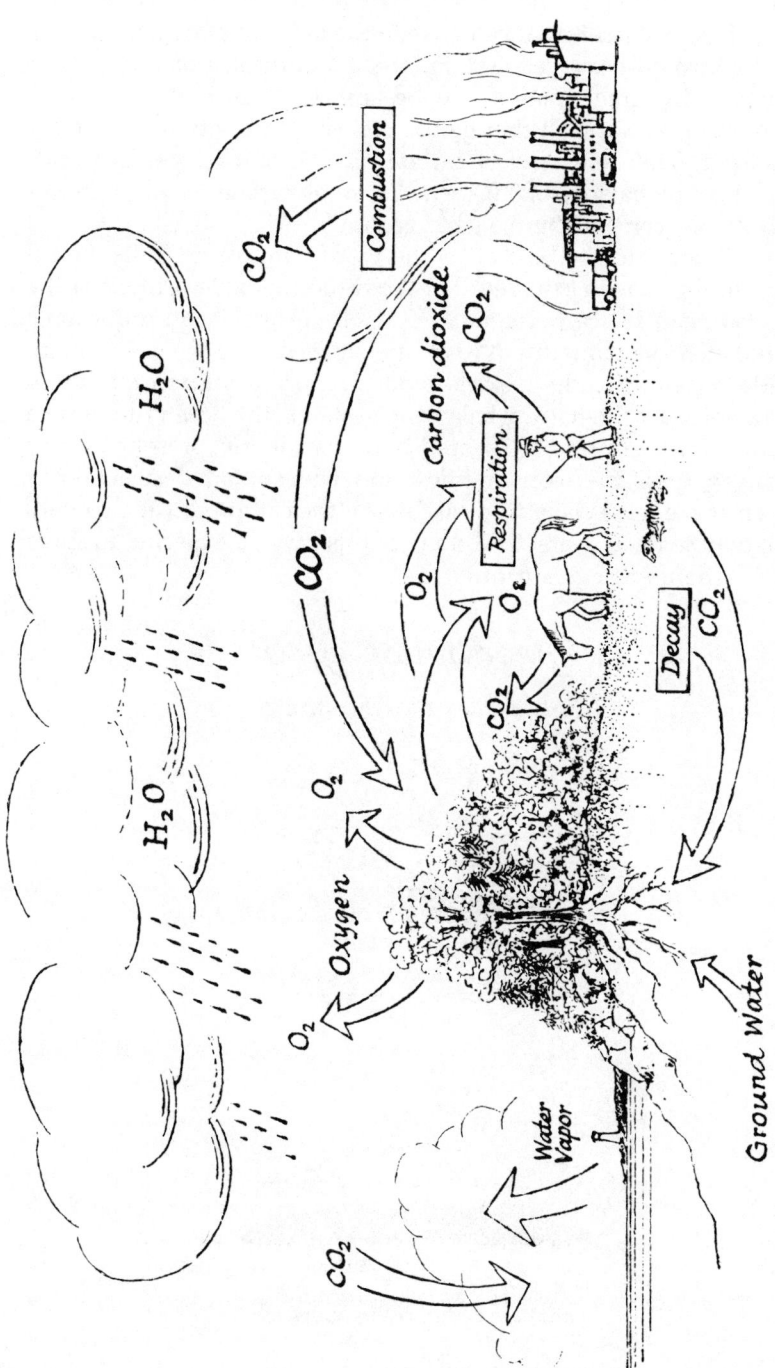

The Carbon-dioxide balance is maintained through Respiration, Combustion and Decay interacting with the oceans and green plants

207

There is a neat balance between the amount of carbon dioxide derived from decay, respiration, and combustion and the amount removed by green plants and oceans. Until recently, the bank account of air showed that global deposits and withdrawals were balanced. The cash flow of carbon dioxide and oxygen currency left a healthy balance of 0.03 per cent in the carbon dioxide account and 21 per cent in the oxygen account.

All appeared to be well in the world, atmospherically speaking, until it was discovered that the carbon dioxide content of the air has risen by 14 per cent since 1850, an increase proportional to the increased amount of fossil fuel burned. The volume of man-made carbon dioxide, experts report, is increasing too rapidly to be handled by the natural balancing systems, the oceans and green plants. Furthermore, it is predicted that at the present rate of growing fossil-fuel consumption and widespread destruction of green space, especially tropical forests, the carbon dioxide content will double in 50 years. The effect of this may be expected to show up by the end of this century.

Greenhouse effect

THE CARBON DIOXIDE SHIELD

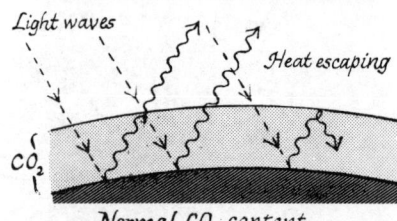

Normal CO_2 content
Light becomes heat in the atmosphere
Some heat escapes; some is absorbed

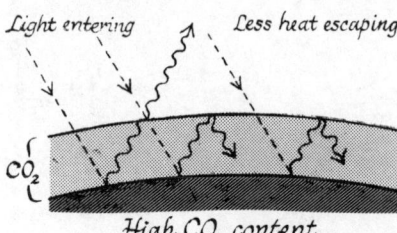

High CO_2 content
Less heat escapes; more heat is
absorbed — the greenhouse effect

The relationship between carbon dioxide and climate may not be readily apparent. Carbon dioxide, the heaviest of the atmospheric gases, blankets the surface of the earth. It acts like the glass windows in a greenhouse, allowing sunlight to pass through and heat the earth while stopping most of the heat from escaping into space. This phenomenon is called the "greenhouse effect." Since the heat is unable to pass out through glass windows, the greenhouse heats up, like the inside of a closed car on a hot day.

Possible Climatic Catastrophe:
Rising World Temperature

What are the possible consequences of increased atmospheric carbon dioxide? Experts are convinced that increasing the carbon dioxide concentration in the atmosphere can trigger major climatic changes by increasing the greenhouse effect. Doubling the content of this insulating, heat-trapping layer could cause the average global temperature to rise by 6° Fahrenheit (3°Celsius). This warming trend is enough to melt the polar ice caps and raise the level of the oceans by as much as 20 feet, flooding huge coastal areas and cities. It can also cause shifts in climatic zones and agricultural areas. It could conceivably also lead to hotter summers in the midwest transforming farmland into deserts and deserts into farmland. In short, burning more coal may lead to an environmental catastrophe of world-wide proportions.

Consider the possibility that as the carbon dioxide level of the air rises, the earth may return to the climate of the Carboniferous period and to the life that existed hundreds of millions of years ago. Higher forms of life—reptiles, birds and mammals—may be unable to survive in a high carbon dioxide atmosphere and a hot, muggy, swampy environment. Perhaps ferns would again take over and rule the world.

SUMMARY:

The Coal Controversy

Ferns did not relinquish their former position as the dominant land flora without leaving their mark. Mountains and plains of coal scattered over the world, half in North America, are testimonials to their former greatness.

Coal is largely the fossil remains of ferns and their allies. During the great coal forming period starting 350 million years ago, layers of fern vegetation accumulated in shallow swamps. The lower layers escaped decay and were compressed into peat. Thick layers of sand and mud buried the peat beneath the surface of the earth and preserved it. The resulting pressure and heat squeezed the moisture and gases out of the peat and compressed it into coal, increasing its carbon content.

This fossil fuel which powered the industrial revolution has been both a blessing and a blight since 1300 when wood became scarce and was being replaced by coal in England. King Coal ruled our industrial society until the 1940's and was then deposed by the two competing fossil fuels, natural gas and oil. The growing energy demands of expanding industries coupled with the increased cost of these fuels and their growing scarcity, are being offered as reasons for recalling coal as king again. Potentially there is sufficient coal to meet our energy needs for several hundred years. The question of the day is "Can we increase the use of coal in view of the innumerable environmental problems it creates?" From mining to burning, coal is the "dirtiest" of the fossil fuels and a polluter without a rival. Mining is a dangerous, unhealthy occupation. Underground mining causes cave-in of surface land and is the source of acid run-off which destroys water life in neighboring streams. Strip mining has converted millions of acres of green landscapes into barren moonscapes.

The burning of increased amounts of fossil fuels, especially coal, is creating two serious worldwide environmental problems of growing proportions. The first is acid rain and snow caused by oxides of sulfur and nitrogen, highly toxic pollutants, released into the air when fossil fuels are burned. These oxides combine with water vapor forming tiny droplets of sulfuric and nitric acids respectively. Carried by air currents, they fall as acid rain or snow sometimes hundreds or even thousands of miles from their place of origin, across state lines and national boundaries. The sharp increase in the acidity of these atmospheric fallouts is killing and crippling wild life, eroding buildings and undermining health.

Equally threatening and a cause for serious concern is the growing carbon dioxide content of the atmosphere and its possible effects on world climate. Carbon dioxide normally serves as a thermal blanket which allows sunlight to pass through it and heat the earth but does not let all the heat escape; this is called the "greenhouse effect". It is predicted that the carbon dioxide concentration will double within the next 50 years; this may increase the temperature of the earth enough to melt polar ice caps and flood coastal areas, turn farmlands into deserts and deserts into farmland. In short, increased carbon dioxide generated by increased coal and oil burning may lead to catastrophic climatic changes and dislocations.

Before irreparable damage is inflicted upon our planet and its inhabitants by mounting fossil fuel fumes, particularly coal, these prime polluters must be "cleaned up" or "cleaned out": Time is no longer a luxury we can afford. At the present rate of consumption, cost and pollution contamination, the days of fossil fuels are numbered. Solutions being shouted and whispered are "cleaner fossil fuels", "conserve, conserve, conserve", "out with nonrenewable fouling fading fossil fuels; in with clean, safe natural renewable energy sources".

CHAPTER XVIII

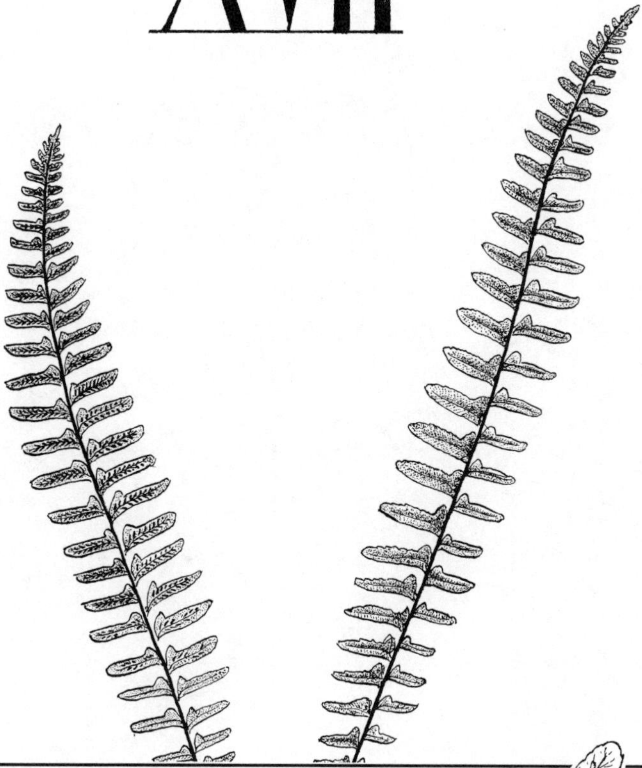

CHAPTER XVII

Ebony Spleenwort

Sterile frond short, sprawling;
fertile frond erect; pinnae eared;
sori in herring-bone pattern

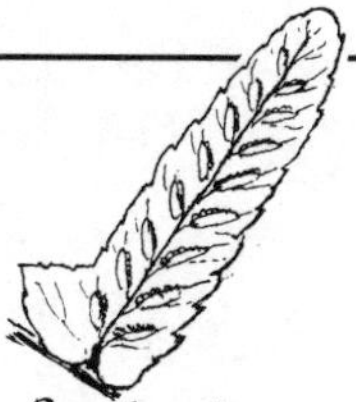

fertile pinna

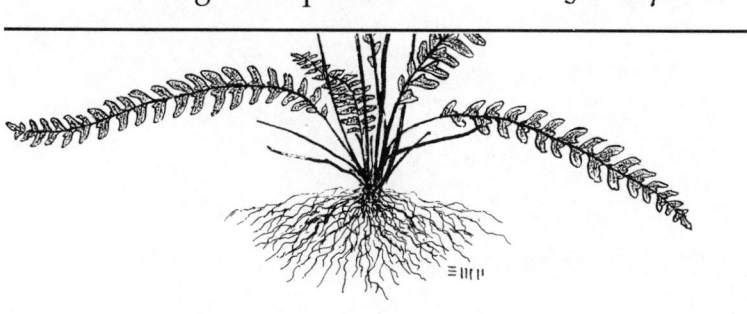

XVII

Ferns, Fuels, and the Future: Energy Alternatives

*I*t seems ironic that coal, the great legacy left us by ferns, is both the boon and the bane of our existence. Having sparked the industrial revolution, power from coal ran our society until it was replaced by power from petroleum (gas and oil). Now that the future of our petroleum supply is in question, coal is again making a bid to regain its place as the number one fuel.

Despite its abundance, versatility, and availability, there is general reluctance to return to a world ruled by King Coal. This deposed monarch has a reputation as the "dirtiest" and most "disliked" of the fossil fuels, a prime polluter of the environment capable of destroying the world with its poisonous fumes and ashes. Petroleum is also a polluter, but somewhat less so. In addition escalating gas and oil prices are rocking our petroleum-powered economy and generating enough heat to ignite a World War III. There is no real choice when coal and petroleum are offered as the only practical, viable options.

More and more we are turning to other energy alternatives by necessity; the wood-to-coal forced-choice drama of the past is being reenacted. The search for power sources follows many pathways from atoms to zephyrs (gentle breezes). Each source has its defenders, doubters, and disclaimers, and each power proposal is surrounded by confusion, contradiction, and controversy. There are no simple yes or no answers.

Power Sources:
Fossil Fuels, Atoms and the Sun

The energy that powers our industrial society flows from three major sources: fossil fuels, atoms, and the sun. The largest stream of energy comes from the fossil fuels—oil, natural gas, and coal— in that order. They supply about 95 per cent of our present power needs, 75 per cent from oil and natural gas, the remainder from coal. The geological forces and conditions that created the fossil

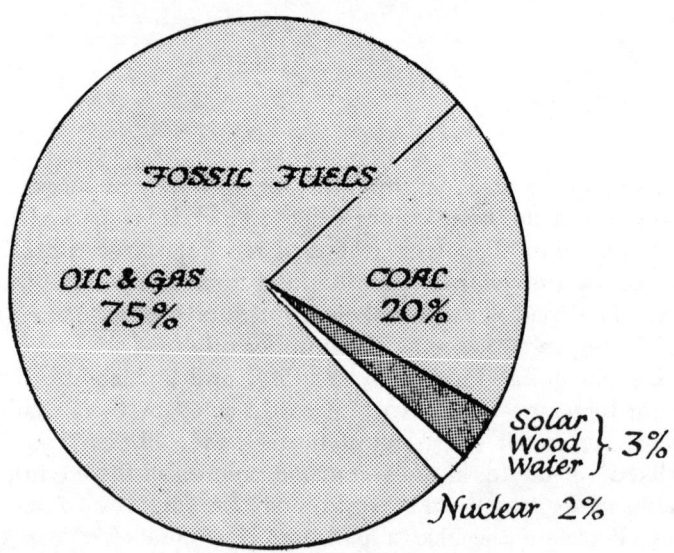

MAJOR U.S. ENERGY SOURCES

fuels are still operating today. However, Mother Earth cannot keep pace with the frantic rate at which we are digging, scraping, draining, and burning these nonrenewable deposits of stored solar energy. Despite periodic oil and gas gluts, these sources are evaporating and will eventually leave us high and dry.

King Coal II:
Revival

The courtiers of King Coal do not give up easily. They are busy trying to change the public image and chemical composition of coal to make it environmentally and economically more acceptable. "Dirty" coal and its fumes can be cleaned up by washing and scrubbing, but at a price. This black "devil" can be converted to liquids and gaseous fuels that imitate its more successful competitors, oil and natural gas.

Coal-derived fuels are not new; they have been around for some time. Water gas, made by passing steam over hot coal, was in use as a cooking and lighting fuel for a century, until it was replaced in the 1930's by cheap natural gas. Kerosene, or coal oil, a coal-derived fuel, was also widely used during the water-gas light era. During World War II, blockaded Germany produced liquid and gaseous fuels on a large scale from coal. South Africa is doing the same thing today. Coal-based synthetic fuels are still too expensive to compete with natural products. However, continued shortages and rising costs may price these synthetic fuels into the marketplace sooner than we think or would like.

Nuclear Energy:
Power from Atoms

The second power pathway is the atomic energy route, once regarded as the fuel of the future and heralded to replace the fossil fuels as the major power source. Despite the publicity and support it received, this power prodigy of the 1950's has failed to live up to expectations. Nuclear power has become the most controversial and contested alternative among the contending energy candidates. The record shows that nuclear energy has been frightfully more "successful" as a weapon of war than a patron of peace.

Today power from the atom supplies roughly 2 per cent of our total energy needs, used almost exclusively in fueling power stations that generate electricity. Safety, cost, pollution by long-lived radioactive wastes and fear of the known and unknown are unresolved complex issues of debate in our society that make the future of nuclear power uncertain—power from atoms certainly is not a quick answer to the present energy crisis.

Nuclear Energy Alternatives:
Fission and Fusion

Nuclear energy can be released by both fission and fusion. In the fission process, when the nucleus of a fissionable atom is split into smaller fragments, a tiny part of the atom is converted to energy. Fissionable fuel is a rare form of uranium (U-235). This is the fuel of the atomic bombs of World War II vintage. It is also the current fuel for the nuclear power plants which generate about 10 per cent of our electricity. The "ashes" of nuclear fission are fragments which are radioactive and remain "hot" for a very long time, some for thousands of years. Preventing pollution and disposing of deadly debris are among the major pending problems blocking the future of atomic energy as a prime power source.

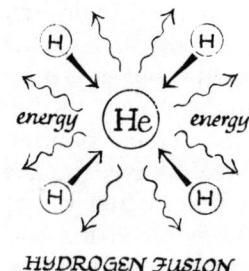

HYDROGEN FUSION

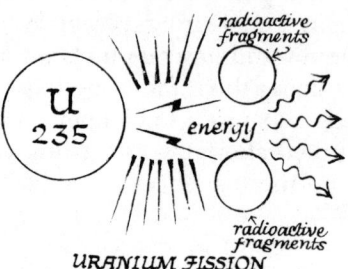

URANIUM FISSION

Breeder Reactors: Fissionable Fuel Fabricators

The latest model of nuclear-fission devices that has been developed is the breeder reactor, so named because it produces more fissionable fuel than it burns. These "second generation" breeder reactors do what conventional reactors do—release energy by splitting fissionable atoms. At the same time they create more fissionable fuel from nonfissionable atoms. Nonfissionable uranium (U-238) is transformed into fissionable plutonium (PU-239). The breeder backers in the nuclear industry are pushing this reactor as the ultimate answer to the energy crisis. Breeders get fifty times more energy out of uranium than do the conventional reactors. By "breeder" magic, present stockpiles and reserves of uranium, a nonrenewable mineral, would be sufficient as breeder reactor fuel for hundreds of years.

218

However, breeders are being confronted with the same kinds of opposition and problems as the original reactors: cost, safety, and pollution. A breeder program requires a tremendous financial investment, and there are questions about its environmental and social costs as compared to economic benefits. Safety issues are likely to intensify; plutonium is far more poisonous than uranium. Protection against reactor accidents, pollution, and sabotage require answers. The future of the breeder reactor program in this country is cloudy and uncertain.

Nuclear Fusion:
Hydrogen to Helium

The second source of atomic energy is nuclear fusion. Basically, the fusion process is the opposite of fission. In nuclear fission, energy is released when the nucleus of a large atom, uranium, is split into smaller ones. In fusion, there is a burst of energy when the nuclei of four very small atoms, hydrogen, fuse into one larger atom, helium. In both fission and fusion, a tiny bit of the reacting nuclei, 0.1 per cent, is completely turned into energy. The energy potential of fusion is best illustrated by considering the sun and the hydrogen bomb. Hydrogen fusion reactions are the source of solar energy and have been going on without interruption for 10 billion years. It is estimated that the earth receives only the tiniest portion of the total solar radiation, one-half-of-a-billionth part. The only man-made fusion reaction to date has been the explosion of the hydrogen bomb, the most powerful and destructive weapon of war yet conceived. The fusion fuels are rare forms of hydrogen, deuterium (do-TIER-ee-yum) and tritium (TRIT-ee-yum), of which there is an abundant supply.

"Success" in creating the H-bomb for war has not led to success in containing and controlling hydrogen fusion for peace. It is not for the lack of effort. For more than 30 years scientists have tried in vain to imitate solar fusion by holding mixtures of deuterium and tritium close enough and long enough together to get the atoms hot enough to fuse. Unlimited energy from hydrogen fusion is an idea whose time has not yet come, but may arrive before the end of this era. This dream has prompted the United States government to adopt a $20 billion national plan to develop by the end of this century a nuclear fusion technology that it hopes will provide future generations with an almost inexhaustible source of energy. Let us hope that these billions for fusion are not a delusion.

Solar Energy:
Salvaging Sunshine

The third major power pathway is the sun. It is the oldest, cleanest, safest, most abundant, and least developed source and has the brightest future. At present, only a trickle of our energy needs are fulfilled from direct solar sources. Yet, except for nuclear and geothermal energy, (heat from the earth: hot springs and geysers) the sun is the ultimate provider of all earthly energy, past, present, and in the future, for as long as it shines.

About half the solar radiation reaching the earth is reflected by its surface and lands back into space. The other half is absorbed by water, air, exposed soil, and green plants. Only 1 to 2 percent of the solar energy is captured by green plants during photosynthesis and is stockpiled as food and fuel. The sun also provides indirectly the energy behind the wind and rain that turns turbines, windmills, and waterwheels. Direct solar energy is being harvested to heat homes and generate electricity.

Solar Houses:
Basking in the Sun

Heating a house with direct solar radiation is an old idea whose time has come again. Over 3,000 years ago, the Chinese built entire villages facing the sun. Today, the energy crisis is reviving this old Chinese custom; we are building houses that bask in the sun. Solar architects are designing houses with glass south walls and solid, well-insulated, or nearly windowless north walls. An overhang on the south side shields windows from the high summer sun but admits the low winter sun. The north side is protected against cold winter winds by evergreen shrubbery or outbuildings, which act as buffers and insulators. Shades and drapes can also go a long way inside windows, keeping the summer heat out and the winter warmth in. To paraphrase an old American proverb, "make heat while the sun shines."

Solar Heating and Cooling:
Warm Water and Cool Air

Solar heating and cooling systems can offer comfort and financial relief during the growing energy crunch. The basic principle behind solar heating is the greenhouse effect. The blackened underside of transparent glass or plastic can absorb sunlight and convert it to heat energy with 85 percent efficiency. Solar collectors are located in sunny spots, usually on the roof of a house. Heat is absorbed by water or air circulating through the collectors and can be stored in a storage tank. From here, hot water or warm air can be sent through the house by conventional plumbing systems. Homes in the South and Southwest are now being built with plumbing systems for solar water and space heating. The growth of these solar systems is being encouraged in several states through tax exemptions.

THE SOLAR WATER HEATER

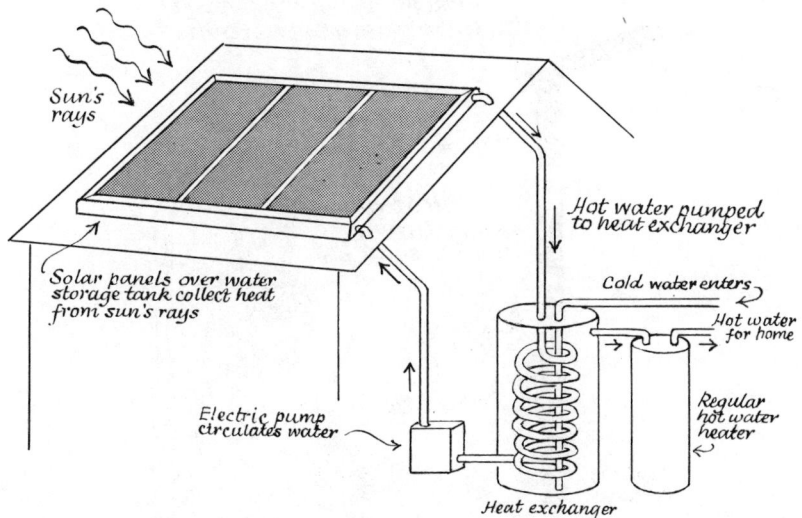

Sun's rays

Solar panels over water storage tank collect heat from sun's rays

Hot water pumped to heat exchanger

Cold water enters

Hot water for home

Electric pump circulates water

Regular hot water heater

Heat exchanger

Solar energy can also be used in cooling systems. For water to evaporate, heat is required; as water evaporates, it absorbs heat from the air and so cools the air. People perspire and plants transpire to keep cool. The cool of the forest is due to transpiring trees, nature's air conditioners.

221

Evaporation water coolers are still in use in hot, dry climates and work very well. In solar coolers, water is evaporated by the heat of the sun as it runs over pipes. Evaporation cools the water in the pipes and the cooled water is circulated through the house. This principle is being applied to solar air conditioners, but not with the same success as solar space and water heaters.

Solar Greenhouses:
For Plants and People

A greenhouse is a glass-covered solar-heated space in which plants grow year round. The idea of people sharing greenhouse heat with plants, although not entirely new, is nevertheless catching fire. Solar greenhouses capable of yielding food, flowers, ferns, and heat are hot items.

THE GREENHOUSE ENERGY SAVER

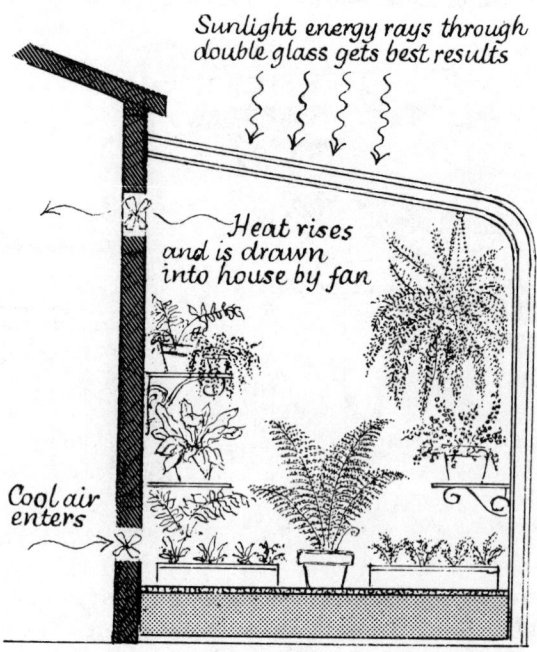

Sunlight energy rays through double glass gets best results

Heat rises and is drawn into house by fan

Cool air enters

Glass allows light to enter trapping resultant heat

Plans for solar greenhouses as additions to homes and on terraces of city apartments are being made available by builders and suppliers. The basic elements in the construction of such solar heat collectors are southern exposure, tilted, tight-fitting, double-glazed walls, a ventilation system for heat distribution, and heat-holding materials for the nights and sunless days.

The most efficient solar greenhouses follow the design principles of solar architecture: solid, well-insulated walls on all but the south side and a roof with an overhang to exclude the high summer sun and admit the low winter sun.

Concentrated Sunshine:
From Sunlight to Electric Light

It is a long way from starting a fire with a magnifying or burning glass to collecting enough heat energy to operate a solar electric-generating station. But this is exactly what is being tried. Such tests are being conducted in the Southwest; huge fields of movable mirrors focus the rays of the sun on a boiler mounted on a central tower housing an electric generator. Temperatures high enough to turn a turbine with heated helium or air can be produced. Fields of mirrors may be part of the future landscape, where electricity is generated by solar energy.

Solar Cells:
From Photons to Electrons

The technology of photovoltaic cells is very promising. These are devices that generate electricity from direct sunlight. The light meter on a camera is a photovoltaic cell. Spacecraft and satellites are powered by such solar cells. These cells are semiconductors composed of two very thin layers of unlike materials, most commonly forms of silicon. Photons, the energy particles of which light is composed, collide with the electrons of the silicon atoms, causing electrons to flow in one direction across the cells, providing a source of electricity. Solar cells have a great future, but are beset by many technical problems and high cost. These problems must be overcome before photovoltaic cells become a significant source of energy. Getting electricity from sunlight has "turned on" many people and solar cells may appear more quickly and burn more brightly than anticipated. Experimental solar-powered airplanes and automobiles are here, foreshadowing the vehicles of the 21st century.

Wind, Water, and Watts:
Windmills and Waterwheels

The air and water of the world absorb most of the solar energy that reaches the earth. The sun heats water causing it to evaporate; water vapor rises into the atmosphere, cools and condenses, form clouds, or falls back to the earth as snow, hail, and rain. Flowing

and falling water turns waterwheels and turbines of electric generators, satisfying about 2 percent of our energy appetite. Increasing hydroelectric power sources by building more giant dams is not a good prospect for the future since such constructions are opposed by many because of their undesirable environmental effects. However, abandoned mini-hydroelectric plants (waterwheels) are now being restored in many parts of the United States.

The sun also heats the air causing it to expand, rise, cool, and flow back to the earth as air currents, winds. Moving air may be a gentle zephyr or a terrifying typhoon or tornado. Winds whirl windmills, a seventh-century Persian invention, brought to China by Ghengis Khan and then to Europe by the Crusaders. In the seventeenth century. Wind power made the Dutch the commercial leaders of the world by sailing their ships, turning their grinding mills, and expanding their coasts by pumping water from the land under the sea. Windmills, picturesque relics of the past, are being revived as supplementary power sources in windswept parts of this country.

Water power in tides, waves, and ocean currents is also being explored as a source of energy. The oceans cover two-thirds of the world's surface and are tremendous thermal reservoirs. Differences in temperature between tropical surface water and cold,

deep ocean currents can be as much as 20°C. This energy differential is being tested experimentally as a way to produce electricity.

Pond Power:
Solar Salt Pools

Another promising path being pursued by many countries around the world is solar salt pools, in which solar heat is collected and converted into electricity. Ordinarily, the water of a shallow pool heated by the sun circulates, making its temperature almost uniform from top to bottom. In a solar salt pool, the top layer of water is fresh or nearly so while the bottom layer is very salty. Sunlight passes through the top fresh water and heats the salty bottom layer. Since the bottom salt water layer is heavier than the top fresh water layer, there is no circulation and the heat accumulates, bringing the temperature of the bottom layer almost to boiling. This heat may be used to cool or heat homes, or to turn an electric generator.

Plant Power:
"Now" Fuel

The search for fuels to fill the growing energy gap has led back to plants, with stores of solar energy. Solid nonfossil substances of organic (plant and animal) origin contain about half as much energy as hard coal. Materials from which energy can be extracted are called biomass; they are looked upon as the potential source of huge quantities of renewable energy which has not been properly exploited. The energy in biomass can be released by burning, fermenting, or reacting these materials with chemicals. Potential biomass power is found in such diverse materials as food crops, wood, corn husks, hay, seaweeds, garbage, waste paper, and manure.

Wood Power:
For Work, Warmth, and Watts

The best-known nonfossil fuel is wood, a product of photosynthesis, which has been used as a source of energy since the discovery of fire thousands of years ago. Until the middle of the last century, the United States was a wood burning country; 90 percent of the fuel came from forests. Wood was displaced by a fossil forebear, coal, which in turn was replaced by oil and gas. Despite these fossil-fuel substitutes, wood burns brightly again in homes and factories, supplying more energy to homes than nuclear power stations. Fast rising fossil-fuel costs are making wood an economically attractive power source, especially in heavily wooded areas. Wood-burning stoves and fireplaces, industrial plants, and power stations are becoming more common especially in New England.

In addition, scrap wood and industrial wood wastes from lumber and paper mills and furniture factories are biomass fuels. Fuel farming of fast-growing trees, and new methods of harvesting entire trees, leaves and all, are added fuel for the fire. Overall, wood is making a modest but meaningful contribution to the power pool.

Fuel Farming:
Energy Agriculture

In addition to foraging in forests, farms, fields, and streams are being explored for biomass fuels. Scientists are experimenting with fuel farming—raising flora for fuel instead of food. A wide variety of land and water plants, some noxious weeds, are being studied. For example, water hyacinth, a costly nuisance clogging southern waterways and giant kelp, a fast growing brown seaweed inhabiting west coast water, are promising sources of methane, the principal constituent of natural gas.

Alcohol and Gasohol:
Cocktails and Cars

Food crops such as sugar cane, wheat, corn, and other cereals can be converted to alcohol by fermentation, a practice, as old as civilization, for brewing alcoholic beverages. Mixed with gasoline as gasohol or by itself, alcohol has the potential of replacing gasoline as the source of automobile power. At present, Brazil, with an enormous sugar cane supply, can make alcohol cheaper than it can buy gasoline. Although Brazilian cars travel on either gasoline or gasohol, there is the expectation that they will be fueled by pure alcohol in the near future. In this country, a very limited supply of 10 percent gasohol mixtures is available and consumed by 1 to 2 percent of our cars. It seems that for American farmers, it is more profitable to raise biomass for food and drink than for fuel. Considering our annual agricultural surplus, there seems to be bountiful biomass, enough to satisfy our appetite for dining, drinking, and driving.

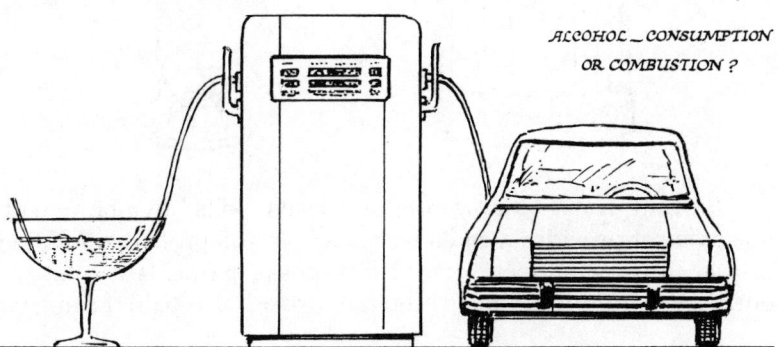

ALCOHOL — CONSUMPTION
OR COMBUSTION ?

Trash Power:
Wastes to Watts

A new Eldorado has been found, "gold" in them there garbage dumps. Power prospectors struck it rich when they discovered that three-quarters of municipal solid wastes are combustible, rich in "trash" power. As the cost of collecting, processing, and disposing of urban wastes mounts, as landfill and dumping sites disappear, and as the cost of fossil fuels escalates, garbage becomes an asset instead of a liability. Wastes are being burned by power stations and turned into watts. Landfill and garbage dumps along with sewage sludge and animal manure are being tapped for methane and burned as an industrial fuel. Add to this the mountains of agricultural and lumber wastes which are also energy rich, and trash power looms large.

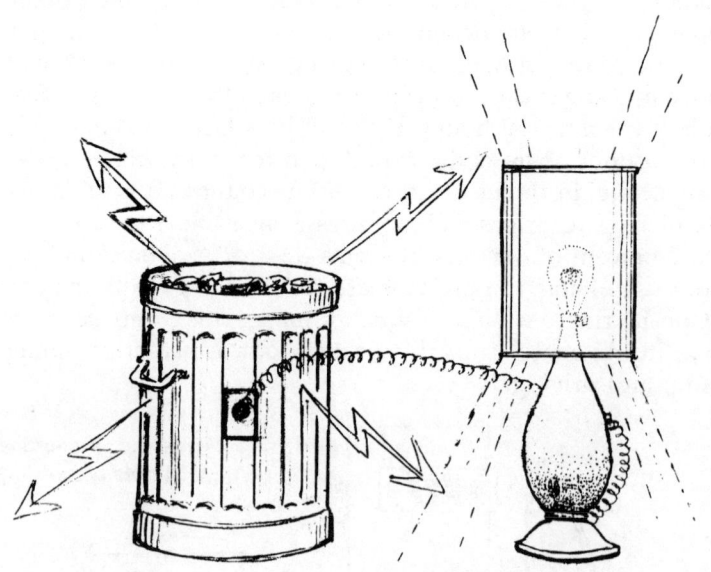

Burning wastes for warmth and watts "kills" two birds with one stone: it provides wanted watts and offers a profitable solution to the growing problem of waste disposal, particularly acute in our "use once and dump," "replace instead of repair" economy.

Fuels and the Future:
Diversification and Decentralization

As one reviews the spectrum of energy alternatives, it becomes painfully clear that there is a plethora of proposals but a scarcity of solutions to the fossil-fuel famine. Neither coal, gas nor oil, nor atomic energy, nor solar energy, nor conservation alone are the answer. An international game is now being played with fossil fuels as the gambling stakes. The name of the game is COG, the first letters of the "big three", coal, oil and gas. It is the old shell game in which you try to pick the winner. Switching back or forth from oil to gas to coal makes it a grim guessing game of Russian roulette. Oil and gas fields are the potential battle grounds in an all-out clash between OPEC, the "have" oil countries and NOPEC, the "have not" oil countries. There is the real possibility that oil may set off a world-wide conflagration, a war in which the H-bomb would be the final arbiter resolving this conflict to no-body's satisfaction, a war without winners or survivors.

On the other hand, this crisis has provided very powerful incentives for curbing and taming the "big three" and seeking alternatives that imitate natural recycling, self-renewing systems. COG is not the strongest nor the most durable cog in the wheels of progress. The only realistic approach is to diversify and not put all our energy eggs in one basket. Variety is the spice of life; diversification is a sound biological and economic strategy. The more energy options open, the more likely are we to ride out this storm and come out on top with power for a better and brighter future. The key is diversification and decentralization. Breaking the monopoly of the petroleum power potentates, nationally and internationally, may provide incentives for the growth and de-velopment of energy alternatives. Sun power in the South, wood power in the North, water power in the mountains, biomass power in the Midwest, wind power on open plains, wave and tide power in coastal areas and trash power in large cities should be nurtured.

229

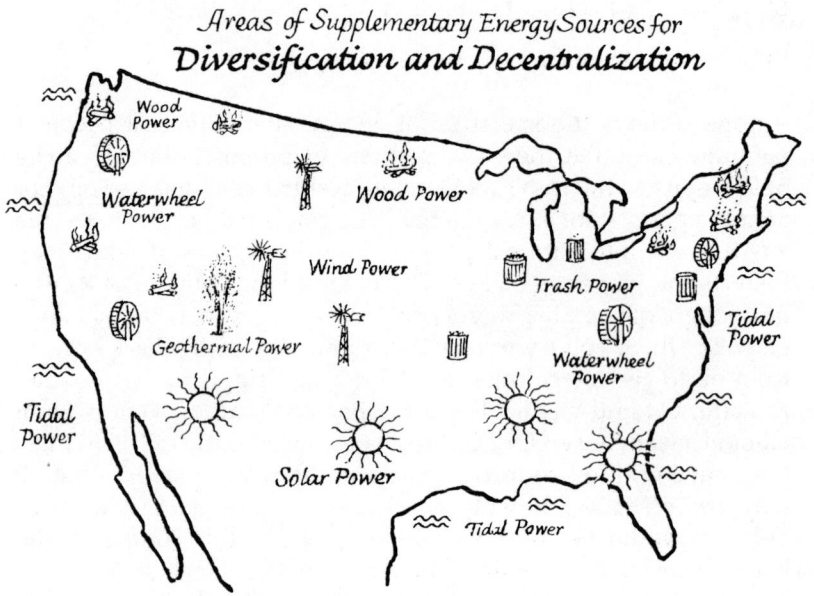

Areas of Supplementary Energy Sources for
Diversification and Decentralization

Ferns and Photosynthesis:
Storing Energy

This brings us full circle back to ferns, fuels and photosynthesis. The past half century has witnessed great strides in understanding photosynthesis and attempting to duplicate in the laboratory what green plants have been doing so well for billions of years.

Ferns, as representative of green plants, provide a living model for seeking solutions to problems of energy storage. The success or failure of alternatives depends upon mechanisms of stockpiling energy. Except for the fossil fuels, which are shining examples of packaged power, effective alternatives must have systems for storing energy. Electricity, for example, is produced and consumed almost simultaneously, moving from the generator to the electric appliance with lightning speed. It can be changed to chemical energy and stored in batteries, then changed back to electricity when needed. But batteries have a limited capacity and a limited life and are more expensive as an energy source than generators.

Plant Power Packs:
ATP

The chlorophyll-containing bodies in green plants have solved the problem of capturing and storing solar energy. Not only do they absorb energy from photons, but they store it as chemical energy in special molecules from which this power is released on demand. These special storage molecules found in the cells of all living things are called ATP, Adenosine Triphosphate. They are the universal power currency involved in almost every energy transaction of life. The stored solar energy in food released by respiration is also transferred and held by ATP until needed. We are in the process of solving the secret of energy storage in plants with the silicon solar cells that can absorb photons and generate a flow of electrons, a phenomenon that takes place in photosynthesis.

Synthesizing an "ATP" all-purpose energy storage molecule should not be impossible for a world with the ability and knowhow to launch men and machines in space and maintain communication with spacecraft millions and billions of miles from earth. A breakthrough in solar energy storage technology would be the answer to both the food and fuel problem. It would free the world from starvation and the dirt and danger of fossil and atomic fuels. It would enable us to live in and by sunlight. Ferns, which played such a vital role in ushering in the industrial era, may hold the key to the door opening the solar century.

SUMMARY:

Energy Alternatives

Energy to power our industrial society comes from three major sources: about 95 percent from fossil fuels, 2 percent from atomic energy and the remainder from the sun. Environmental pollution, political and economic problems created by rising costs and growing shortages are providing powerful incentives for seeking energy alternatives. To make "dirty" coal and oil ecologically more acceptable, by "cleaning" them up to increase present fuel supplies, by converting coal into liquid and gaseous fuels and by squeezing liquid fuels out of oil shales are at present more costly than natural products and not meeting our growing energy needs.

Nuclear sources have failed to live up to promises and expectations as a major source of power. Atomic power plants which supply electricity by nuclear fission are the targets of great controversy. Safety, cost, disposal of long-lived dangerous radioactive wastes and fear, are issues of public debate which is halting the operation and expansion of these facilities. Breeder reactors which also release energy by fission but produce more fissionable material than they burn, are meeting the same kind of opposition as reactors currently in use. The future of breeder reactors is in doubt.

Fusion reactors which release energy by the fusion of hydrogen atoms are being promoted as the source of practically unlimited energy and the solution to the energy crisis. Atomic fusion is the source of solar energy. The only man-made fusion reaction has been the "H" or hydrogen bomb, the most powerful and destructive weapon of war yet conceived. Energy for peacetime by nuclear fusion is still a dream on the drawing board; the success of the investment by our government of billions of dollars for fusion has been described as wishful thinking.

The ultimate source of all energy on earth except for atomic and geothermal energy comes from the sun. And yet it provides only a trickle of our power needs despite the predictions that this safe, renewable and unlimited resource will be the chief source of energy in the next century, the solar century. Old solar sources such as wind, water, and wood are being reexamined and new ones developed.

Direct sunlight is being used in solar homes and greenhouses to heat and cool especially in the sun belt where it can compete successfully with the traditional fuels. By concentrating sunlight with movable mirrors enough heat can be collected to generate steam and turn a turbine in a power plant. Shallow salt pools are being employed by several countries to absorb and collect solar energy as heat and used in homes and power plants.

Solar energy can be converted directly into electricity by photovoltaic cells. They are presently powering spacecraft and satellites and have a future in solar powered airplanes and automobiles. The sun is the power behind the winds that turn windmills, waters that turn waterwheels and the turbines of hydroelectric stations. These are being considered as energy source alternatives.

About one to two percent of the solar energy reaching the earth is captured and stored by green plants during photosynthesis. Solid substances of organic origin (plants and animals) hold about half as much energy as hard coal. Such materials which are renewable, are an excellent source of energy, the potential of which has not been fully exploited. Wood, garbage, industrial and agricultural wastes, giant kelp, food crops and the products of fermentation such as methane and alcohol are some of the sources of energy being explored and used.

Research and development of solar energy sources are not receiving the financial support, encouragement and incentives accorded fossil fuels and nuclear energy. Billions of dollars are being spent on coal and nuclear energy development and very little by comparison on solar energy research. A basic area begging for intensive study is photosynthesis and energy storage mechanisms of ATP. Ferns are living examples of how to capture, store and use solar energy, and as such are models worthy of intensive research efforts.

Appendixes

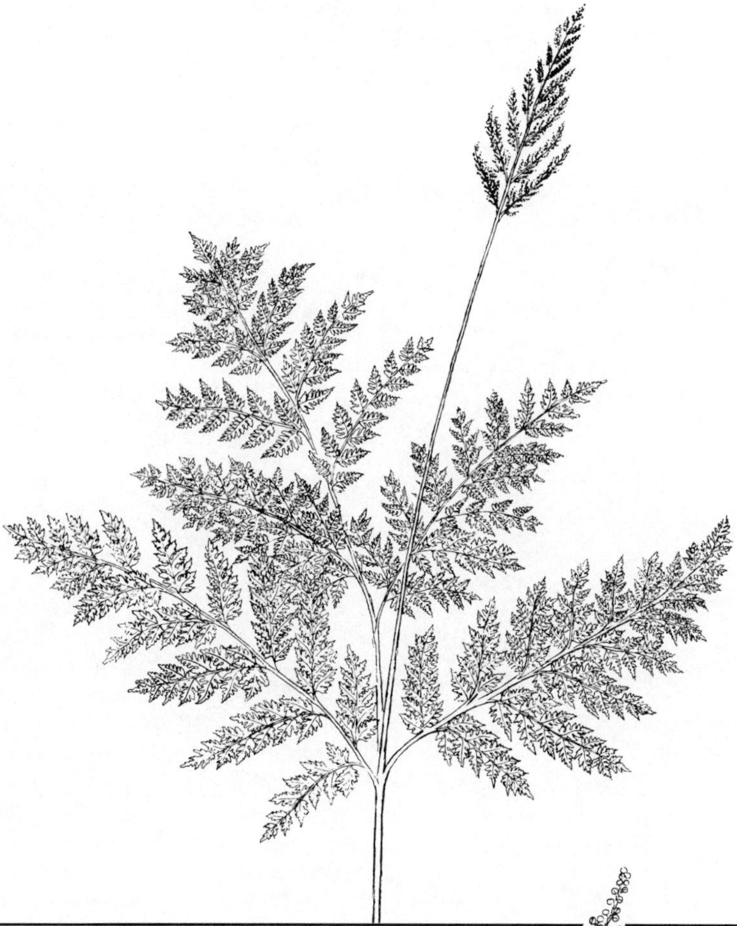

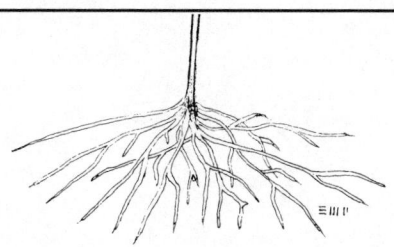

Rattlesnake Fern

Fertile spike rising from a
three-part thrice-cut sterile frond

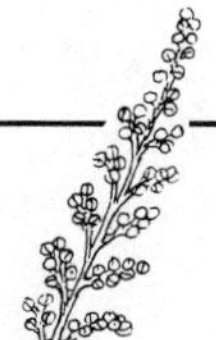

fertile tip

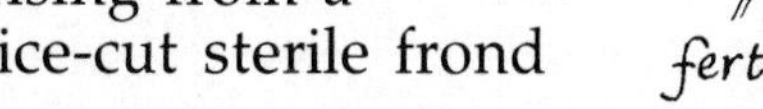

DESCRIPTIVE GUIDE
TO SOME FERN GENERA AND
REPRESENTATIVE SPECIES

There are about four hundred species of ferns native to the continental United States. As an introduction and overview of this population, 25 species, each representing a different fern genera, have been selected for inclusion in a descriptive guide for study and identification.

The descriptive guide presents diagnostic frond and sori characteristics for easy and fast identification of these ferns. However, before using this guide, it may be necessary to review the structure of ferns and the language used in describing them. This guide is based on frond forms supplemented by sori structure. Knowing the meaning of such terms as simple, compound, cut, uncut, once cut, twice cut, and thrice cut as well as pinna, pinnule, rachis, indusium, stipe, and the like is essential. It will be worth your while to look at Chapters III and IV and the glossary of fern terms.

The following hints are offered in using this or other guides to identify ferns:

1. Study a mature fern, that is, one that shows spores. Having both fronds and sori increases the speed and accuracy of identification.

2. A 10-power magnifying lens increases the accuracy of your observations, particularly for sori structure, which is most important and helpful in correctly naming ferns.

3. Be aware of the habitat, geographic range, and frequency of the fern. Don't look for the curly grass fern in a grassy meadow; it is rare and lives only in acid bogs. The hay-scented fern is abundant and lives in open fields and clearings.

4. Compare your specimen with illustrations, herbarium specimens, or any other source that positively identifies it.

5. Join a fern foray or find a friend who is a friend of the local ferns and is willing to reveal the secrets of identification.

6. Keep a record of the ferns you find with the characteristics by which they are identified; include date, place, and identifying data.

KEY TO FERN GENERA, WITH REPRESENTATIVE SPECIES

Key I. Ferns with Unusually Shaped Fronds

A. Fronds Uncut: Simple Entire

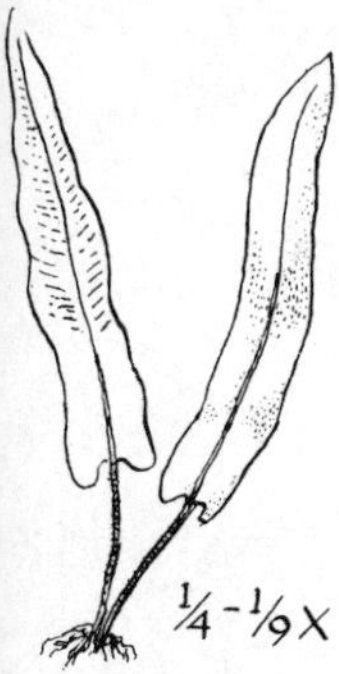
$\frac{1}{4}$-$\frac{1}{9}$X

1. Fronds evergreen, **strap-shaped,** blunt-tipped; margin wavy, entire; base heart-shaped.

Sori on underside, narrow and of **varying** lengths; in pairs along the veins.

Hart's Tongue
(Phyllitis scolopendrium)

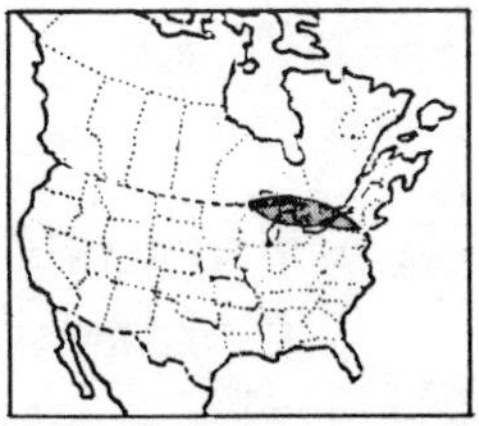

Distribution
rare; moist limestone ledges

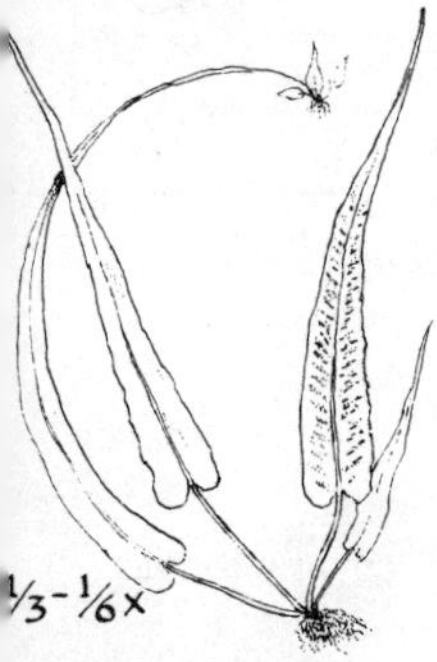
$\frac{1}{3}$-$\frac{1}{6}$X

2. Fronds evergreen, long, triangular with **tapering** tip; heart-shaped base; new plants grow where tip touches ground.

Sori on underside, **scattered** along veins; irregular in shape and pattern.

Walking Fern
(Camptosorus rhizophyllus)

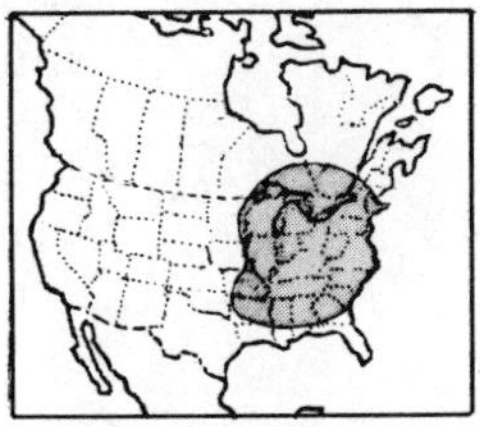

Distribution
rare; moist, limestone rocks

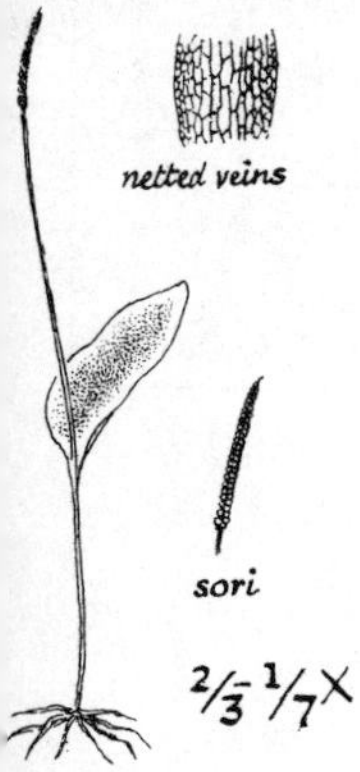
netted veins
sori
$\frac{2}{3}$-$\frac{1}{7}$X

3. Frond single, **spoon-shaped,** fleshy; attached to middle of stalk.

Fertile stalk arises from **base** of sterile part of frond; sori beadlike in two rows at tip.

Adder's Tongue
(Ophioglossum vulgatum)

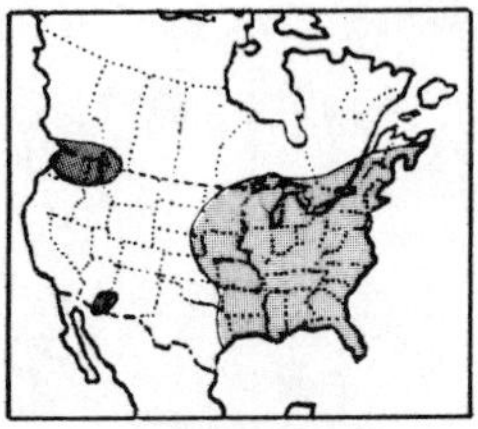

Distribution
rare; wet meadows

A. Fronds Uncut: Simple Entire (*continued*)

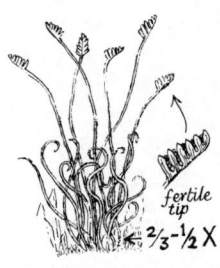

2/3-1/2 X

4. Sterile frond, **grasslike,** very short twisted spirally; evergreen.

Fertile frond separate, taller, erect; sori in fingerlike projections at tip **on one side.**

Curly Grass Fern
(*Schizaea pusilla*)

Distribution
rare; acid bogs

B. Fronds Cut with Unusual Shape: Compound

1/2 X

5. Fronds **vinelike;** long, twisting, climbing; bearing sterile pinnae hand shaped in pairs; evergreen.

Fertile pinnae, smaller, **at end** of rachis bearing double row of sori on constricted fingerlike projections.

Hartford Climbing Fern
(*Lygodium palmatum*)

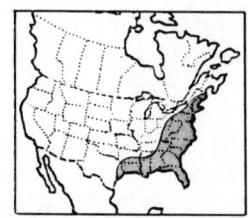

Distribution
rare; sandy bogs and swamps

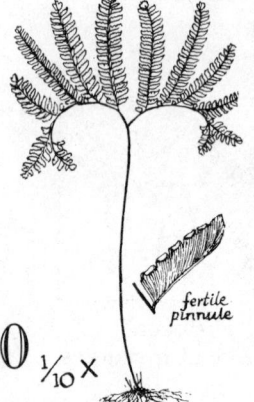

240 1/10 X

6. Fronds with **black,** wiry stipe and rachis curved, divided into two spreading rachises bearing pinnae on outer rim forming **fan-shaped** blade.

Sori on underside along upper margin of pinnulets, covered by curved-under tooth-shaped edge.

Maidenhair Fern
(*Adiantum pedatum*)

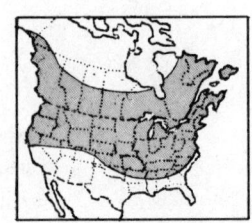

Distribution
common; moist woods

Key II. Ferns with Once-Cut Fronds

A. With Lobes Joined to Winged Rachis

⅟₇–⅟₁₅ X

fertile pinna

7. Sterile frond with several pairs of opposite lobes, wavy-edged; lowest pair separate, stemmed.

Fertile frond separate; shorter, woody, tipped with small, brown **bead-shaped clusters** enclosing sori.

Sensitive Fern
(Onoclea sensibilis)

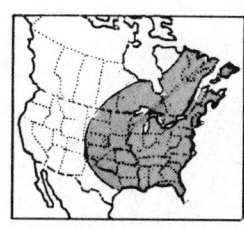

Distribution
very common; open fields and swamps

⅟₆–⅟₁₂ X

fertile lobe

8. Sterile frond with alternate, sharp, pointed narrow lobes; middle ones longest; **netted** veins.

Fertile frond taller with narrower, linear lobes; edges rolled over **chainlike** rows of sori on either side of midrib.

Netted Chain Fern
(Woodwardia areolata)

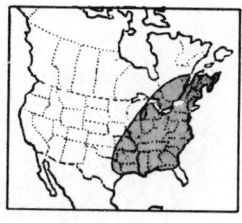

Distribution
common; moist woods and swamps

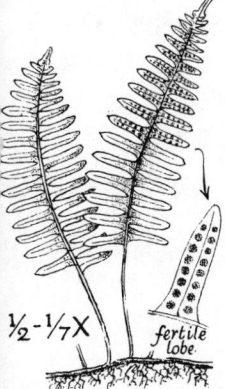

½–⅟₇ X

fertile lobe

9. Fronds leathery, evergreen; lobes alternate, cut almost to rachis, **rounded** tips.

Sori on underside of upper lobes; large, round; indusium absent.

Common Polypody
(Polypodium virginianum)

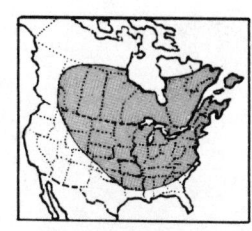

Distribution
common; rocky woodland

241

Key II. Ferns with Once-Cut Fronds (*continued*)

B. With Pinnae Eared at Base and Stalked to Rachis

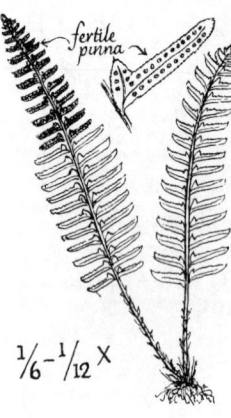

¹⁄₆–¹⁄₁₂ ×

10. Fronds leathery, ever-green; pinnae **ear-shaped,** spiny-tipped; stipe and rachis very scaly.

Fertile pinnae sharply reduced in size, limited to top pinnae; sori on undersides, red-brown, crowded, large; indusium circular, fixed at center.

Christmas Fern
(*Polystichum acrostichoides*)

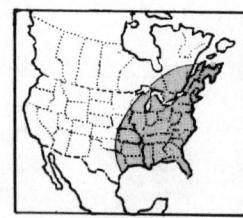

Distribution
common; rocky woodland

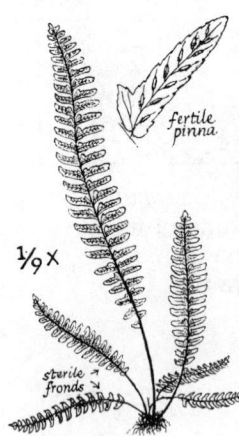

¹⁄₉ ×

11. Sterile fronds short, sprawling, with dark brown stipe and rachis; pinnae alternate, **winged,** gradually reduced below, blunt-tipped.

Fertile frond taller, erect; pinnae distinctly eared; sori on underside on either side of midvein in **herringbone** pattern.

Ebony Spleenwort
(*Asplenium platyneuron*)

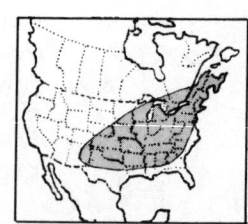

Distribution
common; rocky woods and walls

Key III. Ferns with Twice-Cut Fronds

A. Sterile and Fertile Fronds Separate and Distinctly Different

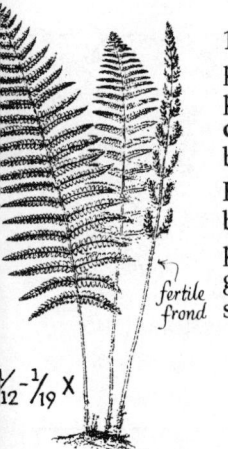

fertile frond

$\frac{1}{12}-\frac{1}{19}$ X

12. Sterile fronds tall, pointed; in circular clusters; pinnae lance-shaped with **cinnamon tuft** of hairs at base.

Fertile frond cinnamon brown; fertile pinnae in pairs, **club-shaped**, hugging rachis, sori in large, spherical clusters.

Cinnamon Fern
(Osmunda cinnamomea)

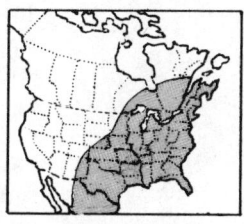

Distribution
common; swamps and wet woods

$\frac{1}{30}$ X

fertile frond

13. Sterile fronds tall, plume-shaped blade; pinnae widest near top, gradually tapering toward base; lower pinnae winged, clasping base; stipe short.

Fertile frond, short, **plume-shaped;** cut into hardened pinnae that clasp dark brown clusters of sori; woody; persists through winter.

Ostrich Fern
(Matteuccia struthiopteris)

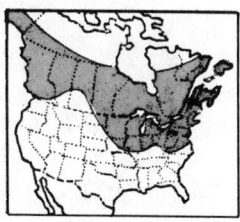

Distribution
common; swamps and wet woods

Key III.   Ferns with Twice-Cut Fronds (*continued*)

B.   Fertile Fronds Taller and Somewhat Like Sterile Fronds

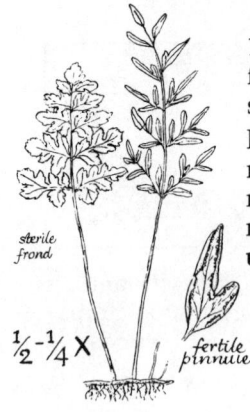

sterile frond

½-¼ X

fertile pinnule

14.   Sterile fronds tiny, fragile, with crinkly, fan-shaped pinnae.

Fertile fronds taller with narrow, lance-shaped pinnae; sori along edge of pinnule covered by **curved under-margin.**

Slender Cliff Brake
(*Cryptogramma stelleri*)

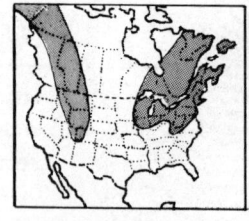

Distribution
rare; moist limestone cliffs

fertile pinna

⅒ X

sterile frond

15.   Sterile frond with dark purple, stiff, brittle stipe; pinnae variable, roundish, elliptical, spear-shaped; hairy.

Fertile frond taller; pinnae more elongated with 2 to 5 pairs of pinnules; sori along edge covered by **curved under-margin,** pod like.

Purple Cliff Brake
(*Pellaea atropurpurea*)

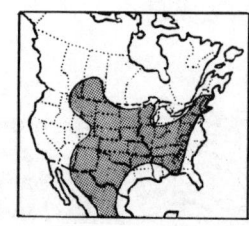

Distribution
common; dry, exposed limestone

16.   Sterile frond thin, delicate; pinnae opposite cut into rounded or blunt-tipped pinnules, veins simple.

Fertile frond taller; pinnae narrower, **pointed** because **pinnule** edge curves under partially covering sori on underside; indusia kidney-shaped.

Marsh Fern
(*Thelypteris palustris*)

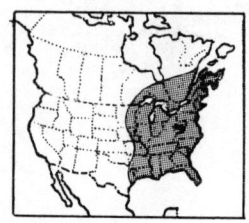

Distribution
very common; moist meadows and swamps

244

⅑-1/15 X

fertile pinnules

Key III. Ferns with Twice-Cut Fronds (*continued*)

C. Sterile and Fertile Fronds Very Much Alike in Appearance

17. Fronds large, leathery, evergreen; stipe scaly; pinnae lance-shaped; pinnules **blunt-tipped.**

Sori located on **margin** of pinnule; large, round covered by shield-shaped indusium.

fertile pinnule

Marginal Shield Fern
(*Dryopteris marginalis*)

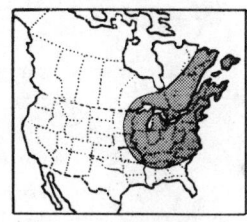

Distribution
common; rocky woodland slopes

18. Fronds small, evergreen, narrow, hairy; pinnae underside densely hairy; cut into roundish pinnulets.

Sori marginal, dark brown, partially covered by turned over edge of pinnules; no indusium.

underside of pinnule

Hairy Lipfern
(*Cheilanthes lanosa*)

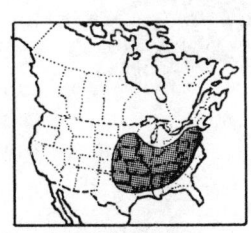

Distribution
frequent; rocky slopes

Key IV. Ferns with Thrice-Cut Fronds: Lacy Ferns

A. Fronds Triangular, Divided into Three Pinnae: Almost Parallel to Ground

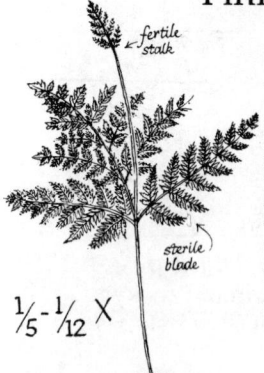

fertile stalk

sterile blade

$\frac{1}{5} - \frac{1}{12}$ X

19. Sterile blade triangular; **divided** into **three** pinnae, subdivided into pinnules bearing pinnulets with round edges; papery.

Fertile stalk arising from base of blade; sori at tip in **spherical clusters** in widely spreading branches.

Rattlesnake Fern
(Botrychium virginianum)

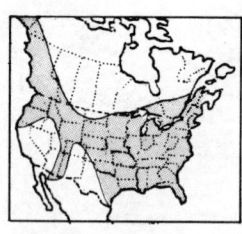

Distribution
common; moist woods

fertile pinnule

$\frac{1}{9} - \frac{1}{18}$ X

20. Blade **triangular,** very large, coarse, leathery; pinnae divided into oblong, blunt-tipped pinnules.

Sori a **continuous** line around underside; edge of pinnule covered by curved under-margin.

Bracken Fern
(Pteridium aquilinum)

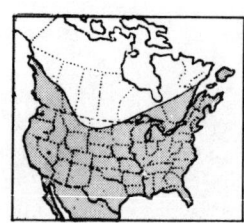

Distribution
very common; open fields and woods

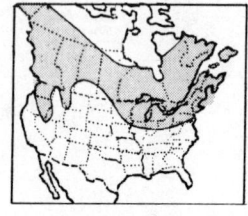

$\frac{1}{5} - \frac{1}{10}$ X

fertile pinna

21. Fronds tiny, a delicate **"baby bracken"**; pinnae divided into blunt-tipped pinnules.

Sori on underside of pinnule, small, round few, **near edge;** no indusium.

Oak Fern
(Gymnocarpium dryopteris)

Distribution
common; moist woods

246

Key IV. Ferns with Thrice-Cut Fronds: Lacy Ferns (*continued*)

B. Fronds Long, Lacy, Upright, Lance-Shaped

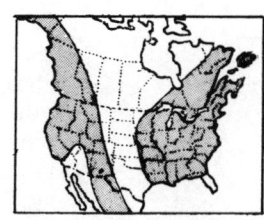

22. Fronds with pointed lax tips; growing in circular clusters; pinnae with narrow, pointed tips; pinnules deeply cut into toothed pinnulets.

Sori on underside, short, straight, or curved; indusium **crescent-shaped;** between midvein and margin.

Lady Fern
(*Athyrium filix-femina*)

Distribution
common; moist semishade woods and fields

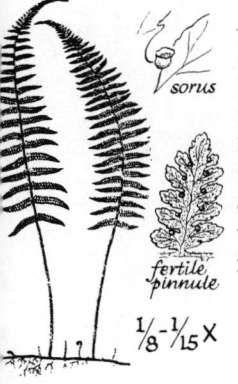

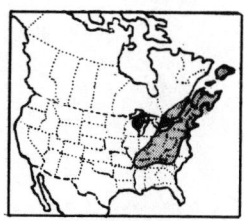

23. Fronds narrow with pointed lax tip, grows singly; hairy; pinnules divided into round pinnulets.

Sori on underside at edge of toothed, lobed margin; very small; in **cup-shaped** indusium.

Hay-scented Fern
(*Dennstaedtia punctilobula*)

Distribution
very common; meadows and forest clearings

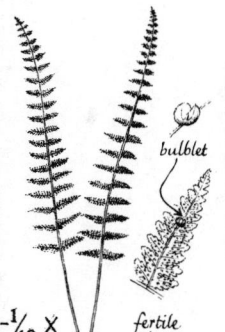

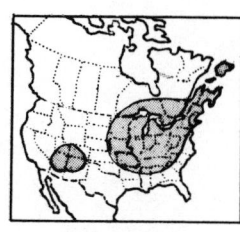

24. Frond tapering to a long point, narrowly triangular; **bulblets** on underside at base of pinnae.

Sori on underside; few scattered; indusium **hood-shaped.**

Bulblet Bladder Fern
(*Cystopteris bulbifera*)

Distribution
common; moist limestone ledges

247

Key IV. Ferns with Thrice-Cut Fronds: Lacy Ferns (*continued*).

B. Fronds Long, Lacy, Upright, Lance-Shaped (*continued*)

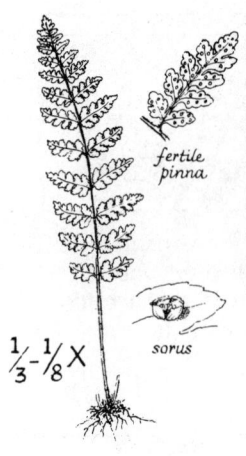

fertile pinna

sorus

$\frac{1}{3}$-$\frac{1}{8}$ X

25. Fronds evergreen; stipe straw colored, few scales; pinnules cut into rounded pinnulets: covered with tiny, **white hairs** and glands.

Sori on underside in cup-shaped indusium which produces **starlike** effect when split.

Blunt Lobed Woodsia
(Woodsia obtusa)

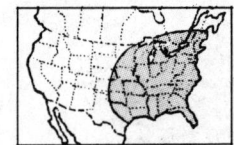

Distribution
common; shaded cliffs and ledges

248

Glossary of Fern Terms: "Fernese"

aerial stem: a vertical stem growing above the ground or water from a rhizome; in horsetails.

alternate: arrangement of pinnae at different levels along the rachis of a frond.

alternation of generations: stages in the life cycle of a plant in which there is a spore-producing sporophyte plant and a separate alternating gamete-generating gametophyte plant.

annulus: a ring of cells partially or completely surrounding the spore case which splits open at maturity and scatters the spores.

antheridum -pl. antheridia: male sex organs of a pteridophyte located on the underside of the prothallus which produces sperm cells.

apogamy: no gametes; prothallus produces buds which grow directly into sporophytes without fertilization.

apospory: no spores; sporophytes produce prothalli directly without going through the spore stage.

archegonium -pl. archegonia: female sex organ on the notch of the prothallus that produces egg cells.

blade: the leafy expanded part of a frond.

bract: a small scalelike modified leaf in whiskbroom ferns.

bud: tissue on roots, rhizomes or fronds capable of growing into a new plant.

bulblet: a budlike body growing on the underside of a frond that can grow directly into a new plant.

compound: referring to a frond consisting of several separate pinnae.

cone: a structure holding clusters of sporangia found at the base of leaflets or at the tip of fertile stems of horsetails and clubmosses.

eggs: female gamete (sex cell) produced in the archegonium of the prothallus.

elaters: ribbon-like structures attached to the spores of horsetails helping in their dispersal.

entire: referring to the margin of a frond lacking teeth, lobes or divisions.

epiphtye: plants that grow on other plants without being parasitic.

evergreen: plants holding on to their fronds throughout the year.

family: a category of classification consisting of a group of genera.

female gametophyte: the small plant in the life cycle of spike-mosses and quillworts that develops from megaspores and produces archegonia.

fern: a flowerless, seedless green plant that reproduces by alternating generations; its fronds contain branching veins.

fern allies: pteridophytes with scale or needle-like leaves bearing a single unbranched vein.

fertile: fronds or parts of fronds that produce spores.

fiddlehead: the uncoiling frond of a young fern that resembles the head of a violin.

flora: the species of plants growing in a given locale.

frond: a fern leaf including stipe and blade.

gametes: sex cells, sperms and eggs.

gametophyte: the small, independent plant in the life cycle of a pteridophyte that produces gametes, sex cells; the prothallus.

genus -pl. **genera:** a category of classification composed of a group of closely related species.

habitat: the natural environment of a plant.

indusium -pl. **indusia:** the thin membrane covering a sorus.

lobe: a more or less rounded part of a simple frond that does not extend to the rachis.

male gametophyte: the small plant in the life of spikemosses and quillworts that develops from a microspore and produces antheridia.

margin: the edge of a frond, pinna or pinnule.

megasporangium: the spore case in which megaspores develop.

megaspore: a relatively large spore that gives rise to the female gametophyte.

microsporangium: the spore case in which microspores develop.

microspore: the small spore that generates the male gametophyte.

opposite: referring to the arrangement of pinnae along the rachis of a fern at the same level.

parasite: an organism living on or in another living thing.

pinna -pl. **pinnae:** a division of a once-cut fern, a leaflet.

pinnule: a division of a pinna in twice-cut ferns, a subleaflet.

pinnulet: a division of a pinnule in thrice-cut ferns; a segment.

prothallus -pl. **prothalli:** the product of a spore; a small plant that contains both sperm-producing and egg-producing organs; the gametophyte.

pteridophytes: the ferns and fern allies as a group.

rachis -pl. **rachises:** the portion of the blade to which the pinnae are attached; the central axis or midrib.

rhizoids: hair-like rootlets found on the underside of a prothallus for absorbing soil water.

rhizome: the horizontal or underground stem, rootstock.

roots: thin, wiry, black, forking structures growing out of a rhizome.

segment: the ultimate division of a dissected (cut) frond.

simple: an undivided frond.

sorus -pl. **sori:** a group of sporangia, fruit dots.

species: Closely related plants in the same genus.

sperms: male gametes produced in an antheridium.

sporangium -pl. **sporangia:** saclike structures in which spores are borne, spore case.

spore: a single cell produced asexually by the sporophyte plant which grows into a gametophyte.

sporophyte: the large spore-producing plant in the life history of a pteridophyte.

sterile: sporeless fronds or pinnae.

stipe: a stalk portion of a fern bearing the frond, petiole.

stolon: a slender stem that produces new plants along its length and tip, runner.

terminal: the end of the stem.

terrestrial: growing on the ground.

vascular: conducting tubes that transport materials.

veins: fine threads of vascular tissue of fronds.

Selected Books for Pteridophiles

* For Beginners *

GINN, W. C. and M. J. CRAIG
  The Wonderful World of Seedless Plants
  (New York: Bobbs-Merrill, 1973)

GUILCHER, J. M. and R. H. NOAILLES
  A Fern Is Born
  (New York: Sterling, 1971)

KOHN, BERNICE
  Ferns: Plants without Flowers
  (New York: Hawthorne, 1968)

SHUTTLEWORTH, F. S. and H. S. ZIM
  Non-Flowering Plants
  (New York: Golden Press, 1967)

STERLING, DOROTHY
  The Story of Mosses, Ferns and Mushrooms
  (Garden City: Doubleday, 1955)

* Cultivation *

FOSTER, F. GORDON
  Ferns to Know and Grow
  (New York: Hawthorne, 1971)

HOSHIZAKI, BARBARA J.
  Fern Growers Manual
  (New York: Alfred A. Knopf, 1975)

MICKEL, JOHN T.
  The Home Gardener's Book of Ferns
  (New York: Holt, Reinhart and Winston, 1979)

* Selected Readings *

North America

MICKEL, JOHN T.
How to Know the Ferns and Fern Allies
(Dubuque, Iowa: Wm. C. Brown, 1979)

Northeast

COBB, BOUGHTON
A Field Guide to the Ferns and Their Related Families
(New York: Doubleday, 1975)

DURAND, HERBERT
Field Book of Common Ferns
(New York: Putnam, 1949)

WHERRY, EDGAR T.
The Fern Guide: Northeastern and Midland United States and Adjacent Canada
(Philadelphia, Pa.: The Morris Arboretum, 1975)

WILEY, FARIDA A.
Ferns of Northeastern United States
(New York: Museum of Natural History, 1948)

Southeast

SMALL, JOHN K.
Ferns of the Southeastern States
(Lancaster, Pa.: Science Press, 1938)

WHERRY, EDGAR T.
The Southern Fern Guide
(New York: Doubleday, 1964)

West

DORN, R. D. and J. L. DORN
> *The Ferns and Other Pteridophytes of Montana, Wyoming and the Black Hills of South Dakota*
> (Laramie, Wyo.: the Authors, 1972)

Northwest

TAYLOR, THOMAS
> *Pacific Northwest Ferns and Their Allies*
> (Toronto: University of Toronto Press, 1970)

The Pteridophyte Test

Before you close this book and rush off into the fields and forests or to gardens and nurseries in search of members of the pterid-ophyte tribe, turn to the pages introducing each of the chapters of this book. They are full-page portraits of some common mem-bers of the fern fraternity, eighteen in all. These drawings are intended to familiarize you with the characteristics which will enable you to identify each of the plants illustrated. If you can identify each plant from the drawings your success in the field will be greatly enhanced. One can enjoy and admire an anony-mous fern, but there is greater pleasure and satisfaction in know-ing exactly what is being admired.

Go back and study each of the eighteen drawings with their names and characteristics and when satisfied that you have made some new fern friends, turn to the next two pages. There you will find a duplication of these eighteen drawings but in an order different from the one that appears in the book. In the space provided under each illustration, write the name of the plant.

Using the key on page 258, check your answers. The Fern Familiarity Scale will tell you how well you have done. Don't be discouraged if you find that you know less than half by name. These plants are not easy to identify unless you have seen them many times, in the field, or herbarium sheets or as drawings. Fern friendship develops slowly but lasts a lifetime.

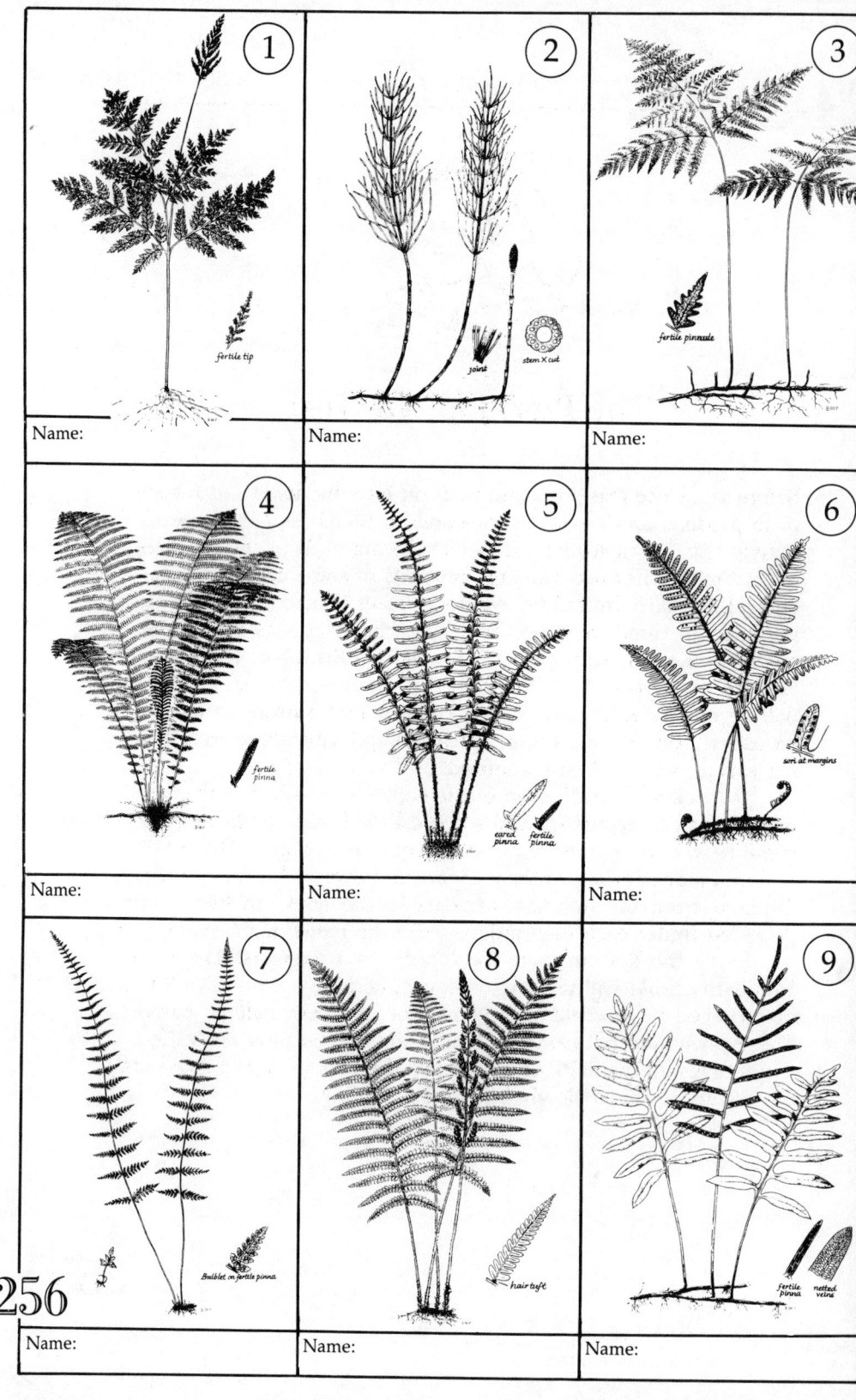

①

fertile tip

Name:

②

joint

stem X cut

Name:

③

fertile pinnule

Name:

④

fertile pinna

Name:

⑤

eared pinna

fertile pinna

Name:

⑥

sori at margins

Name:

⑦

Bulblet on fertile pinna

Name:

⑧

hair tuft

Name:

⑨

fertile pinna

netted veins

Name:

256

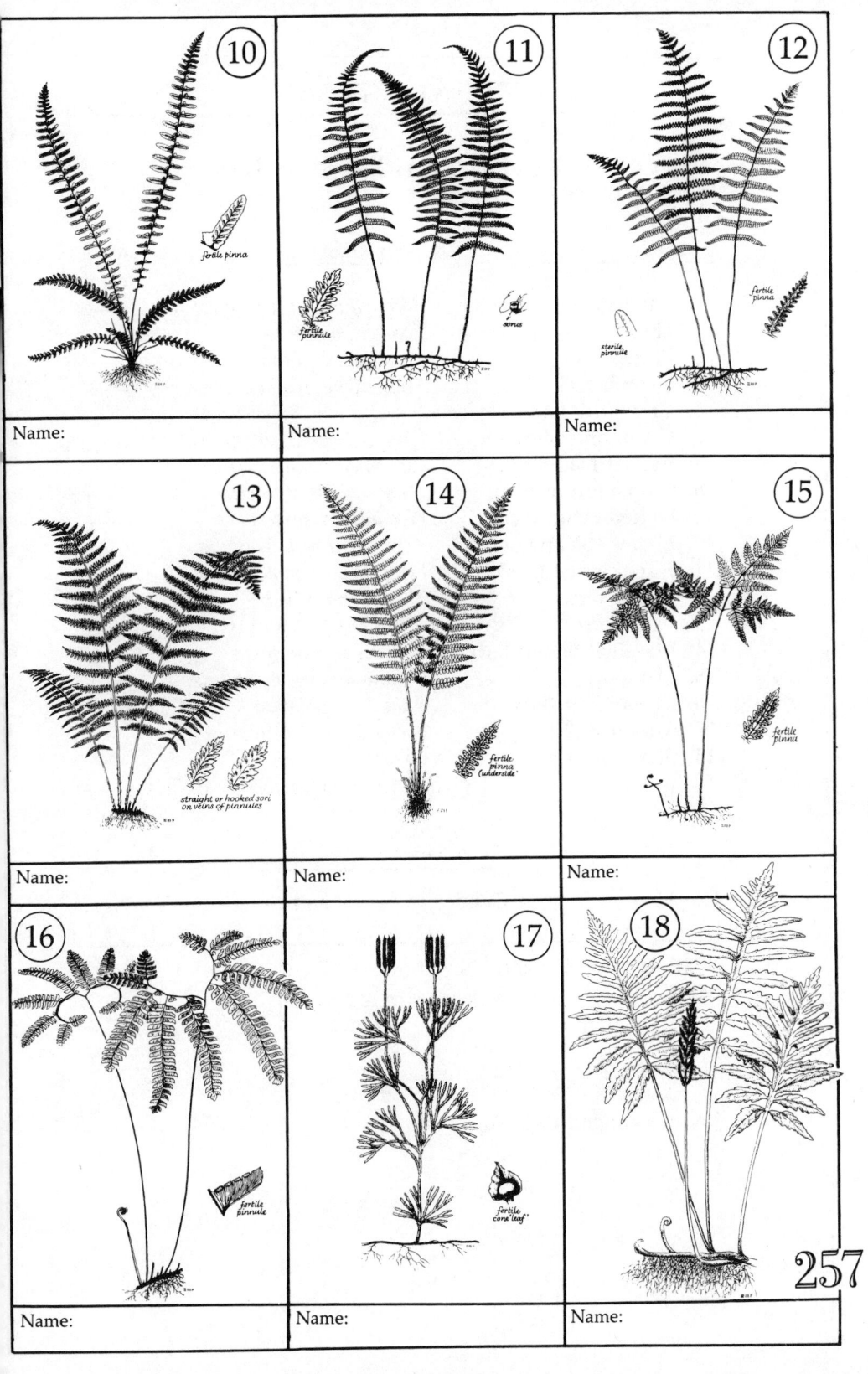

Name:

Name:

Name:

Name:

Name:

Name:

Name:

Name:

Name:

257

Key to Pteridophyte Test

No.	Common Name	Scientific Name	Correct Name (check)
1.	Rattlesnake fern	*Botrychium virginianum*	___
2.	Field horsetail	*Equisetum arvense*	___
3.	Bracken fern	*Pteridium aquilinum*	___
4.	Ostrich fern	*Matteuccia struthiopteris*	___
5.	Christmas fern	*Polystichum acrostichoides*	___
6.	Common polypody	*Polypodium virginianum*	___
7.	Bulblet bladder fern	*Cystopteris bulbifera*	___
8.	Cinnamon fern	*Osmunda cinnamomea*	___
9.	Netted chain fern	*Woodwardia areolata*	___
10.	Ebony spleenwort	*Asplenium platyneuron*	___
11.	Hay-scented fern	*Dennstaedtia punctilobula*	___
12.	Marsh fern	*Thelypteris palustris*	___
13.	Lady fern	*Athyrium filix-femina*	___
14.	Marginal Shield fern	*Dryopteris marginalis*	___
15.	Oak fern	*Gymnocarpium dryopteris*	___
16.	Maidenhair fern	*Adiantum pedatum*	___
17.	Running cedar	*Lycopodium flabelliforme**	___
18.	Sensitive fern	*Onoclea sensibilis*	___

Total number of correct names ___

Fern Familiarity Scale

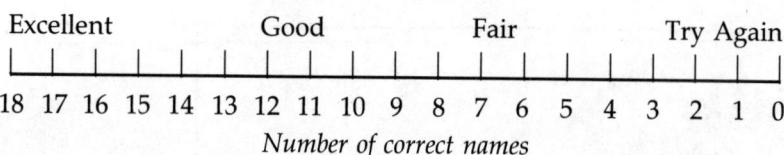

Excellent		Good		Fair		Try Again

18 17 16 15 14 13 12 11 10 9 8 7 6 5 4 3 2 1 0

Number of correct names

* Now changed to *L. digitatum*

Index

*Numbers in **boldface** refer to illustrations*